Mr. Monk Goes to the Firehouse

"The first in a new series is always an occasion to celebrate, but Lee Goldberg's TV adaptations double your pleasure. . . . *Mr. Monk Goes to the Firehouse* brings everyone's favorite OCD detective to print. Hooray!"
—*Mystery Scene*

"It is laugh-out-loud funny from the get-go. For *Monk* fans, this is a must. Totally enjoyable. Lee Goldberg has expertly captured the nuances of what makes Monk, well, Monk." —Robin Burcell

"Lee has found the perfect voice for Natalie's first-person narration—sweet, exhausted, frustrated, exasperated, and sweet again. None of these feelings has to do with the mystery. They're all reactions to Monk's standard behavior as he wars with all the ways nature is trying to kill him. Lee Goldberg has managed to concoct a novel that's as good as any of the *Monk* episodes I've seen on the tube." —Ed Gorman

The Monk Series

Mr. Monk and the Dirty Cop

Mr. Monk Is Miserable

Mr. Monk Goes to Germany

Mr. Monk in Outer Space

Mr. Monk and the Two Assistants

Mr. Monk and the Blue Flu

Mr. Monk Goes to Hawaii

Mr. Monk Goes to the Firehouse

MR. MONK
AND THE DIRTY COP

A Novel by
Lee Goldberg

Based on the USA Network television series created by
Andy Breckman

AN OBSIDIAN MYSTERY

OBSIDIAN
Published by New American Library, a division of
Penguin Group (USA) Inc., 375 Hudson Street,
New York, New York 10014, USA
Penguin Group (Canada), 90 Eglinton Avenue East, Suite 700, Toronto,
Ontario M4P 2Y3, Canada (a division of Pearson Penguin Canada Inc.)
Penguin Books Ltd., 80 Strand, London WC2R 0RL, England
Penguin Ireland, 25 St. Stephen's Green, Dublin 2,
Ireland (a division of Penguin Books Ltd.)
Penguin Group (Australia), 250 Camberwell Road, Camberwell, Victoria 3124,
Australia (a division of Pearson Australia Group Pty. Ltd.)
Penguin Books India Pvt. Ltd., 11 Community Centre, Panchsheel Park,
New Delhi - 110 017, India
Penguin Group (NZ), 67 Apollo Drive, Rosedale, North Shore 0632,
New Zealand (a division of Pearson New Zealand Ltd.)
Penguin Books (South Africa) (Pty.) Ltd., 24 Sturdee Avenue,
Rosebank, Johannesburg 2196, South Africa

Penguin Books Ltd., Registered Offices:
80 Strand, London WC2R 0RL, England

Published by Obsidian, an imprint of New American Library, a division of Penguin
Group (USA) Inc. Previously published in an Obsidian hardcover edition.

First Obsidian Mass Market Printing, December 2009
10 9 8 7 6 5 4 3 2 1

Copyright © 2009 *Monk* © USA Cable Entertainment LLC. All Rights Reserved.

The Edgar® name is a registered service mark of the Mystery Writers of
America, Inc.

OBSIDIAN and logo are trademarks of Penguin Group (USA) Inc.

Printed in the United States of America

To Valerie & Madison . . .
and to Oreo for keeping me company
while I wrote late into the lonesome hours
of the morning.

ACKNOWLEDGMENTS
AND AUTHOR'S NOTE

This is the first *Monk* novel in several years that wasn't written on different computers in various cities, countries, and modes of transport. I wrote the entire manuscript at my desk in Los Angeles.

I would like to thank my friend author Michael Connelly and cops-turned-authors Lee Lofland and Paul Bishop, for their advice on police matters.

And, as always, I am indebted to Andy Breckman, the creator of *Monk*, for entrusting me with his characters and for his unwavering support and enthusiasm.

I also would like to thank Gina Maccoby, Kristen Weber, and Kerry Donovan for making it all possible.

While I try very hard to stay true to the continuity of the *Monk* TV series, it is not always possible given the long lead time between when my books are written and when they are published. During that period, new episodes may air that contradict details or situations referred to in my books. If you come across any such continuity mismatches, your understanding is appreciated.

I look forward to hearing from you at www.leegoldberg.com.

1

Mr. Monk and the Old Lesson

My name is Natalie Teeger. I've spent a good chunk of my life trying to figure out who I am, who I want to be, and what I want to do.

Although I don't have the answers to those questions, I've pretty much reconciled myself to the fact that I'm not going to be a rock star, a U.S. senator, or an international supermodel.

I'm also probably not going to discover the cure to some horrible disease, host my own TV talk show, bring peace to the Middle East, or come up with a handy invention that completely changes the way we live.

Not that I necessarily aspired to any of those things in the past, but now I've officially stopped searching for a career and dreaming of lofty achievements.

I've set more modest goals for myself—like finding a steady boyfriend, doing the laundry before I run out of clean underwear, and paying off my credit cards in full each month.

There was a time when I was desperate to define myself through a career, but I couldn't seem to find one that suited me (not that I was ever entirely sure who "me" was). Along the way, I tried all kinds of jobs, from blackjack dealer to yoga instructor, but nothing stuck; nothing felt right.

Who I turned out to be, and what I've ended up doing, found me rather than the other way around.

I certainly didn't plan on being a widowed single mother with a teenage daughter, or working as the assistant to a brilliant, obsessive-compulsive detective.

Yet here I am.

If who we are is a reflection of what we do, how we perceive ourselves, and how others see us, then I suppose I am a loving, supportive mother to Julie and a capable, reliable, and hardworking assistant to Adrian Monk.

I've been fulfilling those roles comfortably, and more or less happily, for many years now, and yet I still feel as if I haven't found myself.

I guess it's because I'm not doing something that I always dreamed of doing or that feels like the perfect expression of who I am and my natural talents, not that I have a clue what they might be.

I envy people who don't have those problems—and that seems to be just about everybody I know.

Take my late husband, Mitch, for example. From the time he was a kid, he always wanted to be a fighter pilot, a husband, and a father. So that was what he set out to accomplish, and he succeeded.

Mitch died being the man he wanted to be and doing what he knew he was meant to do. I'm sure that even in his last moments, he never doubted that. When I think about him and how he died in Kosovo, that certainty, along with the knowledge that he knew how much he was loved by me and Julie, gives me a measure of peace.

Adrian Monk is another good example of what I mean. He craves order, predictability, symmetry, and cleanliness. Early in his life, he longed to be an inspector for the California State department of weights and measures, but that soon changed. As early as grade school, he exhibited an amazing knack for solving little mysteries, like who stole the money from the bake sale or who was responsible for vandalizing a locker.

He wasn't driven by nosiness, or curiosity, or a need for attention, or a quest for justice, but rather an overpowering compulsion to restore balance and order to the world around him.

To him a mystery is a form of chaos, a mess that has to be cleaned up or an imbalance that has to be corrected. It's his uncontrollable need to literally straighten up, to put things back where they belong, that enables him to see the little details everyone else misses and solve the crimes that boggle everybody else.

Justice isn't a philosophical, moral, or ethical ideal for him. It's a balance that must be maintained. In a way, he became an inspector of weights and measures.

There's absolutely no doubt that Adrian Monk was meant to be a detective. It is the natural extension of his personality, his talents, and his psychological disorder.

Everybody knows it. And he does, too. There are a thousand things he is insecure about (exactly a thousand, by the way, he has them cataloged and indexed) but being a great detective isn't one of them.

That's why he won't give up trying to get back on the San Francisco Police Department, even though they fired him after he suffered a complete mental and emotional breakdown in the wake of his wife Trudy's murder.

And that's why his friend Captain Leland Stottlemeyer hired him as a consultant to the Homicide Department, despite Monk's many phobias and behavioral peculiarities.

Stottlemeyer knew that being a detective was an essential part of Monk's character and that working was the only thing that would begin to make him whole again—at least until the day he finally finds whoever put a bomb in his wife's car.

But doing that favor for Monk came at a huge price, and I don't mean the countless things that Stottlemeyer, and his right-hand man, Lieutenant Randy Disher, have to do to keep Monk happy. (Like making sure there are no black-and-white police cars in sight at a crime scene because it will ruin his concentration. He believes that if cars are painted two colors, it must be done symmetrically, black on one side and white on the other. Anything else would violate the laws of nature.)

Monk is called in to consult whenever there is a crime that totally stumps Stottlemeyer and his detectives. He inevitably solves the mystery so easily that the captain feels stupid for not seeing the clues himself. I know this because the captain has said so on many occasions.

That's one thing I really like about Stottlemeyer. He always expresses his gratitude and gives Monk all the credit he deserves. But I know it takes a toll on him. Relying on Monk implies that the captain and his men weren't good enough to solve the crime on their own . . . or at least not as quickly.

What's got to make it even worse is that even on the homicide cases that Stottlemeyer and his detectives *could* and undoubtedly *would* solve on their own, Monk often figures out the solution while they are still taking out their notebooks.

The fact is that every time Monk performs brilliantly at a crime scene, he's unintentionally demonstrating that Stottlemeyer isn't as good at the job as he is.

Monk is oblivious to that, of course. But I'm not.

It's been going on like that day after day, year after year, and it's got to be hard on the captain's self-esteem.

I know it's hard on mine, and I don't even want to be a detective.

Witnessing Monk's natural ability and affinity for his work over and over again only reminds me that I've yet to demonstrate anything like that in my own life.

It's got to be much worse for Stottlemeyer, who is not only in the same profession, but in a leadership position.

All those conflicts were on my mind the morning we walked into the lecture hall in one of the newer buildings at the University of California, San Francisco's law school.

We were supposed to meet Stottlemeyer at headquarters to pick up Monk's paycheck and, by extension, my own, but the captain and Disher got called away to investigate a shooting at the university. Since we were desperate for the money, and Monk couldn't resist visiting a crime scene, we went out there, too.

It was a big lecture hall with dry-erase boards and flat-screen monitors behind the lectern. Pretty soon, chalkboards and erasers will be as extinct as typewriters, vinyl records, and carbon paper.

All the seats in the room had power plugs and tables for laptop computers. I imagined that being a student here was like listening to lectures in the business-class section of a British Airways jet. The only thing missing was someone pushing a cart down the aisles serving beverages and snacks.

I did a rough head count of the students in the room. There were about a hundred of them and they were still in their seats, fidgeting nervously as a handful of detectives questioned them one by one.

The questions probably had to do with the dead guy.

The victim looked to me like one of the students, except that unlike the others he had a gunshot wound in his chest and he was dead.

His body was sprawled at the bottom of the aisle that ran down the left side of the room. There were streaks of blood on the floor that indicated he'd rolled halfway down the aisle before his foot snagged one of those fancy seats.

I could see a gun lying in the blood. A numbered yellow evidence cone marked the spot in case nobody had noticed the weapon, the blood, or the body.

Lieutenant Disher was in front of the lecture hall, pencil poised over his notebook, interviewing a jowly man who had gray hair and wore a suit and tie.

The jowly man had a short beard that I figured he grew to give his first chin more definition and distract attention from his second one.

He held his chins high, his back straight, and stared down his long nose at Disher as if regarding a misbehaving child. I wondered if he had that posture before he became a professor, if it came with the job, or if it was a vain attempt to stretch his flabby neck taut.

Lieutenant Disher was in his midthirties, eager to please, and surprisingly friendly for a homicide detective, which put most people at ease and got them to open up to him, revealing far more than they would to anybody else with a badge. But from what I could see I didn't think the man Disher was talking to then was one of those people.

There were a couple of crime scene technicians taking pictures and gathering forensic evidence and trying very hard to look as cool as David Caruso and Marg Helgenberger while they worked. They weren't succeeding. They were too self-conscious about striking poses, and they didn't have the wardrobe, the stylists, or the buff bodies to pull it off.

Stottlemeyer wasn't trying to impress anyone. In fact, he looked wearier and more haggard than usual. His jacket and slacks were wrinkled and his bushy mustache needed trimming. He was standing with his hands on his hips, staring down at the body as we approached.

He acknowledged us with a quick glance and a nod.

"You didn't have to come all the way down here," Stottlemeyer said.

"We came for Mr. Monk's check," I said.

"It's back at the office," he said. "Stop by later this afternoon and I'll have it for you."

Monk crouched down to examine the body, holding his hands out in front of him like a movie director framing a shot with his thumbs.

"Mr. Monk thought if he helped you out here, we wouldn't have to wait until this afternoon."

He eyed me suspiciously. "It was Monk's idea."

"I might have given him some advice on the matter," I said. "The check is a week late as it is."

"The department keeps slashing my budget and I have to prioritize my spending," Stottlemeyer said. "I'm afraid consultants are at the bottom of the list."

"Then you can forget about getting any help from Mr. Monk today," I said. "He doesn't work for free."

"I don't need his help right now," Stottlemeyer said. "There's no mystery about what happened here."

"The guy on the floor burst into the room in the middle of class and pointed a gun at the professor," Monk said, standing up. "The gunman was about to shoot but the professor shot him first."

"That's exactly what happened," Stottlemeyer said. "It was a clear case of self-defense and we've got a lecture hall full of eyewitnesses to back it up."

"What was the professor doing with a gun?" Monk asked.

"He's a former federal prosecutor who put a lot of scary people away in his day," Stottlemeyer said. "He's licensed to carry a concealed weapon."

Monk looked to the front of the room. "Is that Professor Jeremiah Cowan?"

"Yeah, you know him?" Stottlemeyer said.

"I took his Introduction to Criminal Law class when I was at Berkeley."

"That's the class he was teaching today," Stottlemeyer said. "But I don't think the lesson the students got was on the syllabus."

Monk rolled his head as if trying to work out a kink in his neck. But I knew it wasn't his neck that was bothering him. The kink was in his mind. There was some detail that wasn't fitting where it should and that worried me.

"You're not working today, Mr. Monk," I said. "You haven't been paid."

"I'm not working," he said.

"Then what was this?" I rolled my head the way he did.

"It was nothing," he said.

"Of course it was nothing," Stottlemeyer said. "This case was closed before you got here. There's nothing left to do now but the paperwork."

"Good, then there's no reason you can't hurry back to the office to sign Mr. Monk's check."

Monk headed straight for Professor Cowan, who seemed to recoil at the sight of him approaching.

Stottlemeyer and I followed Monk, neither one of us too happy that he was getting himself involved in this.

"Oh my God," Cowan said. "It's Adrian Monk."

"You still remember me after all these years?" Monk said.

"Before each class, you drew lines on the chalkboard for me to write on," Cowan said. "You insisted that I use a fresh box of chalk. And you'd never let me erase the board; you had to do it yourself. It took you hours."

Monk looked at Stottlemeyer and me and shrugged

with false modesty. "I was kind of a teacher's pet. The entire faculty loved me."

"You're fortunate I wasn't carrying a gun in those days," Cowan said.

"Why were you carrying a gun today?" Monk asked.

"I always carry it," Cowan said. "But I had it within easy reach today because I've been getting these crazy, threatening e-mails lately from a student who believes I destroyed his life by giving him bad grades. He said that I would die for it."

Disher tipped his head towards the victim. "Was it him?"

"I presume so," Cowan said.

Disher narrowed his eyes. "Why?"

"Because he screamed, 'You ruined my life,' and then aimed his gun at me."

"Maybe there is more than one student who hates you," Disher said.

"There could be," Cowan said tightly.

"We don't make assumptions," Disher said. "We deal in facts."

"Of course," Cowan said. "How reckless of me."

"The guy who sent you the e-mails could be hiding behind a bush outside right now, waiting to leap out and garrote you as you leave the building."

"You should go check, Randy," Stottlemeyer said.

Disher stood there for a moment. "Really?"

Stottlemeyer glared at him.

"I'm going to go check the bushes." Disher pocketed his notebook and hurried away.

Stottlemeyer sighed and turned to Cowan. "Did you report the threats?"

"I informed the campus police and showed them the threatening e-mails," Cowan said. "But there wasn't much they could do. They traced the e-mails to the public computers at the campus coffeehouse. Anybody could have sent them."

Stottlemeyer gestured to the victim. "Do you recognize him? His name is Ford Oldman."

"He looks vaguely familiar but I have nearly a hundred students in this class alone, not counting the others that I teach," Cowan said. "I can't be expected to remember them all, semester after semester, year after year. There must be thousands."

"You remembered me," Monk said.

"You stood out," Cowan said. "Besides, this is only the second week of the class. I'm just getting to know the faces."

Monk rolled his shoulders. Another kink. Not a good sign. Stottlemeyer caught it, too.

"Yes, that makes perfect sense," Monk said in a robotic, completely unnatural way. "I couldn't be more convinced that what you are saying is true. There are no doubts in my mind. Captain, could I please speak to you for a moment about something that has nothing whatsoever to do with the murder of this student?"

"It wasn't murder," Cowan said. "It was self-defense. That's an important legal and moral distinction."

"You're right," Monk said in that same stilted voice. "I should have said self-defense murder."

"It wasn't murder at all," Cowan said, raising his voice an octave in exasperation.

Stottlemeyer took Monk by the arm and dragged him out of earshot of the professor. I tagged along because that's what I do. It's in my job description.

"What has gotten into you, Monk?" the captain asked.

"He's the guy," Monk said. "He's the killer."

"Yes, Monk, we know that," Stottlemeyer said. "That's not in dispute."

"It was murder, Captain."

"It was self-defense," Stottlemeyer said. "We've got a hundred eyewitnesses and they all tell the same story."

"That proves it," Monk said.

"That I'm right," Stottlemeyer said.

"That this was *premeditated* murder," Monk said.

I had no idea why Monk believed this shooting wasn't what it appeared to be but I'd long since learned he was always right when it came to murder.

"Mr. Monk doesn't work for nothing," I said. "If you want to hear more, you'll have to sign his check."

"But I don't want to hear more," Stottlemeyer said.

"When I took Introduction to Criminal Law, someone ran in, fired a shot at Professor Cowan, and ran out again," Monk said. "It scared everyone and was over in about ten seconds. He then questioned the students about what they saw and got all kinds of contradictory information. The shooting was just a dramatic stunt to demonstrate the unreliability of eyewitness testimony. But I got it right, of course."

"That was twenty years ago, Monk," Stottlemeyer said. "It's a coincidence."

"The shooting happened during the second week of my class, too. I can pull my lecture notes out and show you if you want."

"You still have them?" I asked.

"Of course I do," he said. "I've kept all my schoolwork, from nursery school through college."

"Why?"

"In case I need to refer back to it in situations like this."

"Do lots of your former teachers shoot people?" I asked.

"It happens," Monk said.

"I'm surprised none of them shot you," Stottlemeyer said.

"I'm also keeping them so I can donate my papers to the university when I die."

"I didn't know you had papers," I said.

"Everybody has papers," Monk said. "Mine have the advantage of already being indexed and cataloged according to the Dewey decimal system, which is why I could find my lecture notes for this class very easily if the captain wants them."

Stottlemeyer rubbed his temples. He was getting a Monk-ache.

"But this shooter wasn't firing blanks, Monk," Stottlemeyer said. "There were real bullets in his gun. Maybe the shooter picked this week on purpose as some kind of sick joke."

"Here's what happened—" Monk began, but I interrupted him.

"He doesn't get to hear what happened, because he hasn't paid you for last month's consulting," I said. "If you give him the benefit of your skills for free, he has no incentive to pay you in a timely fashion."

"You're right," Monk said, bit his lip, and then gave in to temptation anyway. It wasn't much of a battle. "Professor Cowan asked the student, Ford Oldman, to take part in his usual eyewitness stunt. But what Ford didn't know was that his gun was loaded and that he was being set up for his own murder. It was a nearly perfect and very risky plan, because if Professor Cowan hadn't shot first, he might have gotten himself killed."

"What was Professor Cowan's motive for murdering Oldman?" Stottlemeyer asked.

I spun Monk around and gave him a shove towards the door.

"That's all you get for free, Captain," I said. "You're on your own."

Before Monk could turn back, I grabbed him by the arm and practically dragged him out of the lecture hall.

"Do you want to get evicted from your apartment?" I asked. "Do you want to lose your assistant? You don't give away your expertise for free. You're running a business, Mr. Monk."

"But I don't know what the professor's motive is yet," Monk said.

"It doesn't matter," I said. "Let the police do some detective work for a change. They could use the practice."

2

Mr. Monk Picks Up His Check

When Monk doesn't have a case to investigate, he likes to clean his apartment and straighten up his belongings. The problem is that there is no cleaner, straighter place on earth than the twelve hundred square feet of San Francisco that he occupies. You're more likely to find microscopic signs of life on the surface of Mars than on his countertops. And you could use his apartment to calibrate every level-measuring device on earth.

So when he runs out of things to disinfect or balance at home, which happens within minutes, he'll start pleading with me to let him clean my house instead.

I know what you're thinking: You're wondering why I bother fighting with him about it. You would immediately say yes if your boss volunteered to thoroughly clean your house and pay you to sit around while he scrubbed.

But we're not talking about just anybody. We're talking about Adrian Monk. When he cleans your place, he practically strips it down to the studs and then puts everything back according to his arcane rules of order.

That may not sound so bad to you unless you've actually experienced it.

For example, after he empties and polishes my refrigerator, he puts all the leftovers, meat, fruit, and vegetables into individual plastic containers and Ziploc bags, labels them, and arranges them on the shelves by food group, size, and expiration date. (Call me crazy, but I don't see the point of putting an apple in a transparent bag and sticking a label on it that says, *Apple*.)

There is no food, not even a slice of chocolate cake, that looks appetizing once it's been air-locked in a Tupperware container and labeled. It becomes a scientific sample, and who wants to eat that?

He also rearranges all my furniture, all the decorations on my walls, and all the books and knickknacks on my shelves so that everything is centered, balanced, and symmetrical, regardless of what my personal tastes might be.

I think some casual disarray demonstrates character and makes a place feel lived-in.

But if Monk comes across something that doesn't fit in as he thinks it should, he throws it out, regardless of its monetary or sentimental value to me.

When he's done, it's still our stuff but the house doesn't feel like we live there anymore. It looks like a model home for a family of androids.

That's not even the worst of it.

As part of his cleaning, he goes through all my clothes, jewelry, medications, and toiletry items in detail, making me account for everything and justify its reason for being in my life, much less in my room, closet, or drawer.

I'm a pretty liberal and open person, and I spend most of my time with Monk, so it's not like there's much about me or my past that he doesn't know anyway. But everybody likes to keep a part of themselves to themselves, no matter how small or insignificant that part might be. That's impossible if you let Monk into your house, much less let him root around in your drawers.

My daughter, Julie, is at an age when she's especially protective of her privacy and refuses to allow me into her room unless she's in it, and even then I practically need to submit a request in writing along with a photo ID. She'd never forgive me if I let Monk into her room, though it's not likely to happen. She has a hamster, and even though it's in a cage, Monk is not about to enter her room unless he's wearing a haz-mat suit with its own air supply.

Despite all the problems and aggravations that come with letting Monk clean my house, sometimes I give in to his nagging anyway. It happens when I've been really busy or really lazy or both, the dirty dishes and laundry have piled up, and there's enough dust on the shelves that housecleaning would qualify as an archaeological dig.

The day after our visit to the university was one of those times.

The key to surviving a Monk housecleaning is not letting him do everything all at once. I strictly limit him to certain tasks or areas of the house, like cleaning the kitchen or doing the laundry. But even so, I still have to spend an agonizing amount of time and energy justifying things, like why I didn't incinerate a stained blouse instead of keeping it in my closet, where it could contaminate my other clothes.

"It's an old stain," I said. "It's not transferable."

I was sitting at the kitchen table, doing some important reading in the *Enquirer*. I was catching up on which stars were "flabulous" without makeup and photographic trickery to hide their belly fat and cellulite.

"Once a piece of clothing is stained, it attracts other stains," Monk said. "And insects. If you wear this, you're just asking to be infested with lice."

Monk was in the adjacent laundry room, wearing an

apron and dishwashing gloves as he folded my clothes. He wore the gloves in case he accidentally came into contact with bras or panties. It took me months to convince him he didn't need to wear protective goggles as well.

He pinched my blouse between his thumb and index finger and held it at arm's length, his head turned away from the garment as if it had been soaked in urine and infected with smallpox.

"It's one of my favorite blouses," I said. "I've had it for years. I wear it when I'm hanging around the house or doing messy projects because I don't have to worry about ruining it."

"With that insane attitude, why even bother washing it at all? Why don't you just roll around in dirt and excrement all day and hang it up again when you're done?"

"Maybe I will," I said, just to needle him a bit.

A moment later, I smelled smoke.

"What are you doing?" I whirled around to see him holding a lit match to the shirttail of my blouse, setting it aflame.

"Staging an intervention," Monk said, dangling my burning shirt over the laundry room sink. "You'll thank me later."

"You can't come into my house and burn my clothes," I told him. "How would you like it if I did that to you?"

"I begged you to burn a pair of my pants last week and you refused." He dropped the burning blouse into the sink before the flames could singe his fingers.

"I'm not going to incinerate a perfectly good pair of slacks because you found a cat hair on them," I said.

"That hair could have been home to a thousand fleas," Monk said.

"It wasn't."

"What if they are Africanized killer fleas? They could swarm my bed tonight and kill me in my sleep."

"There is no such thing as Africanized killer fleas," I said.

"There are Africanized killer bees," he said. "Who knows how many other insects have been Africanized? When you take me home tonight, we have to stop on the way and get some mosquito netting to put around my bed."

"Maybe you should get steel mesh instead."

"Good thinking," he said.

"What if poultry and livestock have been Africanized, too? How will you protect yourself from the hordes of Africanized killer chickens and Africanized killer cows?"

"Don't be ridiculous," Monk said.

"You're the one who brought up Africanized killer fleas," I said.

"Only to make an important point," he said.

"That it's okay for you to burn my stained clothes."

Monk sighed with relief. "I'm glad you're finally seeing reason."

The phone rang and I reached for it desperately, like a drowning woman grabbing a life preserver.

"Hello, this is Natalie," I said.

"It's me," Stottlemeyer said. "I've got Monk's check if you want to come down and get it. Otherwise, I can stick it in the mail to him."

"Don't move," I said. "We'll be right there."

"There's no hurry," he said.

I turned my back to Monk, cupped a hand over my mouth and the receiver, and whispered, "If we leave right this second, I think I can stop Mr. Monk from incinerating all of my clothes."

"You're not letting him do your laundry, are you?"

"It's your fault for not keeping him busy," I said.

"That's a big mistake. Let him wash your car or cut

your grass instead," Stottlemeyer said. "Otherwise, he could burn your house down."

Lieutenant Disher was standing at the Mr. Coffee machine, staring forlornly into his open wallet as we walked into the Homicide Department squad room. He brightened when he saw us.

"Hey, can either of you break a twenty?" he asked.

"What for?" I replied.

"I need some change to buy a cup of coffee."

"It's free, Randy."

"Not anymore," he said.

I glanced past him at the coffee machine on the table. There was a collection box now amidst the dozens of stained and chipped mugs that belonged to the detectives. A sign on the box said, COFFEE: $1.50.

"The department is imposing budget cuts across the board," Disher said. "It's getting brutal. They're even rationing our pens and pencils."

"There's a coffeehouse across the street," Monk said.

"Have you seen what they charge? It's cheaper to buy a tank of gas than a cup of their coffee," Disher said. "That's why I need some change."

"I'm sorry; I can't break a twenty," Monk said. "Not in good conscience."

I didn't get it, so I gave him a look.

"Randy gives you a twenty and you give him the same amount back in smaller bills," I said. "What's immoral or unethical about that?"

"Because I would have to give him a ten, eight singles, and eight quarters, just to keep the things even. I don't carry any five-dollar bills, of course."

"Of course," I said.

Monk once wrote a petition demanding that the U.S.

Mint remove the five-dollar bill from circulation and replace it with a four- or six-dollar bill. He'd stood for a week outside of a Wells Fargo bank soliciting signatures and got only one: mine. And that was given under extreme duress, so it doesn't count.

"Then Randy will use six of the quarters, or one of the dollar bills and two quarters, for the cup of coffee," Monk said. "That will leave him with eighteen fifty, an uneven amount composed of an uneven mix of bills and coins. It's anarchy."

We both stared at him. After a long moment, I turned to Disher.

"I can give you a dollar fifty, Randy."

Disher shook his head. "No, thanks. I think I need something stronger now than a cup of coffee."

"You can't," Monk said. "You're on duty."

"Then maybe I'll just shoot myself," Disher said, as he shoved his wallet in his pocket, and walked back to his desk outside of Stottlemeyer's office.

Monk looked after him with befuddlement. "What's his problem?"

There was no point in trying to explain it to him, so I simply headed for Stottlemeyer's glass-walled office, which gave the captain a commanding view of the squad room and no privacy whatsoever unless he closed the blinds.

Stottlemeyer was at his desk, doing some paperwork as we came in.

"That was quick," Stottlemeyer said, looking up at us. "How many traffic laws did you break getting down here?"

"I refuse to answer on the grounds that it might incriminate me," I said.

"Eight," Monk said.

I turned to him. "Eight?"

"Actually, it was seven, but since that's an uneven

number, I included the red light you drove through yesterday on the way to the university."

I leaned out the door of Stottlemeyer's office and called out to Disher, "After you shoot yourself, do you mind if I borrow your gun?"

"Be my guest," he said.

"Thanks." I turned back to Stottlemeyer. "Are you going to ticket me now?"

"Did you run over anybody?" he asked.

"No," I said.

"Then it's not my department." Stottlemeyer reached for an envelope on his desk and handed it to Monk. "Here's your paycheck, along with my personal apology for the delay."

"You've included a written apology?" Monk asked.

"No, I didn't," Stottlemeyer said. "I'm offering it to you now, in person."

"I'd prefer it in writing," Monk said.

Stottlemeyer glanced at me. "Could I have that gun when you're done with it?"

"You have your own," I said. "Speaking of guns, what's happening with that professor who shot a student?"

"We arrested him for murder this afternoon," Stottlemeyer said. "Ford Oldman, the student that he killed, was working on his dissertation and stumbled across some obscure paper that a legal scholar wrote in the early nineteen hundreds. The student noticed some similarities between passages in the paper and a chapter in one of Cowan's books, so he sent the professor a friendly e-mail asking him about it. There was no implied threat. All the kid was looking for was some additional insight."

"Instead he got a bullet," I said, pleased with myself for sounding so hard-boiled. Cops respected that. "Cowan didn't want to be outed as a plagiarist."

"It would have been especially embarrassing because Cowan wrote an opinion piece last year for the *San Francisco Chronicle* chastising politicians, students, and authors for passing off other people's work as their own." Stottlemeyer referred to a clipping on his desk. "Cowan called it 'an unacceptable erosion of academic standards that's led to the rampant intellectual dishonesty of public discourse.'"

"Hoist with his own petard," I said.

"Shhhhhh." Monk waved his hands frantically in front of my face. "How can you talk like that in front of an officer of the law! You should be ashamed of yourself. I hope you don't use that kind of profanity around your daughter."

"*Petard* isn't a profanity," I said.

He shushed me again with more waving.

"We don't use the 'p' word in civilized conversation," Monk said. "In fact, we don't use it at all. It's been banned."

"A petard is an explosive charge," I said. "It's not part of a man's anatomy."

That led to more red-faced shushing and hand waving from Monk.

"This is what happens when you wear dirty clothes," he said. "Pretty soon, you start talking dirty, too. Before you know it, you're smoking hashish, drinking hooch, and selling your body to sailors."

"I always wondered how women ended up that way," Stottlemeyer said. "Now I know."

"What about the threatening e-mails Cowan claimed that he got?" I asked.

"Cowan probably sent them to himself from the public terminals at the university's Internet café. We found witnesses who say he was in there all the time." Stottlemeyer turned to Monk. "The truth is, Cowan probably would have gotten away with the perfect murder if it weren't for you."

"You would have caught him," Monk said.

"I don't think so," Stottlemeyer said. "We're under-staffed and underfunded, so when an open-and-shut case comes along, we don't try to pry it open again; we just move along."

"I haven't seen you do that," Monk said.

"You're not here in the trenches every day, Monk. There's a lot you don't see."

"I see more than most people do," Monk said.

"That's true and it's that skill that brings up something else I need to talk to you about," Stottlemeyer said. "The department would like a favor from you."

"You're not asking me to deliver a baby, are you?"

"No," he said.

"Or shave the hair on somebody's back?"

"No," he said.

"Or milk a cow?"

"I have a suggestion, Monk. Instead of going through the endless list of things you don't want to do, how about letting me tell you what the favor is?"

"It doesn't involve chewing gum or spitting tobacco, does it?"

"The Conference of Metropolitan Homicide Detectives is being held in San Francisco this year and they want to interview you and me onstage tomorrow morning about our working relationship."

"Why?" Monk asked.

"Because we end up solving a lot of murders together," Stottlemeyer said.

"Would I have to be in front of an audience?"

Stottlemeyer nodded. "Just a couple hundred cops from around the country. But you won't be alone. I'll be up there with you."

Monk squirmed. "I'm not comfortable with public speaking."

"And I'm not comfortable rubbing other cops' noses

in our high case-closure rate," Stottlemeyer said. "But this request comes directly from the chief. I think he wants to gloat."

I spoke up. "Look at the bright side, Mr. Monk."

"There's never a bright side," he said.

"This means the police chief knows about your achievements and respects your abilities. He's proud of the work you are doing and wants to show you off," I said. "Speaking at this conference could be a big step towards getting reinstated to the force."

Monk looked at me and then at Stottlemeyer. "Do you think so?"

Stottlemeyer shrugged. "It never hurts to kiss up to the boss."

"Okay, I'll do it," Monk said. "As long as there isn't any actual kissing involved."

"There won't be," Stottlemeyer said. "And if any women go into labor, I'll deliver the baby."

3

Mr. Monk Answers Questions

The Dorchester Hotel was built in the 1920s by a particularly greedy and egotistical land baron named William K. Dorchester, who lived atop the twenty-story building in a ridiculously Gothic penthouse apartment and was known to use Powell Street below as his personal spittoon.

As a nod to Dorchester's British heritage, he insisted that the bellmen dress in the bright red beefeater uniforms with ruffled white collars and gloves worn by the guards of the crown jewels. The doormen still wear those uniforms today. They'd look classier dressed as SpongeBob SquarePants.

Once you get past them, there's a certain amusing and historically appropriate gaudiness to the place that is an accurate reflection of when it was built and the man who funded it.

The lobby has a vaulted gold-leafed ceiling and crystal chandeliers. The walls are covered with enormous murals that chronicle the arrival of the Spanish explorers, the Gold Rush, and maritime trade in San Francisco

Bay, with Dorchester himself looking down upon it all from the heavens like some benevolent god.

There's French and Italian marble on the floors, the columns, and the grand staircase. Supposedly, even the urinals in the men's room are carved from marble, though I have never seen them for myself. However, I can tell you that the women's room doesn't have marble toilets.

The Conference of Metropolitan Homicide Detectives was being held on the second floor, so Monk, Stottlemeyer, and I climbed the grand staircase and discovered that the gaudy grandeur ended at the top step.

The second floor looked like it had been renovated in the early seventies in garishly bright colors and hadn't been updated since. The Brady Bunch would have felt right at home there.

Monk, Stottlemeyer, and I made our way to the ballroom. It looked like we'd walked into a reunion of JCPenney men's department customers. The room was filled with potbellied men wearing off-the-rack suits, wide ties, and yellow crime-scene-tape-style name-tag lanyards around their necks.

We were greeted at the door by a man who looked like a cinder block that had magically come to life. He seemed square everywhere, from the flat-top buzz cut atop his head to the square-toed shoes on his feet. Even his hands looked square.

He introduced himself to us, even though his name was written on his lanyard and Stottlemeyer appeared, judging by the scowl on his face, to already know him and not like him much.

"I'm Detective Paul Braddock, Banning PD. I'll be your moderator," he said as he shook our hands in turn. "It will just be a simple Q and A. I'll start things off with a question or two and then open it up to the floor."

Monk motioned to me for a wipe. I took out a bottle

of instant hand sanitizer from my purse instead. I figured he'd be shaking a lot of hands and I didn't want to lug around a huge box of wipes or end up with a purseful of Baggies containing used ones.

"I'm Natalie Teeger, Mr. Monk's assistant," I said.

I squeezed a shot of disinfectant gel into Monk's right palm and he rubbed his hands together so briskly he could have lit kindling.

Braddock watched him, amused. "My God, you really do that. I thought it was just an urban legend. I guess I can scratch that question off my list."

"I'd like to see the others," Stottlemeyer said.

Braddock grinned. "That would be cheating, Leland."

"Since when do you have a problem with that, Paul?" Stottlemeyer asked pointedly.

"I wouldn't want to undercut the spontaneity of the discussion," Braddock said, his grin unfaltering. "See you up on the dais."

The detective walked away. Stottlemeyer glared after him.

"What was that all about?" I asked.

"He used to work for SFPD," Stottlemeyer said. "Now he doesn't."

"Are you the reason why?"

Stottlemeyer shook his head. "He's only got himself to blame for that."

We headed up to the dais, which was a raised platform with a table set against a backdrop of four potted plants.

The table was covered with a white cloth. There were three chairs behind the table and three glasses, one pitcher of water, and two microphones on top of it.

I saw disaster looming. I excused myself and sought out Braddock in the crowd.

"Excuse me," I said. "You're going to need to invite

another guest up to the table, and add another chair, glass, and two more microphones. Or you're going to have to remove a chair and a glass, add a microphone, and moderate standing up."

Braddock looked at me like I had a bug crawling out of my nose. "Why would I want to do that?"

"Because Mr. Monk won't sit at a table for three guests. He likes even numbers. So you can have two guests or four, it's up to you, but they each need to have their own microphone."

"You're joking," he said.

"I'm afraid not," I said.

"Is he nuts?"

"Mr. Monk likes things to be a certain way," I said. "You want him to be comfortable up there, don't you? Because if he's not, he won't answer any questions; he'll just obsess about everything that's wrong and try to fix it."

Braddock sighed. "I'll have the extra glass and chair taken away. I'll stand with a microphone."

"Thank you," I said, and went back to the table, where I discovered that Monk had already removed the extra chair and set the extra glass on top of it for the workers to take away.

Monk was now arranging the two chairs, the glasses, and the microphones so everything was evenly spaced, centered, and symmetrical.

Stottlemeyer was busy chatting with some other cops and trying hard to disassociate himself from what Monk was doing.

I couldn't blame him. I would have done the same thing if I weren't being paid not to.

The hotel workers showed up and took the extra chair away and set up a microphone stand for Braddock.

Monk was measuring the ends of the tablecloth with his pocket tape measure to make sure it draped evenly on all sides just as Braddock climbed up onstage.

"Okay, everyone, please take your seats," Braddock said into the mike. "We'd like to get started."

Monk and Stottlemeyer sat down at the table. I took a seat in the front row so I could jump onstage in an instant if there was a major emergency, like a wrinkle in the tablecloth or a spilled glass of water.

Braddock turned to Stottlemeyer and Monk. "Shall we begin?"

"We can't," Monk said.

"Why not?" Braddock replied.

"Everybody isn't here yet," he said.

Braddock looked out across the large conference room. "The room looks packed to me."

"There are three people missing."

"Friends of yours?"

"No," Monk said. "I don't know who they are. I just know they aren't here. There are two hundred and one people in the audience."

"That seems like a good size to me," Braddock said.

"Two hundred and two or two hundred and four would be better," Monk said. "Or you can ask one person to leave."

"I'll leave," Stottlemeyer said.

Braddock grimaced, waved over a busboy, and whispered in his ear. Within a few moments, the empty seats were filled with three busboys. He turned to Monk.

"Happy now?" Braddock asked.

"Aren't you?" Monk replied.

Braddock forced a smile, turned to the audience, and introduced himself. He then explained that for the last eight years the San Francisco Police Department had employed Adrian Monk as a special consultant, working exclusively with Captain Leland Stottlemeyer, the man who brokered the arrangement.

"What makes this consulting arrangement even more unusual is that ten years ago, Adrian Monk was an

SFPD homicide detective himself, until he was declared psychologically unfit for duty and forced to turn in his badge," Braddock said, then looked at Monk. "Are you still suffering from those problems?"

"I've been suffering since I was born," Monk said. "Life is suffering."

"He's got things under control," Stottlemeyer said, and took a sip of water. "Let's move on, Paul."

"How would you describe your working relationship?" Braddock asked.

"Professional and productive," Stottlemeyer said. "When we have a case that strikes me as particularly complex or unusual, I'll call him in for his unique perspective. Nobody analyzes a crime scene the way he does."

Monk took a sip of his water, placed his glass next to Stottlemeyer's, and squinted at the water level in each.

Braddock looked at Monk. "And you? How would you describe it?"

"It looks even to me," Monk said, double-checking the level in the water glasses with his tape measure.

"He means our working relationship," Stottlemeyer said, snatching the tape measure from his hand.

"That, too," Monk said.

"I'm an old-fashioned cop. I focus on standard investigative procedure, gathering the facts and the evidence," Stottlemeyer said. "Monk takes a different, more personal approach. He has an instinctive sense of how things should fit together, and when they don't, it really, really bothers him. He tries to organize things and along the way he finds clues that might get overlooked by traditional methods."

"How does he get paid?" Braddock asked.

"They issue me a check," Monk said. "It's in an envelope but I can assure you that nobody licks the seal, which, as you all well know, is an unsanitary and sickening practice engaged in by psychopaths, degenerates, and lunatics."

There was a long moment of silence as everyone stared at him.

Stottlemeyer took another sip of water and cleared his throat. "We guarantee him a minimum of eighteen cases a year and pay him on a per-case basis on anything beyond that."

"Not every case," Monk said.

"Every case that we call you in on," Stottlemeyer said.

"There are others?" Braddock asked.

"Sometimes Monk shows up at crime scenes without being called. I'm talking about routine cases that don't really require his expertise."

"You mean that you can handle on your own," Braddock said.

"We can handle any case on our own," Stottlemeyer said. "But there are some that are more difficult than others, and in those instances, we appreciate qualified help wherever we can get it, whether it's from other law enforcement agencies, journalists, civilian experts in various fields, or anybody else with relevant information or special insight."

Monk sipped his water, set his glass down next to Stottlemeyer's, and compared the two. He didn't like what he saw, though they looked even to me.

"And what happens when Mr. Monk shows up uninvited at the scene of one of these routine cases?" Braddock said.

"I solve them." Monk took another sip of water, so small it could have counted as evaporation. But this time when he compared the two glasses, he seemed satisfied. He sat back in his seat and relaxed.

Braddock looked at Stottlemeyer. "So he does your job for you even on the small cases and doesn't charge you for it. Lucky you."

"When Monk solves a murder, it's good for the citizens of San Francisco whom we protect and serve," Stottlemeyer said. "It's not about me."

Stottlemeyer took another sip of water, much to Monk's obvious consternation.

"In fact, Mr. Monk solves a lot more murder cases than he's paid for," Braddock said. "In the last seven years, Mr. Monk has personally solved nearly a hundred and fifty homicides and your department's closure rate has reached an incredible ninety-four percent."

"That's all?" Monk said. "We should be ashamed of ourselves."

Monk narrowed his eyes at his glass, picked it up, and took a carefully measured sip, then set it back down next to Stottlemeyer's.

The captain glared at Monk. "Most police departments are lucky if they can clear half their murder cases. Our closure rate is thirty percent higher than the national average."

"Explain the six percent of murders in San Francisco that haven't been solved," Monk said.

Stottlemeyer motioned to Braddock. "He's asking the questions, Monk."

"They must have been cases nobody showed me," Monk said. "If you give them to me now, I'll solve them."

"They're not for you. They're mostly gang shootings and drug-related murders," Stottlemeyer said. "We've got detectives with a thorough understanding of gang culture and a lot of experience on the streets handling those cases."

Stottlemeyer picked up his glass, drank all of the water, and slammed it back down on the table so hard I thought it might break.

"But they're not solving them," Monk said. "I will. I'm streetwise. I'm down with those hepcats."

Laughter rippled through the audience. Stottlemeyer was visibly embarrassed for Monk and shifted uncomfortably in his seat. So did I but there wasn't anything either one of us could do to help him.

"Are you saying that you're infallible, Mr. Monk?" Braddock asked.

"No," Monk said. "There is one case I haven't been able to solve."

"Next question," Stottlemeyer said bluntly, and looked out into the audience. "I'm sure somebody out there has a question they'd like to ask."

I could have hugged him for that. He always tried to protect Monk from pain, self-inflicted and otherwise.

A detective stood up. "I'm Zev Buffman, Owensboro, Kentucky, PD. I got one. What was the department's homicide closure rate before Monk began consulting with you?"

"I'm afraid I don't have those figures in front of me," Stottlemeyer said.

"I do," Braddock said. "It was forty-three-point-five percent. How do you explain that, Captain?"

I think Stottlemeyer would have liked to explain it by punching Braddock in the face. Instead, he took a more diplomatic approach.

"There were lots of factors, Paul. Violent crime and homicide rates in the city were way up and at the same time we were understaffed and underfunded. The department cut four million dollars from the overtime budget, resulting in a hundred and ninety-five thousand fewer overtime hours, and forty-eight officers either quit or took early retirement. You can't solve crimes without time and manpower. The city eventually restored our overtime budget and the homicide rate fell, but history is repeating itself now. Murders are up twenty percent from last year and our budget is being slashed."

Monk took the pitcher and carefully poured enough

water into Stottlemeyer's glass to bring the water level even with his own glass.

"You can't recall the stats but you've got all the excuses down cold," Braddock said.

"I easily forget statistics but I never forget when my detectives are treated badly."

"Do you know what the SFPD's homicide closure rate was when Mr. Monk was still on the force?" Braddock asked.

"No, but I bet you do," Stottlemeyer said.

"It was seventy-seven percent," Braddock said. "And Mr. Monk himself had a hundred and twenty percent closure rate."

"A hundred and twenty percent?" a female detective said from the audience. "How is that even possible?"

"I solved my own cases and ones that weren't assigned to me," Monk said.

"Like you do now," Braddock said.

"I like to keep busy," Monk said.

"How interesting," Braddock said. "What is your personal case-closure rate, Captain?"

"I don't know, but I'm sure it's less than his and I am not ashamed to admit that," Stottlemeyer said. "Monk is the best detective I have ever known, perhaps the best ever. He could outperform anybody in this room. We're lucky to have him."

"That's an understatement," Braddock said. "Right now, your closure rate is the envy of every department in the country. But without Adrian Monk, what would it be?"

Monk leaned close to the captain. "Would this be a bad time to ask for a raise?"

He didn't mean it as a joke, because he doesn't have a sense of humor, but that was how the audience took it anyway. They broke into uproarious laughter that

drowned out the exchange between Monk and Stottlemeyer that followed. But I heard it.

"I don't get it," Monk said. "What's the joke?"

"Me," Stottlemeyer said. He picked up Monk's glass
and drank all of his water.

4

Mr. Monk Has Good Friends

There was no way Monk could drink out of his glass again and Stottlemeyer knew it. The only recourse Monk had was to keep both glasses filled at the same level no matter which glass the captain drank from.

That plan might have worked if Stottlemeyer hadn't taken the pitcher of water and emptied it into one of the potted plants behind them.

Now all Monk could do was pray that the captain wouldn't dare knock the entire universe out of balance by taking a sip of water from either glass.

But the fear that Stottlemeyer might do it anyway virtually paralyzed Monk, who couldn't take his eyes off the glasses, as if he were willing the water to harden into solid ice.

Luckily, someone in the audience stood up and asked Monk and Stottlemeyer to talk about some of their most unusual and puzzling cases, so the interview ended on a more or less positive note before Braddock could get another dig in.

"All in all, I think that went well," Monk said as we left the hotel and stepped onto Powell Street.

Stottlemeyer nodded. "Compared to being burned at the stake, tarred and feathered, or stoned to death, I suppose it did."

"You seemed a bit edgy," Monk said.

"Did I?"

"Things got a little dicey with the water but I had your back," Monk said. "You could have been humiliated in front of all your colleagues."

"I'm glad that didn't happen," Stottlemeyer said. "Thanks for sparing me any embarrassment."

Monk was oblivious to the captain's sarcasm, so it was probably unavoidable that whatever he said next would only make things worse.

"Think nothing of it," Monk said. "That's what friends are for."

Stottlemeyer turned to me. "I appreciate you asking that question about our most interesting cases."

"It was either that or throw something at your moderator," I said. "What was Braddock's problem?"

"He was only asking what most of the cops in the room were already thinking."

"It was personal, Captain," I said.

"I didn't take it that way," Stottlemeyer said.

He was lying, of course. But there was nothing to be gained by challenging him on it and I didn't have the time. We were running later than I'd anticipated and I'd already have to break a few traffic laws if Monk was going to make it on time to his appointment with his shrink. So we went our separate ways.

Ever since Dr. Kroger passed away, Monk had been seeing Dr. Neven Bell. They weren't quite as close as Monk and Dr. Kroger had been but I saw that as a good thing. It seemed to me that the less dependent Monk was on his shrink, the closer he was to being a rational, independent person.

While Monk unloaded his troubles on Dr. Bell, I took a

walk up the street, which was so steep that steps were cut into the sidewalk. I liked the walk; it got my blood pumping and I was rewarded with a nice view of the city when I got to the top.

Monk hated the street, and all the others like it in San Francisco, because the Victorian houses were staggered against the incline. But at least he no longer insisted on being blindfolded to avoid the sight. I guess that was progress.

I thought about the flaying that Stottlemeyer endured at the conference and felt bad that we hadn't done a better job of defending him (though I knew Monk would have argued that he'd done his share by maintaining the water level of the glasses).

Braddock didn't say anything that was untrue but he could have made the same points without turning it into an attack on Stottlemeyer's character and competence.

Monk wouldn't have been working for the SFPD at all if not for Stottlemeyer. The captain didn't bring Monk in to boost his case-closure rate, or to make himself look good. He did it because he was the one person in San Francisco who cared about Monk, regardless of his psychological problems.

Stottlemeyer hired him as a consultant to save Monk from a life of isolation and misery. It was a wonderful act of friendship and kindness, and probably cost the captain whatever political capital he'd saved up during his career. So it infuriated me to see what he did for Monk used as a weapon against him.

I couldn't undo the damage that was done to Stottlemeyer at the conference but at least I could offer him some friendly consolation. So on the way back to Dr. Bell's office, I called the captain and invited him for coffee after we both got off work.

Neither one of us had a significant other waiting at home, so I knew he didn't have any real excuses to decline my invitation. Call me immodest, but I was pretty sure that spending time with me had to be better than going home to an empty apartment and leftovers in the fridge.

Besides, after what he'd endured today, he probably needed someone to talk to, whether he admitted it or not.

Stottlemeyer met me at a Starbucks near my house in Noe Valley, a quirky neighborhood that had upscaled around me since I bought my fixer-upper that I never got around to fixing up. I kept waiting for the Neighborhood Watch Committee to march on my house with torches to drive me away because I don't have breast implants, a German car, or an iPhone. What saved me was that I was a thin, natural blonde with a perky smile, but I knew that wouldn't hold them off for much longer.

The captain and I forked over an inordinate sum of money to the barista for two cups of coffee and settled into two lumpy, mismatched, wing-backed chairs.

He'd taken off his tie and opened the top two buttons of his shirt, exposing the collar of his V-neck undershirt. He looked terrible.

"So what's the occasion?" Stottlemeyer asked.

"I thought you might want to talk after what happened today," I said.

"There isn't really anything to talk about."

"We could talk about the lie you told me," I said.

"Which one?" he said with a smile. "I lose track."

"When you said that you didn't take Braddock's questions personally," I said. "He was out to get you. What happened between you two?"

"We have a different approach to policing. I follow the law and he'll do whatever he has to do to make a case, even if it means trampling over people's rights. Or over the people themselves," Stottlemeyer said. "I gave him a choice: He could quit the SFPD or I would go to Internal

Affairs with what I knew about him and he could take his chances with them. So he left for a job in Banning. That was eight years ago."

"So this was his opportunity to finally get even with you," I said.

"Then he blew his shot. All he said was that Monk is a better detective than I am. That's not exactly a revelation."

"But it must hurt anyway," I said.

"I'm proud of Monk's success," Stottlemeyer said.

"Even if it overshadows your own?"

"I'm the captain of the division, Natalie. It's my job to bring out the best in the people who work for me and that includes Monk. I get the blame when they screw up and the chief gets the credit when they succeed. That's the nature of the job. The important thing is that the bad guys are getting caught."

"You *do* bring out the best in Mr. Monk. It's because of you that he's able to solve crimes at all," I said. "But I wonder if you really give yourself the credit you deserve."

"Sure I do," Stottlemeyer said. "Every time Monk outsmarts some clever killer with an airtight alibi I congratulate myself for not listening to the bureaucrats and shrinks who wanted to write him off."

"Yeah, but I've seen your face when Mr. Monk solves a case on the spot," I said. "I've also heard you beat yourself up for not seeing the clues yourself. You did it again yesterday over the Professor Cowan case."

"I wish I were as sharp-eyed as he is. I'm not. So I'm glad Monk is there to catch the crooks who might've walked because I'm not the detective that he is," Stottlemeyer said. "But the truth is, I wouldn't want to be. The price is too high."

"You mean his obsessive-compulsive disorder."

"I mean all the things that Monk is missing out on,"

Stottlemeyer said. "Simple pleasures like licking an ice-cream cone, swimming in a lake, going to a ball game, laughing at a good joke, petting a dog, smoking a cigar, playing with your kids, camping in the woods, driving a car, or having coffee with a friend. I have a life. What does Monk have?"

"You and me and his brother, Ambrose," I said.

"It's sad," Stottlemeyer said.

"But his inability to enjoy the things you mentioned, and to establish relationships, that's all a symptom of his disorder."

"And it's the disorder that makes him a great detective," Stottlemeyer said. "It's all he's got in his life besides his constant cleaning and organizing. I have a family. I know I am good at what I do but my self-esteem isn't wrapped up in how many cases I solve. I measure myself by the kind of men my sons are growing up to be, by the strength of my friendships, and by the respect of my peers."

"They weren't showing you much respect today," I said.

Stottlemeyer shrugged. "They may have been onto something. Maybe I've become overdependent on Monk. Maybe I've gotten lazy knowing he's there to back me if I screw up. Maybe so have my men. I don't know."

We sipped our coffees for a moment in silence. Stottlemeyer regarded me with a curious look on his face. I met his gaze.

"What?" I asked.

"Is everything okay with you?"

"Why do you ask?"

"Because of this sudden concern over whether my self-esteem is taking a beating."

"I only asked because of the grilling you took today," I said.

"We've known each other a long time, Natalie. I

didn't tell you anything about myself tonight that you didn't already know. So I've got to wonder if this has less to do with me and more to do with something you're trying to work out about yourself."

"Are you a detective or a shrink?"

"In my job, you have to be a little bit of both," Stottlemeyer said. "And I spent a lot of time in marriage counseling."

I set down my coffee cup and looked him in the eye.

"Who am I, Captain?"

"I don't know what you're getting at."

"When you look at me, who do you see?"

"A confident, independent woman who knows how to take care of herself and others."

"Gee, if I could sing, I'd be Mary Poppins."

"So who do you want to be?" he asked.

I sighed, suddenly feeling very tired, despite the high-priced caffeine surging through my veins. "Someone who knows the answer to that question."

Stottlemeyer nodded.

"I've got an old friend I haven't seen in a while. His name is Bill Peschel. I'm going to visit him tomorrow," he said. "If you really want to help me out, you'll come along."

I couldn't see what visiting his friend had to do with my concern over how Stottlemeyer felt about being negatively compared to Monk in front of his peers. But I couldn't turn him down.

"I'd have to bring Mr. Monk," I said.

"The more the merrier," he said.

When I got home, Julie was sitting cross-legged at the kitchen table, going over a social sciences textbook with a yellow highlighter and eating Wheat Thins out of the box.

I bought the Wheat Thins for Monk so he'd have

something to nosh on when he visited. He likes them because the crackers are perfectly square.

"Those are for Mr. Monk," I said. "And he'll never eat them if he knows your hand was inside the box."

"Don't tell him," she said.

"He'll know," I said.

"How?"

"He's a brilliant detective. And he's probably counted the crackers that were left in the box. And he's probably measured the opening he cut into the bag. And he can probably correlate that opening with the width of your hand and deduce that you were the one who breached it."

"He's a nut job," Julie said.

"I thought you liked Mr. Monk and admired his abilities," I said, and reached into the box for a few crackers. The damage was already done.

"I do," she said. "But c'mon, Mom, he's seriously messed up."

"Aren't we all," I said.

"I'm not," she said.

"Give it time," I said.

"Gee, thanks."

"Face it, honey. No one gets out of childhood unscathed, though you have a better shot than most, since you are being raised by the most loving, understanding, and, dare I say it, coolest mother on earth."

"If that were true, you'd let me get a tattoo."

"There is no artist good enough to use you as his canvas." I didn't want her walking around with a tramp stamp on her lower back.

"You have a tattoo," she said.

"And I regret it," I said. "I'm just glad it's where no one can see it."

"Not lately," Julie said. "Speaking of which, how was your date with Stottlemeyer?"

I couldn't believe how sassy and presumptuous Julie

was getting with me. Then again, she wasn't a little girl anymore. She was a woman. And she wasn't stupid, either. Julie knew I wasn't celibate.

Refusing to let her get a tattoo was my last, desperate stand for parental control. In a few months, she'd be an adult as far as the State of California was concerned and wouldn't need my permission for anything. She could tattoo her entire body, color her hair purple, drop out of school, join the French Foreign Legion, or run off and marry a guy she'd known for only an hour.

Her imminent freedom to make all kinds of mistakes was something I tried not to think about or I might start hyperventilating. It was better to concentrate on the subject at hand, which was my completely innocent and chaste encounter with Captain Stottlemeyer.

"It wasn't a date," I said. "It was two friends having a cup of coffee and it was very nice, thank you. He's really a sweet, sensitive man under that gruff-cop exterior."

"He's too old for you, Mom."

"I'm not interested in him romantically. He's someone I can talk to."

"That's what your female friends are for," she said. "Your posse."

"I don't have a posse," I said. "Besides, he knows better than anybody else the unique problems I have to deal with. We share a common bond."

"You're both over thirty and single?"

"We both care deeply about Adrian Monk," I said.

"You're like two divorced parents who share custody of him," she said.

"We're the closest thing Mr. Monk has to a family," I said.

"What about his brother?"

"He never leaves the house," I said. "We're the ones who see him every day. And with that caring and commitment comes a certain amount of responsibility and aggravation."

"Because he's a nut job," Julie said.

"Because he's special," I said. "Like you."

I gave her a kiss on the head and mussed her hair up.

"I'm nothing like Mr. Monk," she said.

"You don't think you give me aggravation?"

"Not half as much as you give me," she said.

"That's a mother's job," I said.

"Then you're very good at it," she said, gifting me with a big smile.

It was nice to know I was good at something.

5

Mr. Monk and the Bartender

Mill Valley is a bedroom community across the Golden Gate Bridge from San Francisco in woodsy Marin County. For much of the seventies and eighties, the town was known primarily for the swinging that went on in those bedrooms, hot tubs, and any other place any number or combination of consenting adults gathered.

The only thing notorious about Mill Valley now was how expensive the homes were. Everything started at a million. I couldn't even afford a birdhouse there.

Bill Peschel lived with his daughter, Carol Atwater, her husband, Phil, and their two children in a three-bedroom, ranch-style house on a street with landscaping so manicured and sidewalks so clean that they brought a smile to Monk's face.

Stottlemeyer was leaning against the hood of his police-issued Crown Vic at the curb and chewing on a toothpick when we arrived. I parked alongside the gleaming Mercedes SUV in the driveway and got out. On the back window of the SUV was an inscription in stickered white letters that read, IN LOVING MEMORY OF CLARA PESCHEL.

I don't understand the point of those automotive memorials. How does buying yourself a nice car celebrate the memory of a loved one? I almost always see those memorials on sports cars or supercarrier-sized SUVs. Does making your Porsche or Hummer a rolling grave marker for your dead family member somehow justify the gas-guzzling indulgence? Or are those memorials actually for people the driver has killed with his car?

To me, those memorials are even stupider than the yellow BABY ON BOARD warning signs, which imply you might have considered smashing into the car if you weren't alerted that an innocent child was a passenger.

The SUV had one of those signs, too. And two child seats in the back.

"Clara was Bill's wife," Stottlemeyer said, following my gaze.

"So why dedicate a car to her?" I asked.

"Maybe her daughter bought it with her inheritance and wanted to acknowledge the gift," Stottlemeyer said.

"I think it's weird," I said. "So who is this guy we've come to see?"

"Bill was one of my most reliable snitches," Stottlemeyer said. "He used to own a dive bar in the Tenderloin. He sold out ten years ago, retired to Sarasota, and then, after his wife died, he moved back here to live with his daughter."

Monk squatted beside the lawn and admired the neatly trimmed, bright green grass. "I'd like to get the name of their gardener."

"But you don't have a yard," I said.

"I'd just like to compliment him on his fine work," Monk said.

I turned to the captain. "Do you visit Bill often?"

"I try to make it out here once a month or so."

"Are you this close to all your snitches?"

"His tips helped me solve a lot of big cases," Stottlemeyer said. "I might not be a captain today if it weren't for him."

I looked at Monk. "Did you know him?"

"I didn't use confidential informants," Monk said.

"You didn't need to," Stottlemeyer said.

I pointed at him. "There, that's exactly what I was talking about last night."

"You saw each other last night?" Monk asked.

I ignored him and pressed my point. "You make self-deprecating remarks like that about your investigative abilities all the time. It reveals your feelings of insecurity and inferiority."

"I prefer to think of it as stating the facts in a dispassionate and totally candid manner," Stottlemeyer said, then turned to Monk. "Yes, we had coffee last night."

"Why did you do that?"

"Because I like coffee and getting together with my friends," the captain said. "It's something human beings do, Monk. It's called socializing. You ought to try it sometime."

"With other people?" he said.

"That's the idea," I said.

He shook his head. "That's how communicable diseases are communicated. Socializing should be done only under the strict supervision of a doctor in a sterile environment."

"Sounds like fun," Stottlemeyer said, and headed for the door.

It sounded like the creepy pictures I'd seen of Thanksgiving at the Monk household when he was a child. The dining room table, the floor, and the seat cushions were covered with protective plastic. His mother served them turkey cold cuts with a pair of tongs that she held with rubber-gloved hands like either the meat or the children were radioactive.

"More important, it's sanitary," Monk said, and we trailed after the captain.

Stottlemeyer rang the bell and the door was opened by a woman who had the harried look that defines early motherhood. Any mother can recognize it, because she's looked the same way. It's a mix of weariness, confusion, and exasperation that comes from trying to do fifteen things at once while taking care of your inexhaustible, demanding, and uncontrollable kids.

Carol Atwater was in her early thirties, thin but bordering on chubby, still carrying a few of those stubborn pregnancy pounds. She was dressed in designer-label casual clothes that were too expensive to really be casual in.

"Hello, Captain," she said.

"Please, Carol, call me Leland," he said, then tipped his head towards us. "These are my friends Adrian Monk and Natalie Teeger."

"I have to warn you, things are a little crazy here this morning," she said. "Actually, it's been that way ever since Dad moved in."

"Anything I can do to help?" Stottlemeyer asked.

"You're doing it just by being here and getting him off my back for a few minutes," she said, stepping aside to let us in. "It's great when you or some of the other cops come by. I can only sit around drinking with him for so long."

"I hear you," Stottlemeyer said.

I wasn't sure that I did. I'd known her for only five seconds, but she already didn't strike me as the kind of woman who'd hang out with her dad having cocktails all day.

"Dad is where he always is," she said, gesturing ahead of us.

The entry hall led into a family room that was cluttered with children's toys. There was a fireplace, a big-screen TV mounted on the wall, and an overflowing toy box in one corner. A pair of French doors opened to the backyard, where I could see a swimming pool ringed by a wrought-iron fence and the sprinklers watering the impossibly green lawn around it.

A baby girl in a T-shirt and diaper sat on a blanket in the center of the room and teethed happily on a plastic doughnut. She was smiling and drooling all over herself. I wanted to steal her and take her home with me.

Monk kept his distance, as if the child were a ferocious dog.

The family room was separated from the open kitchen by a long counter with four bar stools in front of it.

Bill Peschel stood behind the kitchen counter, drying some glasses with a towel. He looked to me to be in his late sixties or early seventies. He wore an apron over his sunken chest and broad belly. Tufts of hair sprang from his nearly bald head like patches of dry, overgrown weeds. His nicotine-stained teeth were almost the same color as his weathered skin.

Behind him, on the opposite counter, was a row of unlabeled bottles filled with water. He motioned us over with a sweep of his bony arm.

"Howdy, folks, come on in," he said. "There's plenty of room up here at the bar or you can help yourself to a table."

He motioned in the general direction of the baby.

Carol lifted up the baby, sniffed the diaper, and made a face.

Monk gasped in horror. "Are you insane?"

"Did that old drunk wet herself again?" Peschel said. "Show her the door, will you please, Bev? She's scaring away the customers."

The way he said it, he might have been joking. But I had a feeling he wasn't. For one thing, he called his daughter Bev and her name was Carol.

"I'm going to go change the baby and see if I can put her down for a nap," Carol said.

"Take your time," Stottlemeyer said to her, then sat down on one of the stools and smiled at Peschel. "I'd like a gin and tonic, please. My partner here will have a beer."

"You can't do that, Captain. You're on duty and I don't drink," Monk said. "The only alcohol that passes my lips is in mouthwash and I spit it right out again."

Stottlemeyer shushed Monk with a wave of his hand.

"Stuck with another rookie?" Peschel asked Stottle-meyer.

"Afraid so," Stottlemeyer said.

Peschel took a coffee mug from amidst the baby bottles in the dish strainer, filled it up with water at the sink, and set it down in front of Monk, who seemed very confused.

"Drink up, Boy Scout," Peschel said. "Put some hair on your chest."

"I don't want hair on my chest, among other places," Monk said. "But this isn't a beer. It's tap water."

Peschel grinned at Stottlemeyer. "The kid talks tough, but I don't see him drinking it. You want a chaser with that?"

"He's fine." Stottlemeyer glared at Monk, trying to get him to play along. But make-believe wasn't something Monk was good at.

I sat on the stool beside Monk, took a sip from his mug, and wiped away the imaginary foam from my lips. "Tastes fine to me."

Peschel smiled. "Are you a working girl, honey?"

"No," I said. "Just thirsty and lonely."

"I've got nothing against your trade," he said. "But whatever you score in here, I get a ten percent commission."

He winked at me and moved down the counter to Stottlemeyer.

"How's business?" the captain asked him.

"Slow." Peschel reached for one of the unlabeled bottles of water behind him and poured a splash into a glass, then added a shot from another bottle. He put a napkin down in front of Stottlemeyer and set the glass on top of it. "Besides that drooling old drunk, hardly anybody has been in tonight."

"So you called me down here for nothing," Stottlemeyer said. "Except some refreshment."

"I didn't say that." Peschel set a bowl of animal crackers in front of Stottlemeyer and leaned close. "Hy Conrad was in here the other night, shooting his mouth off. He was bragging about the Jewelry Mart smash-and-grab."

"That's small-time stuff. I'm in Homicide now." Stottlemeyer nursed his drink as if it packed a punch. "That kind of news isn't worth the cost of this watered-down booze you serve."

"I'm just getting warmed up," Peschel said. "What if I told you a fancy lady came in here looking for someone to kill her rich husband and make it look like an accident?"

"Why would she come to you?" Monk asked.

"I've been tending bar here for a long time," Peschel said. "I know people who know people."

"In a residential neighborhood?" Monk said. "That can't be legal. Do you have a liquor license to be selling alcohol out of your home?"

"I was tending bar here while you were still sucking your mama's teat," Peschel said.

The blood drained out of Monk's face. "I never did that. What a disgusting, horrible thing to say. Captain, arrest this man."

Stottlemeyer motioned to me to get Monk out of there. I tugged Monk's sleeve.

"I saw some crooked pictures in the hall," I said. "Maybe you could straighten them."

"I'd like to straighten him," Monk said, as I hooked my arm in his and led him away. "He's crazy."

Peschel called after me, "Don't forget my commission, sweetheart."

Once we were in the entry hall, out of earshot, I said, "Mr. Peschel's got Alzheimer's or something like that. He thinks he's still a bartender and that this is the tavern he used to own. You have to play along."

"I don't know how," Monk said.

"Well, for one thing, you don't contradict him."

"Then how is he ever going to learn the truth?"

"He's not, Mr. Monk. This is his truth."

"How sad." Monk glanced at him, then back to me. "At least he still knows who he is."

That was when I realized why Stottlemeyer had dragged me here. It wasn't to help him. It was for me, to put my troubles in perspective.

Peschel knew who he was—he had a vocation that defined him—but in every other way, he was lost. He didn't know where he was in time or space or even who he was with. All he knew was that he was a bartender. But I'm sure he would have traded that certainty for all the other connections that made his life rich and that he didn't have now. I had everything Peschel didn't. So what did I have to complain about?

I guess Stottlemeyer was trying to tell me to be thankful for what I had. Maybe he was trying to tell me I was a self-indulgent whiner. Or was there an entirely different message for me in all of this?

6

Mr. Monk's Life Is Changed Forever

While I was thinking about why Stottlemeyer had brought me to meet Peschel, Monk had worked his way down the hall, methodically straightening the pictures that I couldn't tell were actually crooked.

I caught up with him passing the open door to a boy's bedroom. I peeked inside. The boy had a bed that looked like a racing car, there were plastic racing tracks all over his floor, and every flat surface was covered with toy cars of different sizes. I pegged his age at about five or six, based on his toys and the pajamas that were on the floor.

The next room across was his sister's. The walls were covered with pictures of cartoon characters and there were stuffed animals on the floor around her crib.

Carol stood at the changing table, closing the adhesive on the fresh disposable diaper that she'd put on her squirming baby.

"Your daughter is adorable," I said. "It's such a wonderful age."

"Yes and no," she said. "I am looking forward to the day when I can sleep again and wear blouses that don't have puke on the shoulders."

"At least she isn't asking you if she can get a tattoo," I said. "And you can cuddle her all you want without her trying to escape."

"Would you like to hold her?"

I reached out my arms. "Desperately."

"You should put on gloves first," Monk said. "And a face mask. We all should."

"Why?" Carol asked.

"The baby," Monk said.

"The baby will be fine," Carol said.

"It's not the baby that I'm worried about," Monk said. "It's the rest of us."

"I'll risk it," I said.

Carol lifted the baby into my arms. The child had that wonderful infant scent of talcum powder, baby formula, and pure lovableness that makes me instinctively feel warm all over. I looked into her bright eyes and playfully rubbed noses with her and was rewarded with a big, toothless smile.

Monk cringed and looked away, his gaze locking on something on the floor beside the changing table. He cocked his head from side to side, trying to figure out what he was looking at.

It was a white plastic container that resembled a large thermos. I recognized it immediately, of course, as any parent would.

"What is that?" Monk asked.

"It's a Diaper Genie," Carol said. "You put a disposable diaper inside, twist the dial that's around the opening, and it seals the diaper in a plastic bag."

I had one of those when Julie was a baby. It meant I didn't have to wash cloth diapers like my mother did or deal with a garbage can full of disposables. Even emptying the Genie wasn't too unpleasant. All you had to do was open the bottom of the Genie over a trash bag or your outdoor garbage can, and the sealed diapers came out in one large string resembling plastic-wrapped sausage links.

Now, thanks to the Diaper Genie, my daughter can claim a small measure of immortality—her dirty diapers will endure for centuries in a landfill somewhere for future anthropologists and archaeologists to examine for clues about how she lived.

"How sturdy are the bags?" Monk asked.

"The bags are triple-layered to hold in the smell and the germs," Carol said, handing him one of the cartridges of refill bags. "It's a godsend for mothers."

"For us all," Monk said.

He studied the cartridge with wide-eyed wonder. "So let me get this straight. Are you saying that whatever you put inside this Genie is individually wrapped and sealed?"

She nodded. "I only use it for diapers and dirty wipes."

"But you could use it for other things," Monk said.

"Like what?"

"Everything you throw out," Monk said.

"Why would I want to do that?"

"It would save you the time of manually separating and bagging all the items in your trash."

"Who does that?" Carol asked.

"Who doesn't?" Monk replied, then held his hand out to me. "Wipe." My hands were full with the baby, so Carol handed him a wipe from the box on the changing table.

He cleaned his hands, dropped the tissue into an open bag in the Diaper Genie, and twisted the outer ring, which cinched the bag shut and opened a new one.

His eyes sparkled with joy.

"Wow," he said, then motioned to me for another wipe.

Carol handed him the box and then gestured for me to follow her into the hallway.

"Now I see why the captain brought you," she said.

"Why?" I asked.

She glanced at Monk, who wiped his hands again and dropped the tissue into the Diaper Genie. "You're dealing with the same problem that I am."

I shook my head and bounced the baby. "Mr. Monk isn't suffering from dementia. He's just eccentric."

"That's what we used to say about my dad. He thinks he's still running his bar. Most of the cops he used to know hang up on him when he calls in the wee hours of the night with his tips. The few who visit rarely come back a second time. It's too depressing."

"What about his old customers?"

"They are either dead, in jail, or people I would never allow to set foot in my house."

I thought about how he mistook the baby for an old drunk and me for a hooker. If that was any reflection on his clientele, Carol's unwillingness to invite them into her home made a lot of sense.

"It must be hard on you, taking care of him and your kids," I said. The baby grabbed my nose and gave it a squeeze. I made a face and she giggled with glee.

"The mornings aren't so bad. My son is in preschool until after lunch. When I bring him home, that's when it becomes a menagerie around here," she said. "Dinnertime is especially hard. It's hell to cook dinner with my dad installed in the kitchen, running his bar, and having conversations from twenty years ago with people who aren't there. It entertains the kids, though."

"How does your husband handle it?" I asked, my nose once again in the baby's surprisingly strong grip.

"He's great. Phil sits at the counter and lets Dad make him drinks all night," she said. "But we know soon he will become too much for us to handle and he'll need assisted living. Thank God those huge dividends from Dad's InTouchSpace stocks keep coming in."

"How did he ever get InTouchSpace stock?" I said.

"A tip from one of his customers," she said. "He got in before it became the biggest social network on the Internet."

That was like getting in on Microsoft, Starbucks, and Google before they hit it big. No wonder Peschel and his late wife were able to retire to Florida.

Monk joined us, a huge smile on his face, and held his arms out to Carol. "Could I give you a hug?"

I almost dropped the baby in shock. Monk doesn't hug anybody.

"Why?" Carol asked.

"Because you have changed my life," he said.

She glanced at me and I gave her a nod, letting her know it was all right.

"Okay," she said hesitantly. "I guess so."

Monk placed his hands lightly on her shoulders and tipped his upper body ever so slightly towards her. There was a good foot of space between them and no physical contact besides his hands. It was the strangest hug I'd ever seen. Apparently, it was even stranger for Carol, who looked bewildered.

"I am so glad to have met you," Monk said. "I will remember this day forever."

"Me, too," she said.

That was when Stottlemeyer joined us. "I'd better be getting back to the station."

"Thanks for coming by," Carol said. "I know it meant a lot to my father."

"I enjoy it as much as he does," he said. "It's just like the old days, only in a much more pleasant environment."

"I know it costs you more than just your time, gasoline, and patience to visit with him." She reached into her pocket and held out some wrinkled bills to Stottlemeyer. "This is what you gave him when you were here before."

"It was good information," Stottlemeyer said a bit sheepishly.

"Fifteen or twenty years ago," she said, and forced the cash into his hands. "I'll pay you back whatever cash you slipped him today but I'll make sure to check his pockets this time before I put his pants through the wash."

"Why?" Monk asked.

"So the captain's money doesn't go through the washing machine," she said.

"What would be wrong with that?"

"Because it will get all clumped and mushy."

"That's why you have to iron the bills afterwards," Monk said. "That's what I do when I clean my money."

"You wash and iron your money?" she asked incredulously.

"Don't you?" he said.

"No," she said.

"My God, woman. You have children," he said. "Cash is filthier than your baby's diapers. Think of all the hands that have touched it and all the places it might have been."

Carol turned to me. "He's eccentric, all right."

I gave the baby a kiss and reluctantly gave her back to her mother.

"It was nice to meet you," I said to them both.

She led us to the door. We said our good-byes and Stottlemeyer walked Monk and me to my car.

"I know why you brought me here," I said to the captain.

"Do you?" he asked innocently.

"So do I," Monk said. "Could I give you a hug?"

"No," Stottlemeyer said, and abruptly turned and went to his car.

Monk looked at me. "You knew about the Diaper Genie before?"

"Yes," I said. "I raised a daughter, you know. She wasn't born a teenager."

"Why didn't you ever tell me about them?"

"Because you aren't interested in babies or their diapers," I said. "They scare you."

"Didn't it occur to you that the Diaper Genie is a revolutionary device with many more uses for humanity than only diaper disposal?"

"Millions of people own Diaper Genies, Mr. Monk. It's not like I've been keeping them a secret from the world."

"And nobody has appreciated its full potential?" Monk said. "It's mind-boggling to me. It's like only using electricity for illumination. If the captain hadn't discovered it here, I might never have known about it."

"You think that's why the captain had us come here, so you could see the Diaper Genie?"

"Of course," Monk said. "What other reason could there be?"

"You're right," I said. "It never occurred to me. That must be why you're the detective and I'm the assistant."

I wasn't ready to talk to Monk about my minor identity crisis.

"Do you know where they sell Diaper Genies?" he asked.

"Yes," I said.

"That's our next stop," he said. "I need to buy some."

"Some?"

"One for each room of my apartment," he said. "And a spare for each room of my apartment."

7

Mr. Monk Gets Some Bad News

It was not a good day for any San Francisco parents who happened to be in the market for a new Diaper Genie or who were simply looking for refills.

Monk had me take him to every Babies R Us, Target, and Wal-Mart in the city so he could stock up on all the Diaper Genies and supplies he thought he'd need for the next year. After he was through, the shelves were bare and the nearest available Diaper Genies were either across the bay or down in Daly City.

It took several trips from the car to unload everything into his apartment. I was going back for the last two Genies when Monk stopped me at his door.

"I want you to keep those two," he said. "They're gifts for you and Julie."

"That's very considerate of you, Mr. Monk. But we really don't need Diaper Genies."

"Everybody needs them," Monk said. "I'm going to spread the word."

"I appreciate the thoughtfulness of the gift, I really do, but I don't have a baby and neither one of us wears diapers."

"You're going to replace your trash cans with these," he said. "You can put one in the kitchen and one in Julie's room to get you started."

"Julie won't put a Diaper Genie in her room."

"Why not?"

"Because she hangs out with her friends in her room all the time," I said. "What would they think if they saw a Diaper Genie?"

"That she's a clean, upstanding citizen," Monk said. "And a patriot."

"They'd think she was either pregnant or incontinent and word would get around school. She'd be mortified."

"All Julie has to do is explain to her friends that she's using it to individually seal each item that she throws out."

"Then they'd think she was a geek," I said.

"She will thank me later," Monk said.

"Why would she thank you for being considered a geek?"

"Don't you know anything about teenage life?" Monk said. "It's a badge of respect."

"It is?"

"I was one," he said.

"You don't say."

"A very special one. I was crowned King of the Geeks, not once, but every single year of high school," Monk said. "It's a record that remains unbroken in my school to this day."

"Were there a lot of students who wanted to be King of the Geeks?"

"It's like being homecoming king, only better. You don't have to go to any dances," Monk said. "You aren't even invited."

"Julie likes dances."

"You should put a stop to that before things go too far," Monk said.

I didn't want to know what "too far" meant in Monk-land, so I just dropped the subject. "I'll do that."

I thanked him for the gift and we proceeded to place Diaper Genies in every room in his house and in the corridors and closets, too.

But we were just getting started.

He had me deliver Diaper Genies, with his compliments, to the other tenants in his building, even the guy with a prosthetic leg who lived upstairs (Monk especially wanted him to have one).

He wasn't doing it out of generosity.

Monk wanted to be sure that all the trash from his building was as "clean" as his was.

I didn't bother telling him that, despite his gift, none of his neighbors would ever seal every single thing in their trash cans into bags and sort them according to his specifications (which he'd printed up and passed out to them on numerous occasions over the years). He'd find out on his own soon enough.

When I got home, I put my Diaper Genie in a corner in the kitchen, because I knew it would be the first thing he'd look for every time he visited me. I didn't have to worry about him ever checking Julie's room for hers, though. Because she had put a DANGER—HAZARDOUS WASTE sign on her door and he took her at her word.

Julie didn't notice the Diaper Genie until we were cleaning up after dinner. She glanced at it and gave me a look.

"Is there something I should know?" she asked.

"I'm not pregnant, if that's what you're getting at, and I'm controlling my bladder just fine. Mr. Monk gave that to us to use as a garbage can."

"Why?"

"So we can wrap up all of our trash," I said. "I have one for your room if you'd like it."

"No way. It was bad enough when he gave us Tupperware containers for our toothbrushes, our underwear, and our socks. This is too much."

"It's just his way of showing that he cares about us," I said. "And I show him how much we care about him by letting him think that we follow some of his rules."

She shook her head, grabbed a cookie, and headed for her room. "He doesn't pay you nearly enough, Mom."

"No," I said, "he doesn't."

The next morning I arrived at Monk's apartment promptly at nine, as I always do. He was waiting for me at the door with two Diaper Genies with ribbons tied around them.

"You already gave us Diaper Genies," I said. "Two more would be an embarrassment of riches."

"They aren't for you," he said. "They're for Captain Stottlemeyer and Lieutenant Disher. Let's go deliver them."

He handed me one, he took the other, and we trooped back to my car for the ride downtown.

We got some strange looks as we carried the Diaper Genies through the Homicide squad room and stopped at Disher's desk. Stottlemeyer hadn't noticed us yet; his door was closed and he seemed to be buried in paperwork.

Monk set the Diaper Genie down on Disher's desk. "This is for you."

Disher studied it. "What is it?"

"A Diaper Genie," Monk said.

The detectives nearby started to snicker. Disher reddened with embarrassment and glared at us.

"If this is your idea of a joke, I don't think it's funny. I'm not the baby cop around here anymore and I'm tired of being treated like I am."

"Randy, you get carded every time you try to buy a beer," I said. "Or go to see an R-rated movie. You asked me to go to *The Dark Knight* with you so you wouldn't have to show your ID."

"I've got news for you both—beneath this deceptively boyish exterior is the soul of a battle-scarred, coldhearted cop." He pointed to the detective at the next desk. "I've got three years on Lansdale. Give the diaper can to him."

"I have no idea what you're talking about. This is for your trash," Monk said. "It will change your life."

"How will a trash can do that?"

"It will individually wrap everything you throw away in its own bag so you don't have to."

"I've never done that," Disher said.

"I know, God help me, I know," Monk said, then addressed the other detectives in the room. "You should all use it." They just stared at him. "You'll thank me later."

He knocked on Stottlemeyer's door and walked in without waiting to be invited. I dutifully followed after him, holding the Diaper Genie.

Stottlemeyer didn't lift his eyes from the mess of papers in front of him and tapped numbers into a calculator that was so old, the numbers had worn off the keys.

"Come right in, make yourselves at home," he said. "Don't let the closed door or the guy working at his desk stop you."

"I have a present for you," Monk said and gestured to me to step forward. I did and set the Diaper Genie down on Stottlemeyer's desk as if it were made of gold and covered with diamonds.

He lifted his head and looked at the Diaper Genie. "Do you know something I don't?"

"What do you mean?" Monk said.

"As far as I know, I haven't fathered any children lately," Stottlemeyer said. "Or even gotten close."

"Don't play dumb," Monk said, and pointed to the Diaper Genie. "This is why you brought us with you to see that senile bartender."

"The diaper can?"

"You wanted to introduce me to this wonderful device because you knew that I would recognize its full potential."

"That's a bizarre leap, even for you," Stottlemeyer said. "Does Dr. Bell have you on some new meds?"

Monk wagged a finger at him. "I see right through you."

"Do you?" Stottlemeyer got up and closed the door. "Then you know what I'm going to say."

I didn't like the tone of his voice when he closed the door or the look on his face when he turned around.

"You're going thank me now instead of later," Monk said. "But you don't have to. Just the joy of having this Diaper Genie in my life is thanks enough."

"I was going to talk with you about this later, but since you're here, I suppose that now is as bad a time as any."

"I believe the correct phrase is 'as good a time as any,'" Monk said.

"Not for what I have to tell you," Stottlemeyer said. "The department has cut my budget to the bone. For weeks, I've been looking for ways to save money without having to pass on too much of the pain to my detectives. But I'm out of creative compromises and I've got to make some hard choices."

"I'm sure the men will understand that," Monk said.

"It's you that I'm concerned about. I'm afraid that I have to cancel our consulting agreement."

There was no hint anytime before that Monk's contract was in jeopardy. And yet now, barely more than a day after Braddock used Monk's success to humiliate Stottlemeyer, suddenly the agreement was canceled. I didn't think it was a coincidence.

I felt a flush of anger rising in my cheeks.

Monk blinked hard. "Aren't I doing a good job?"

"You are," Stottlemeyer said. "An exceptional one, in fact."

"Then how can you let him go?" I said.

"Because I have to think of my detectives first," Stottlemeyer said. "How would it look if I kept him on while they lose their overtime and vacation pay?"

"It would look like you were doing what's best for the people of San Francisco," I said. "Or have you forgotten that Mr. Monk is a better homicide detective than all of your detectives combined?"

It was a low blow, but he deserved it. Besides, it was the truth and he knew it, which was the real reason Monk was getting sacked.

And me, too. If Monk didn't get paid, then neither would I.

Stottlemeyer got in my face. It's what cops do to intimidate perps. But I held my ground and my gaze. I was determined that it wouldn't work with me.

"That may be true. But here's the reality: They are cops and he isn't," he said. "And I'll tell you something else. While they were all out there walking a picket line a couple of years ago, Monk was sitting behind my desk, scabbing. Maybe you've forgotten that, but they sure as hell haven't."

"Apparently, neither have you," I said. "This is payback."

We were so close our noses were almost touching.

"What I'm saying is that I can't take money out of their pocket and put it in his. I just can't."

"Oh spare me, Captain. This isn't about the strike or budget cuts; it's about what happened at the conference," I said. "It's about your pride."

"I'm disappointed in you," he said. "I thought you knew me better than that."

"So did I."

We glowered at each other for a long moment, neither of us blinking. I could make out the edges of his contacts.

Monk cleared his throat to get our attention and to remind us that he was still in the room. "The captain is right."

"No, he's not," I said, maintaining my glower. My eyes were beginning to sting from not blinking.

"Hiring me was always an act of charity and pity," Monk said, "and that's not a luxury the police can afford anymore."

"It was never like that, Monk," Stottlemeyer said, breaking his gaze with me to look at him. I stole a few quick blinks in case we had another stare-down. "I brought you in because you're the best detective I've ever known. But unfortunately, the best is out of our price range right now."

"I understand," Monk said. "That's why I'll do it for free until the department can afford me again."

"I can't let you do that," Stottlemeyer said.

"Neither can I," I said.

Stottlemeyer glanced at me. "It's nice to know that we can still agree about something."

The door flew open and Disher practically leapt into the room.

"Judge Clarence Stanton was just gunned down in Golden Gate Park," Disher said. "He's dead."

"And the shooter?" Stottlemeyer asked.

"In the wind," Disher said.

"Damn," Stottlemeyer said. "Get every available man down there now. I need statements from anybody who might have seen anything."

"We'll follow you down," Monk said.

"No, you won't," Stottlemeyer said. "Didn't you hear anything that I just told you?"

"You said you need every available man," Monk said. "I'm available."

"Not to us," Stottlemeyer said. "I'm sorry."

He hurried out with Disher and nearly every detective in the room.

Monk looked at me.

"I feel like a walk in the park," he said. "How about you?"

"You've been fired, Mr. Monk. You're not welcome at the crime scene."

"It's still a public park," Monk said. "And I'm a member of the public."

"You don't want to do this," I said.

But I knew there was no stopping him.

8

Mr. Monk Takes a Walk in the Park

The crime scene was a jogging path located between a small lake and a densely wooded section of Golden Gate Park, which was once a thousand acres of sandy, windswept wasteland before it was transformed in the late 1800s into a lushly landscaped oasis.

With dense groves of pine and eucalyptus trees, several lakes, thousands of flowers, and wide, grassy fields, it's a terrific place to get away from the pressures of urban life, to take long walks, play games, ride bikes, make love, enjoy picnics, and kill people.

I will confess to doing all but one of those activities in Golden Gate Park myself at one time or another.

A strong wind rolled off the ocean and carried the smell of blood and cordite to our noses before we got to the body. There must have been a lot of blood and a lot of bullets.

The officers who secured the crime scene were used to seeing Monk and me, so they lifted the yellow crime scene tape for us to pass through without asking for ID or any explanations. They apparently hadn't gotten the word that we were no longer on the payroll.

The victim was wearing a T-shirt and jogging shorts. He was on his back on the jogging path in a huge pool of blood, his body riddled with bullet wounds. He looked to me to be in his fifties, judging by the few lines in his face and strands of gray in his hair, though he had the well-toned body of a much younger man. His eyes were open and as dull as stone.

"Two witnesses saw a slender person wearing dark glasses and an oversize hoodie come out of those trees and empty his gun into the judge at point-blank range," Disher said, referring to his notebook. "The shooter then ran back into the trees."

"There's a road that runs along the other side of the grove and out of the park," Stottlemeyer said. "He could have had a car parked there or someone waiting in one for him."

Stottlemeyer and Disher had their backs to us as we approached, so they didn't see Monk until he started circling the body, his hands out in front of him, framing his view.

"Why didn't the shooter throw his gun in the lake?" Monk asked.

"Because there were witnesses and he wanted to dispose of the weapon where no one would find it," Disher said.

"What are you talking to him for?" Stottlemeyer scolded Disher. "He's not supposed to be here."

"But isn't there a bigger risk of being caught with the murder weapon on him?" Monk asked as if the captain hadn't spoken at all.

"We'll ask him when we catch him," Stottlemeyer said. "Get out of here, Monk."

"The judge has been shot in the shoulder, chest, thigh, neck, and arm," Monk said, crouching beside the body. "It's as if the shooter was firing wildly or was not very familiar with a gun."

"Or he was just angry and in a hurry," Disher said. "Judge Stanton tries a lot of criminal cases and he's made plenty of enemies. Maybe one of them just got released from prison."

"I told you to stop talking to him," Stottlemeyer said, then turned to Monk again. "You can either leave or I can have you dragged out of here by two officers. It's your decision."

Monk looked from the body to the grove of trees and then back again.

"It's a public park," he said. "You can't throw me out."

"You are welcome to visit the park, but you are to remain outside the police line, just like everybody else," Stottlemeyer said. "Now go. I don't want to see you at another crime scene unless I call you, but I wouldn't sit by the phone waiting if I were you. This budget crisis is going to last a while."

"He doesn't need to wait," I said. "Once word gets out that he's a free agent, police departments all over the country will be clamoring for his services."

"I hope so," Stottlemeyer said. "I really do."

"Let's go, Mr. Monk." I tugged him gently by the sleeve and led him to the police line.

I lifted up the tape to let him through. Monk looked back at the body, then at the grove of trees again and pointed to a spot.

"He must have come from right about there to intersect with the judge here," Monk said.

"It's not your case, Mr. Monk. You aren't being paid. There's no reason for you to get involved."

"The captain needs me," Monk said.

"He doesn't want you," I said.

"He can't afford me," Monk said. "There's a difference."

"It's not just about the money."

Monk moved across the field towards the grove. The

lupine flowers were in bloom, ringing the base of the tall pines with vibrant color.

Some of the flowers had been flattened where someone crushed them underfoot. This was where the killer was hiding before the shooting.

Monk peered into the trees and examined the ground. "There are bicycle tracks from the street into this grove and back out again."

He circled the area, careful not to disturb the secondary crime scene. I followed him. He cocked his head from side to side, crouched and stood and crouched again, doubled back the way he came, and then retraced the way he had gone forward. It was enough to give me motion sickness.

"The killer wasn't a man," he said. "It was a woman."

"How can you tell from looking at the ground?" I said. "Don't tell me you recognize the footprint left by her shoes."

He shook his head. "All I can tell is that they were running shoes. I can't determine whether they belonged to a man or a woman just from looking at the tread. But I'm sure the forensics unit can by comparing the pattern to those in their footwear database."

"So how do you know the shooter was a she?"

"Her bike fell down," Monk said, and pointed to some impressions in the dirt. "There's a fleck of pink paint on the rock over there. It's considered a feminine color. A man wouldn't want to be seen on a bike of that color."

"We're in San Francisco, Mr. Monk. This may come as a shock to you, but there are a lot of men here with feminine tendencies who aren't shy about showing it."

Monk shivered from head to toe. I don't think he's homophobic, per se. He's just phobic in general. His sense of order demands that if something is designed for a woman, or directly associated with femininity, then only a woman should use it.

He would be just as unsettled by a woman wearing a man's tie or using his aftershave instead of perfume.

Come to think of it, a woman doused with aftershave would unsettle me, too.

"There's more," Monk said. There always is with him. "The bike left an impression in the dirt. You can see the shape of the seat and where it was relative to the handlebars. Women are anatomically different from men."

"Are they really? I thought you didn't notice."

"I try not to," Monk said. "But those differences are reflected in how they design women's bicycles. Women have wider hips than men, so their bike seats are different. They also have shorter torsos and longer legs than men, and that's reflected in the distance between the seat and the handlebars. It's also why the top tube of the frame is at an angle."

"I always thought it was to accommodate women who wore dresses and skirts when they rode bikes," I said.

"That too," Monk said. "Can you take a picture of that?"

I had a built-in camera in my cell phone. I took some shots of the ground for him.

"How do you know it wasn't a man riding a woman's bike?"

"The killer wouldn't risk drawing that much attention to himself."

"Let me remind you again that we are in San Francisco," I said. "A man riding a woman's bike wouldn't be that unusual, even if he was wearing a dress."

Monk shivered again. "I should tell the captain what I know."

"He'll figure it out himself from the shoe impressions and an analysis of the paint chip," I said. I looked back and saw the captain and the officers heading our way.

"Do you think so?"

"I'm positive," I said, though I wasn't. But what the

captain did or didn't discover about this killing really wasn't our problem. We weren't being paid to worry about it.

"I'm not so sure," Monk said.

Clearly, drastic action was necessary.

"You have some nature on your shoes," I said. "I think it's pine sap."

Monk let out a little yelp and hurried towards the road. I took my time. I wondered whether we'd have to burn his shoes when we got back to his apartment or if it would be enough to just dump them in his Diaper Genie.

Perhaps we'd have to do both.

I won't hold you in suspense any longer. We did both. After that, he spent the rest of the day in his apartment, frantically looking for excuses to put something, anything, into his Diaper Genie and seal it for eternity.

He created messes just so he could clean them up and dump the remains in the Genie. He "accidentally" dropped a bag of coffee, a box of cereal, and two cups on the floor.

I went outside to empty the Diaper Genie and when I came back I found Monk talking furtively on the phone in the kitchen.

"My name is Anonymous, and I have no relation whatsoever to Adrian Monk," he said in a deep voice. "Here's my tip. The person who shot Judge Stanton in Golden Gate Park was a woman. You can tell from the impression made by her bicycle in the—"

I yanked the phone plug from the wall.

"What are you doing?" I said.

"Calling the police hotline and leaving an anonymous tip. Don't worry, they'll never know it was me."

"It doesn't matter whether they do or not. They fired you, Mr. Monk, and now you're giving them the benefit of your knowledge for free."

"Not everything has a price," he said.

"Your consulting services do and the police aren't paying it," I said. "You're only hurting yourself by doing this."

"But I'm helping to catch a murderer," he said.

"How does that help you?"

"Because I can't just let it go," Monk said. "It's who I am; it's what I do. I would do it for free."

"That's exactly what you're doing," I said.

"But they don't know that," he said. "That gives us the edge in negotiations."

"There won't be any if you keep this up."

"I don't want the captain's case-closure statistics to fall."

"If they don't, Mr. Monk, they have no incentive to rehire you."

"He's a very good detective and people need to know that," Monk said.

"You're right, and it's great that you want to help him, but if you continue investigating crimes for the police for no salary, what are you going to do for a living? How are you going to pay me?"

"It's who you are; it's what you do," he said. "You would do it for free."

"No, I wouldn't," I said.

"Yes, you would."

"Assisting you is my job, and I enjoy it, but it is not who I am; it is not a burning need that I am compelled to satisfy."

"You're just saying that," Monk said. "You're burning."

"I mean it, Mr. Monk," I said. "If you can't pay me, then I will have to get another job. And what about Dr. Bell? How will you pay him?"

"He'll take me on pro bono."

"Why would he do that?"

"Because I'm fascinating," he said. "You should take me on pro bono, too."

"I won't and neither will Dr. Bell. So if I were you, I would stop detecting for free and find someone else who will pay you for it."

"Like who?"

"Like other police departments," I said. "Tomorrow we'll go back to that conference and do some schmoozing."

"What's that?"

"Chatting people up, getting to know them," I said. "But more important, it's getting *them* to know *you*."

Now he looked worried. "Do they have to?"

"To know you is to love you," I said.

"Bring plenty of wipes," he said.

9

Mr. Monk Gets an Offer

The murder of Judge Stanton was front-page news in the *San Francisco Chronicle* the next morning. The article described some of the more notorious criminal cases he judged and that he'd been about to preside over the trial of reputed mobster Salvatore Lucarelli, the West Coast Godfather.

There were other newsworthy crimes in the city, including a hit-and-run death in the marina the previous night and a robbery in Union Square that left a storekeeper dead.

Stottlemeyer would certainly have his hands full. But if he'd kept Monk on, most of those cases would probably have been solved before lunch.

If I sound a little bitter, that's because I was. Not only did I think he'd treated Monk unfairly, but he'd betrayed me as well. He'd sat across from me at Starbucks and claimed he didn't resent Monk at all. He was either lying to himself, or to me, or both.

I had no doubt that Stottlemeyer would come crawling back to Monk eventually; it was just a question of what would break first, the captain or my checking account.

But there was another option. Monk could get a better-paying job with another police department, perhaps as close by as Oakland, Berkeley, or San Mateo.

I knew I'd have to do most of the networking at the conference, so I dressed up a little more than usual and, I'm a bit ashamed to admit this, I chose clothes that accented my curves (such as they were) and showed a bit more skin.

I would be dealing primarily with men, after all, and I needed whatever edge I could get. I couldn't really count on much support from Monk. Luckily for us both, Braddock had done most of the work for me already by touting Monk's amazing case-closure stats during their panel discussion.

I headed over to Monk's place and heard him talking on the phone in the kitchen as I walked in.

"I am a completely anonymous person who knows that the witness to the hit-and-run killing last night is lying," Monk said. "He told the police that the driver nearly ran over him, too, but he jumped out of the way. The witness gave them a detailed description of the driver and a partial plate, which he said he saw because the driver was bearing right down on him."

I walked in and saw the *Chronicle* on the counter in front of Monk. It was open to the article about the hit-and-run. I leaned against the wall, folded my arms under my chest, and glowered at Monk, who turned his back to me.

"But he couldn't have seen any of it. If what he said was true, then the driver's headlights would have been shining right in his face, blinding him. I believe that the witness himself was the hit-and-run driver and that he's trying to mislead the police with false information."

Monk turned back to me, only so he could refer to the newspaper again.

"I also have some anonymous information about the robbery of the electronics store in Union Square—"

That was more than I could take. I unplugged the phone.

"If you're not going to make an effort on your own behalf, then why should I bother?" I said. "Forget going to the police conference today. You can call back the tip hotline and I'll use the time to get a head start looking for my new job."

I plugged the phone back in and reached for the classified section of the newspaper, which I took back with me to the dining room table in a huff. I opened it to the Want Ads.

"It's unfair and un-American for you to penalize me for being a good citizen," he said. "It's my duty to society to tell the police what I know."

"Hey, this sounds good. There's an opening for a personal shopper at Macy's," I said, circling a listing. "I've got lots of experience shopping and I enjoy it. Would you write me a letter of recommendation?"

"No," he said.

"Don't you think that's being petty?"

"You're overqualified for that job," he said.

"Why? I do a lot of your shopping for you."

"And no shopper will ever be as rigorous in his standards as I am," Monk said. "You'd be wasting your talents. It would be like a brain surgeon working as a nurse."

I thought that was a pretty audacious comparison for him to make. Being Monk's assistant wasn't brain surgery, though at times it felt as if someone were drilling a hole through my skull without anesthesia.

I didn't tell him that, of course. I still might need that letter of recommendation.

Monk picked up the phone and started to dial.

"Oh look, a taxi company is looking for drivers," I said. "I could do that. I can drive, I have a bubbly personality, and I know my way around the city."

"It's too dangerous," he said, hanging up the phone.

"Do you know how many times I've nearly been killed helping you catch murderers?" I said. "I'd probably be safer in a taxi."

"You're forgetting all the diseases you will be exposed to in a filthy taxi," Monk said. "When you are with me, you are safe from infection."

"And from making money," I said.

The phone rang, startling Monk. He answered it. He listened. He winced. Then he nodded.

"I'm just being a good citizen," he said, but apparently the caller had already hung up. Monk set the phone back in its cradle.

"That was Captain Stottlemeyer, wasn't it?" I asked.

Monk nodded. "He told me to stop leaving anonymous tips on the hotline and that he was perfectly capable of solving cases on his own."

"That's what this is all about," I said.

"How did he know it was me who left the tips?"

"He's a detective," I said.

"But I was anonymous."

"They have a sophisticated version of caller ID and instantly trace the calls. They knew who you were the instant they answered the phone."

"I'll have to use different phones," Monk said. "Could I borrow yours?"

"No, you can't," I said.

"Why not?"

Hadn't he heard a single thing I'd said? Did he really think I would give him my phone to make the calls I didn't want him to make? How could someone so brilliant be so incredibly dense?

But I didn't ask him those questions. I had a better reply, one that might actually sink into his head: "Because I need it for arranging job interviews."

He let out a little whine of frustration. Score one for Natalie.

There was a knock at the door. He looked at me. I looked at him.

"Aren't you going to answer that?" he asked.

"Are you going to be calling any more tips in to the police hotline?"

"Not at the moment," he said.

I got up, went to the door, and opened it. I was greeted by a well-dressed man with a big smile, big pecs, and a big income. He wore a gray Hermès V-neck sweater over a white T-shirt, which were loose-fitting enough to convey a casual attitude but not so loose that you couldn't tell he was buff underneath. His True Religion jeans hugged him so tight I almost found true religion myself. If you threw in his Armani loafers, his Ray-Ban sunglasses, and his Omega Seamaster wristwatch, he was wearing my annual salary.

He took off his glasses and revealed his emerald green eyes. I held the door and tried not to swoon.

"I'm Nicholas Slade," he said. "Is Mr. Monk available?"

No, but I am, I thought. "What is this regarding?"

"I'm selling magazine subscriptions and, if I get enough, I can win a trip to Mexico," he said with a mischievous twinkle in his eye.

"Oh, in that case, come right in," I said, and stepped aside.

Slade strode in and gave me an unabashed appraisal as he passed me. I was glad that I'd dressed up for the conference instead of wearing my usual attire.

Monk joined us in the living room.

"This is Nicholas Slade," I said. "He's selling magazines. Or was it Girl Scout cookies?"

"Actually, I'm giving away free copies of *The Watchtower*," he said. "So you can keep up on the latest news regarding your immortal soul."

Monk blanched. I smiled.

"He's joking, Mr. Monk."

"Actually, I'm flirting, Ms. Teeger. I can't help myself around beautiful women." Slade turned to Monk. "But it's you that I came to woo, in a professional sense, of course."

"What can I do for you?" Monk asked.

"What you do better than anybody else," Slade said, and handed Monk his card. "I'm the CEO and founder of Intertect, a private security and investigation company based here in San Francisco. I'd like to hire you as an operative, a consultant, or Grand Poobah of Detection, whatever you want. You tell me. I just want you on my team."

"I'm not available," Monk said.

"Has someone beaten me to you already? I knew I should have come over last night, but I thought it would be too aggressive," he said. "I'll top any offer that you've received."

"How did you know that Mr. Monk is no longer consulting for the San Francisco police?" I asked, and motioned to Slade to take a seat on the couch.

"I wouldn't be much of a detective if I didn't," he said, sitting down. Monk sat on the arm of an easy chair across from him. I stood at Monk's side like the dutiful assistant that I am.

"I have lots of sources within the department," Slade continued. "I used to be a vice detective until I got smart ten years ago and went private. I was invited to be a guest on a panel at the homicide detectives' conference, so I happened to be there to see Monk's interview. After witnessing that debacle, I had a feeling Leland might make a change in the consulting agreement."

"Did you really?" I gave Monk a significant look to underscore Slade's remark.

"Do you have something in your eye?" Monk asked.

"No, I don't. Did you hear what Mr. Slade just said?"

"Did he spit in your eye when he said it?"

"No, he didn't," I said.

"Because some people do that," he said. "They spit when they talk. They need to be stopped. Someone could die."

"My eyes are fine," I said.

"Then why were you widening your eyes like that?"

"I wasn't," I said. "Let's just drop it, okay?"

"There was widening," he said, and looked at Slade. "You couldn't see it because her back was to you. Only I could see it."

"Almost like a private expression shared between two people," Slade said.

"Almost," Monk said. "But it was more like she had something in her eye. Did you spit in her eye? Are you a spitter when you speak?"

"I don't think so," Slade said.

"That's a relief," Monk said. "Because I don't have protective goggles."

"I've been waiting for an opportunity to make a play for your services for a long time, Mr. Monk."

"What stopped you from doing it until now?" I asked. "Mr. Monk wasn't under an exclusive contract."

"I didn't want to step on Leland's toes. I have too much respect for him to do that," he said. "But he's made a huge mistake in letting you go. Leland has no one to blame but himself if you come to work for me."

Monk rolled his shoulders. "I don't think I'd be comfortable in a corporate environment."

"You aren't comfortable in any environment," I said.

"You never have to come into the office if you don't want to," Slade said. "We could get you files by messenger or e-mail. We could talk over the phone, in person, via fax or videoconference. Whatever you want. You can pick and choose your cases and clients. You will have free access to all of our resources, which are considerable. I'm talking research, scientific analysis, surveillance, and manpower. We'll give you whatever assistance you need."

"I have an assistant," Monk said.

Slade smiled at me. "Of course you do. My offer to you extends to Ms. Teeger as well, as does our benefits package."

"Benefits?" I think my voice cracked a little when I said that.

"Medical and dental coverage for you and your daughter," he said. "I know you also act as Mr. Monk's driver, so naturally we would cover your gasoline, car insurance, and expenses or, if you prefer, we can provide you with a company car from our fleet."

I could have cried. The only benefit Monk offered me was an endless supply of disinfectants.

Slade turned to Monk. "Our medical plan would also cover your psychiatric care, of course."

"What's the catch?" Monk asked.

"You'd be working .exclusively for Intertect," Slade said. "But if it is intellectual stimulation that you are worried about, let me put you at ease. We investigate all kinds of cases for our individual and corporate clients, including murder."

I cleared my throat and tried to put on my best poker face. "All these benefits are a given, Mr. Slade. What you haven't mentioned yet is the salary that you're offering. If Mr. Monk is going to lend you his international reputation and his perfect case-closure rate, he expects a compensation package that guarantees that he will share in the phenomenal success that he will bring to your firm."

Slade took a card from his pocket and picked up a pen from the coffee table. He wrote something on the back of the card and passed it to Monk.

"This would be your monthly salary," he said. "It's only the floor to get us started. We'll gladly negotiate an escalator clause that will be tied to certain agreed-upon performance levels."

I glanced over Monk's shoulder at the number. I had to look twice to make sure I wasn't imagining the figure. It was a huge bump up from what he was getting paid by the police.

Monk shook his head. "I can't live with this figure."

He wouldn't live at all if he let this job slip away. I'd kill him myself the moment Slade walked out the door.

"What would it take to make you happy?" Slade asked.

"Make it an even number," Monk said.

Slade took the card back and rounded the figure up to a big, fat, whole number with lots of zeros at the end.

"You drive a hard bargain, Mr. Monk," Slade said. "Do we have a deal?"

I looked at Monk. He sighed miserably.

"Yes," Monk said.

Slade smiled. So did I. He had a nice smile. Now Julie and I could afford to have one like his. I made a mental note to get the name of his dentist.

"I am so pleased." Slade held out his hand.

Monk shook it, then motioned to me for a wipe.

"Allow me." Slade reached into his pocket and pulled out a travel packet of Wet Ones and offered a wipe to Monk. Oh, Slade was a smooth one. "When do you think you can start?"

Monk wiped his hand and glanced at his watch.

Slade took a Baggie out of his pocket and held it out to Monk, who dropped his wipe into it.

Slade sealed the Baggie. I took it from him and dropped it into a nearby Diaper Genie, twisted the ring, and sealed the Baggie in another bag. I hoped the anthropologists who examined it centuries from now would appreciate the effort.

"What a great idea," Slade said, admiring the Diaper Genie. "I have to get one of those for my office."

I had to hand it to him: He actually said it with a straight face. But I was worried that it was overkill and that even Monk would find it insincere.

But then Monk did something incredible.

He smiled.

"I can start today," Monk said.

10

Mr. Monk Goes to Work

Intertect was located on the twentieth floor of a high-rise in the financial district. I stopped by to fill out all the paperwork required to get us on the payroll and the health plan as soon as possible.

As I walked down the hall, I saw that each office had a window with a commanding view of the window of the building next door, but I guess that was better than no view at all. By my count, Intertect had at least thirty operatives—and those were just the ones with offices.

I was led to a vacant office that was set aside for Monk if he ever needed it, though I doubted that he would make the long climb up the stairs to see it unless there was a dead body there, too.

The office came with a sleek computer, sleek furniture, and an even sleeker assistant in her early twenties named Danielle Hossack.

She informed me that she'd graduated from McGill University in Montréal with a degree in psychology, spoke three languages, and had a black belt in tae kwon do. She was also blessed with the body of a lingerie model. She didn't tell me that. It was obvious from what she was wearing, which qualified more as underwear than clothes.

In fact, all the women I saw at Intertect were young, gorgeous, and scantily clad.

Slade was in for a big disappointment if he expected me to dress that way.

He hadn't mentioned what my salary would be and I'd forgotten to ask. When I saw the figure on one of the forms, I blinked hard, hoping it wasn't a mirage. It wasn't.

I could almost hear Ricardo Montalban whispering in my ear. Welcome to *Fantasy Island*.

"Is there something wrong?" Danielle asked. I'd been so mesmerized by my salary figure that I hadn't realized that she was still standing beside the desk.

"No, no, everything is wonderful," I said, and I meant it. "Have you worked here long?"

"Two years," she said.

I wondered if she made as much as, or more than, I did, but I didn't ask.

"Do you like it?"

"I love it," she said. "I have learned so much. Nick is an amazing man."

"He must be," I said. "Lots of detectives leave the force to become private detectives but few are as successful as he is. What's his secret?"

"Substantial capitalization and abundant charm," she said. "He made some wise investments in the stock market ten years ago and used his profits to start the company. I've learned that successful detection is a combination of determination, intuition, and getting people to give you what you want. Nick is a real people person. He can win over anybody he meets."

"That's for sure," I said.

She gave me a knowing look. "If you're thinking about hooking up with him, I should warn you that he's very sweet and a great lover, but he's a free spirit. Monogamy is not part of his personality. He wants to enjoy the buffet of life's opportunities."

That sounded like a direct quote. "Does that philosophy factor into his hiring practices?"

"Is that your way of asking if he sleeps with every woman he hires?"

I shrugged. "They all seem to be young and attractive."

"And smart," Danielle said. "There isn't a woman here, whether it's a secretary or an operative, who doesn't have a degree or two under her garter belt."

"They wear garter belts?"

She politely ignored my comment. "Sleeping with him won't get you hired or get you promoted or get you any special treatment, beyond what he does for you in bed, of course, which is pretty exceptional."

I raised an eyebrow. "So you give him two thumbs-up in the sack-a-roo."

"If you get into bed with him, you won't be sorry."

"I'm not big on buffets. I always feel bloated afterwards," I said. "But I appreciate the information. To be honest, I'm surprised by your candor."

"Because I'm not shy about discussing sex?"

"Because you're so open with intimate, and potentially unflattering, details about your boss with someone you just met," I said. "Aren't you being indiscreet?"

She smiled. "I'm an employee of Intertect but I am working for you and Mr. Monk now. You deserve my full honesty if we're going to establish any kind of trust. And besides, Nick doesn't mind my talking about his love life or I wouldn't do it. He's a very open guy."

"In more ways than one," I said.

"You don't need to worry about me breaking any confidences as far as you and Mr. Monk are concerned," she said. "My first loyalty now is to you both. Nick made that very clear and that's fine with me. I consider it an honor to be working with you. I am a big admirer of your accomplishments."

"You mean Mr. Monk's," I said, handing her the sheaf of completed forms.

"Mr. Monk couldn't have done it without you," she said. "Don't sell yourself short."

Just what I needed: advice on self-esteem from a twenty-something with a college degree and a body that could melt the statue of David. What did she know about insecurity?

Danielle went on to tell me that she was at our beck and call any hour of the day or night, seven days a week, for anything we might need.

In other words, I was getting my own Natalie.

I didn't want her to run away screaming on day one, so I decided to give her a quick briefing on Monk's phobias and his obsessive-compulsive disorder.

It turned out that she'd already studied up on his "special needs" and was not the least bit put off by them. She said that one of the reasons that Slade handpicked her to work with us was because of her psychological background.

Danielle went out to her desk, dropped my completed forms in her out-box, and wheeled in what looked like a rolling file drawer.

"What's this?" I asked.

"Open cases for Mr. Monk to review," she said. "Any insights he can give the detectives working on them would be welcomed. Or, if he likes, he can take over any of the cases himself."

It looked like a huge amount of work, but considering what they were paying him, I couldn't blame them for burying him in cases his first week.

Danielle wheeled the cart to the elevator and down to my car in the parking garage for me. Actually, she took it to a brand-new Lexus SUV parked next to my car.

The wheels of the cart collapsed like an ambulance gurney and it slid right into the back of the Lexus. She dangled a set of keys in front of me.

"This is your company car," she said, dropping the keys into my hand. Then she offered me a credit card. "You can use this card for gasoline and any other expenses."

"What about my car?" I asked, tipping my head towards my Buick Lucerne, a sheet-metal catfish that you have to be a card-carrying member of the AARP to drive. It was a gift to me from my clueless father, who also threw in a Ferrante and Teicher CD so I could, and I quote, "crank up the hi-fi and give the stereophonics a real workout."

"You can drive your car back and I can follow in the Lexus," she said, "or vice versa. Whatever you like."

"I think we are going to be very happy at Intertect," I said, and handed her the keys to my Buick.

I hoped she enjoyed listening to Ferrante and Teicher's rockin' piano version of the theme from *You Light Up My Life* while she drove. It was one of Monk's favorites.

Monk got right to work that afternoon and so did Danielle, who stuck around after she delivered the car. They sat on opposite ends of his dining room table. While he went through the files, she read his indexed lists of personal phobias and made copious notes. I read the Lexus owner's manual and *People* magazine.

"The case of the missing diamonds was an inside job," Monk said, closing a file and sliding it down the table to Danielle, who looked up, stunned.

"Was it the cleaning lady, the pool man, their son with

the online gambling problem, her sneaky ex-husband, his bitter ex-wife, or the contractor who was building their home theater?"

"It was none of them," Monk said.

I didn't know any of the facts of the case but I didn't need to. I was more interested in Danielle's reaction to her first experience with Monk's process, which has less to do with deduction and more to do with noticing the mess.

"Who else is left?" she asked.

"The dog trainer."

"But the trainer worked with the dog in the backyard," Danielle said. "He didn't have any access to the house."

"The dog did," Monk said. "The trainer taught the dog to steal the diamonds and bury them in the backyard."

"The dog?" she said incredulously.

"That explains why there was dirt in the house," he said. "The dirt really bothered me."

"That's a surprise," I said.

"I don't remember seeing any dirt," Danielle said.

"There were some grains," he said.

"Grains?" she said.

"Mr. Monk can detect dirt that isn't visible to the naked eye," I said. "Or even the most powerful electron microscopes."

"The trainer plans to retrieve the diamonds the next time he works with the dog," Monk said, and checked his watch. "Which is in two hours."

"Incredible," she said, reaching for her phone. "I need to call Nick so we can catch the trainer in the act."

"While you're at it, you should tell Mr. Slade that the insurance company is right: The tennis pro is faking his arm injury," Monk said, sliding her another file. "His sling is on his right arm."

"That's because that's the arm he injured when he

tripped over the crack in the country club's parking lot," she said. "He can't bend or extend it. His doctors say his arm is locked at a ninety-degree angle."

"And yet in the surveillance photos, you can clearly see his keys are in his right pocket," Monk said. "How does he get them out if he can't straighten his arm?"

She opened the file and squinted at the picture. We both did. If I had a bionic eye, I might have seen the keys, too.

"How could we have missed that?" she asked.

"You'll find yourself asking that question a lot around Mr. Monk," I said. "But there's another question you'll be asking even more often. . . ."

Monk picked up another file. "And you can tell Mr. Slade that the spy at Joha Helicopters who is selling trade secrets to the competition is Ulrich Sommerlik, the disabled engineer."

"How do you know?" she asked.

"That's the one," I said to her. "I'm thinking of putting the question on a little sign that we can just hold up."

Monk opened the file and held up a photograph of a slender man in a cardigan sweater sitting in a manual wheelchair.

"He claims that he's been in a wheelchair since a copter accident four years ago. But in this picture taken for his photo ID when he was hired six months ago, he has blisters on his hands. If he'd been pushing himself in his wheelchair all that time, he'd have calluses by now."

We both squinted at that photo, too. I couldn't see the blisters, but I knew that when it comes to open sores, Monk has an eagle eye.

"My guess is that he's using secret compartments in the wheelchair to smuggle out drawings, disks, and anything else he can get his blistered hands on," Monk said, putting the photo back into the file.

"I'll call the security chief at Joha Helicopters and

have Sommerlik detained and his wheelchair seized," she said. "We'll take it apart."

"Notify them that the entire facility needs to be evacuated and decontaminated," Monk said.

"Why?"

"Because Sommerlik's hands are blistered," Monk said. "God knows what else he's touched. The whole place is probably dripping with his bodily fluids."

Danielle stared at him, not quite sure what to say. I couldn't blame her. I probably looked the same way the first few days I'd worked with Monk.

"You are amazing, Mr. Monk," she said. "You catch details that nobody else sees. You'll have to teach me how you do that."

"It's a gift," Monk said. "And a curse."

"I'll take my chances," she said with a smile, flirting ever so slightly. It was cute and probably calculated to be. The flirtation was wasted on him but not the flattery.

He gave her the file and she added it to the stack in her arms. She took the files and went off to call Slade. Monk turned to me.

"I think we're going to be very happy at Intertect," he said.

11

Mr. Monk Solves a Mystery

Julie nearly fainted when I showed up at home that night with the new Lexus. The first thing she wanted to do was drive it. I let her drive all over San Francisco with the windows rolled up, because we didn't want to lose one precious whiff of that new-car smell.

She also insisted that we cruise up and down Twenty-fourth Street, the main drag of our Noe Valley neighborhood, for an hour on the off chance that one of her friends might see us.

It was the first car we'd ever had that she wasn't ashamed to be seen in, so she wanted to be seen. I did, too. I was hoping word would get around that we had a Lexus and that it might delay any plans to drive us out of the neighborhood with torches.

"Please don't ever lose this job," Julie said as she steered us on our twelfth pass down the street.

"Now that we have two cars, you can have the Buick all to yourself."

She looked at me in horror. "Why don't you drive the Buick and let me drive this?"

"Because this is the company car," I said. "Technically, you shouldn't be driving it now, but I am in a charitable mood."

"I would rather walk to school than arrive there in a Buick," she said. "I might as well show up wearing Grandma's housedress and clutching a colostomy bag."

"Grandma doesn't have a colostomy bag," I said.

"You're missing the point," she said.

"I'm just teasing you," I said. "I totally understand your embarrassment. I'm not thrilled about driving the Buick either. It's not a car that makes men take a second look at you."

"Unless you're driving up to a retirement home," she said.

"I'll drop you off at school in the Lexus," I said. "We can keep the Buick for emergencies."

"Like what?"

I shrugged. "Grandma might want to borrow it to impress a man on a date."

"She's got a BMW," Julie said.

"I'm thinking of a man her own age," I said.

"You may be but she's not."

I was afraid to ask Julie exactly what she meant by that, or what she knew about Grandma's love life, so I didn't.

Sometimes ignorance really is bliss.

The rolling cabinet was nearly empty of files and Monk's dining room table was covered with photos when I walked in the next morning.

He was studying the photographs very carefully, moving methodically from one to another.

I glanced at the pictures. I saw a dead man sitting in a leather easy chair in his home study. There was a knife buried to the hilt in his chest. He looked to be in his forties and well-off, judging by his monogrammed shirt and the wood-paneled study where he'd been killed.

"You've gone through just about all the cases that Danielle brought you," I said.

"This is the last one," he said.

"You must have gotten an early start this morning."

"I didn't stop," Monk said, cocking his head from side to side as he examined the pictures.

"You stayed up all night?"

"I had a lot of work to do," he said.

"But you didn't have a deadline," I said. "There was no reason you had to do an all-nighter."

"I tried to go to bed," Monk said. "But I could feel all those unsolved cases out there. I couldn't leave them like that."

"It was like leaving behind a mess without cleaning it up," I said.

He nodded. I would have to talk to Danielle about giving Monk only a few cases at a time. At this rate, he'd exhaust himself within days.

I gestured to the pictures on the table. "These look like official crime scene photos."

"They are," Monk said.

"Then how did Slade get them?"

Monk shrugged. "I don't know. He must be very well connected."

"So what's the case?"

"A home-invasion robbery and murder that happened six months ago in a mansion off Skyline Boulevard in Oakland. The killers got away with jewelry worth about two hundred thousand dollars. The culprits still haven't been caught, though the police are pretty sure they know who is responsible. The victim, Lou Wickersham, was in considerable debt to a lot of very unfriendly people. The police believe those people lost patience and came to collect."

There were close-up photos of Wickersham's wound, the knife, a cut on his hand, a bloodstained handkerchief on the floor, a broken window, shards of glass on the rug, and his ransacked study. And there were some photos of the rest of the house, which had also been thoroughly ransacked.

"So why don't they arrest the people that Wickersham owed money to?" I asked.

"There's no evidence," Monk said. "The knife was wiped clean of prints. The case has gone cold. So Wickersham's widow, who was in Europe when the killing happened, hired Intertect to investigate."

"What's your theory?"

Before Monk could answer, there was a knock at the door. I went to answer it. Danielle was standing outside with another rolling file drawer.

"Good morning, Ms. Teeger," she said, pushing the cart right past me.

"Danielle," I said, closing the door and catching up to her. "You can't keep wheeling files in here."

"He asked me for more," Danielle said.

"I'm all out," Monk explained.

"But you haven't slept," I said to him. "You can't keep working like this. You have to pace yourself or you're going to get fried and make mistakes."

Monk ignored my comment and turned to Danielle. "Did you get the information on the Judge Stanton case?"

"Of course, Mr. Monk." She took a notebook out of the file drawer and referred to some pages.

"You're not supposed to be meddling in that case," I scolded him.

"Professional curiosity, that's all," Monk said.

I motioned to the new cart full of files. "Don't you have enough to keep you busy already?"

"I just want to make sure the captain is on the right track."

"You don't work for him anymore," I reminded him. "You are under exclusive contract to Intertect."

Danielle spoke up. "The police believe that the killer is a woman, based on the type of bicycle she was riding and the impression left in the dirt by her running shoes. They've identified the shoes as a woman's Nike model that's sold by the thousands in stores all over the country, so that's a dead end. But they have determined the assailant's weight and height based on the measurements taken from the bike and the depth of the shoe prints in the dirt."

Monk nodded. He was impressed, though I wasn't sure whether it was with the progress of the investigation or the confidential information that Danielle was able to dig up.

"Do they have any suspects?" Monk asked.

"They are concentrating on violent offenders that Judge Stanton sent to prison and who have recently been released," she said. "And the possibility that mobster Salvatore Lucarelli had him killed to avoid trial."

Monk frowned. "Why would any of them ask a woman to do their killing?"

"Women kill just as well as men do," I said.

"It could be the mother, girlfriend, or daughter of someone that he sent to prison," Danielle said.

"It's possible," he conceded with a nod.

And my theory wasn't?

Monk had never conceded that one of *my* alternative theories might be possible. But I wasn't a twentysomething hottie who told him he was amazing.

"Did you take care of that other thing?" Monk asked Danielle.

She flipped a page in her notebook. "Of all the Nobel categories, I think the Peace Prize is the one you want."

"You think that you deserve a Nobel Prize?" I asked him.

"Not me," Monk said. "John Hall."

"Who is he?"

"The inventor of the Diaper Genie," Monk said.

"You honestly believe that creating the Diaper Genie deserves the Nobel Peace Prize?"

"I do," Monk said. "Don't you?"

"Unfortunately, Mr. Monk, what you believe won't be enough," Danielle said. "The only people allowed to submit nominees are professors of social sciences, law, and philosophy; government leaders; directors of peace organizations; members of the Nobel committee; and past winners of the prize."

"Who do we know who has won a Nobel Prize?" Monk asked us both.

"No one," I said.

"How about professors?"

"There's Professor Cowan," I suggested flippantly.

"Good idea," Monk said.

"You just proved him guilty of murder, Mr. Monk. I doubt that he's in the mood to do you a favor."

"But it's for a good cause," Monk said.

"Even if he agreed with you about that, I doubt that the Nobel Committee would accept a nomination from a murderer."

"Then let's create a peace organization," Monk said. "How hard could that be?"

"I'll look into it," Danielle said, writing a note to herself. I bet it was something like, *Monk is crazy.*

"I believe in peace." Monk made a peace sign with his fingers. "You can't have peace without cleanliness. The Diaper Genie could unite the world."

"Did you have any luck with the home-invasion murder case?" Danielle asked.

"It's not a home invasion," Monk said. "And it's not a murder."

She looked baffled. "Then what is it?"

"Suicide," Monk said.

He motioned us over to the table and gestured to the photographs.

"Look at this. Lou Wickersham was stabbed in the heart while sitting in his easy chair. That doesn't make any sense."

"Why not?" she asked.

"If he'd walked in on robbers and they attacked him, then his body would be on the floor, not in the chair. And if they came at him from the front, why doesn't he have any defensive wounds?"

"There's the cut on his hand," I said.

"It's on the back of his hand," Monk said. "If he grabbed for the knife, the wound would most likely be across his palm. Besides, the cut is superficial."

"You're saying that Wickersham stabbed himself in the chest?" Danielle said.

"Yes," Monk said. "He sat down in what is probably his favorite chair in his favorite room and plunged the knife into his heart."

"Then why aren't his fingerprints on the knife?" she asked.

"Because he held it with the handkerchief that's on the floor," Monk said. "The police assumed the killers used the handkerchief to grip the knife and that the spot of blood came from the chest wound. It didn't. The blood came from the cut on his hand."

"How did he get the cut?" I asked.

"When he broke the glass on the French doors to his study," Monk said. "Here's what happened. He ransacked the house to hide the fact that he'd sold his wife's jewelry and everything else of value to pay off the loan sharks while she was away. But it wasn't enough and he knew it. All he bought was some time. The best he could hope for was to secure his wife a comfortable life. So he staged a home invasion and made his suicide look like murder so that his wife would get his life insurance money."

"He sacrificed himself for her," I said.

Monk nodded. "And it was all for nothing. She won't see a penny of the money."

"Not necessarily," Danielle said.

"The insurance company won't pay her off for a suicide," Monk said.

"The only way they'll know it was suicide is if she decides to tell them," Danielle said.

"We'll tell them," Monk said.

"We can't. We were hired by the widow and are bound by our contract with her to maintain her privacy," she said. "Nick will give her our report and what happens after that will be up to her."

"If she doesn't inform the police, and cashes the insurance company's check, then we will be accessories to a crime," Monk said.

"Not necessarily, and only if they discover the truth, if that's what it is," she said. "You're the only one who thinks it wasn't murder. With all due respect, what if you're wrong?"

"Mr. Monk is never wrong about murder," I said.

"That's for our client to decide," she said. "As Nick always says, we provide information and our clients decide what to do with it."

"I can't accept that," Monk said.

"Then maybe Intertect isn't the right place for you," Danielle said.

I suddenly had a horrifying vision of my Lexus, my corporate credit card, my comprehensive health coverage, and my big, fat salary evaporating after just one day.

"Let's not overreact," I said sternly to Danielle, then turned to Monk. "Or do anything rash. I'm sure we can smooth this out with Mr. Slade in a way that everyone can live with."

The phone rang. I answered it. It was Nick Slade, as if on cue. But before I could bring up our ethical dilemma, he spoke up.

"Another judge has been gunned down and we've been hired to investigate. The client specifically asked for Monk."

"Who's the client?" I asked.

"Salvatore Lucarelli," he said.

"The mobster?"

"That's yet to be proven in a court of law," he said. "And the judge who was supposed to hear that case is the guy who was just killed."

"Wait a minute," I said. "I thought Judge Stanton, the judge who was killed in Golden Gate Park, was supposed to preside over that case."

"He was," Slade said. "Judge Carnegie was next in line, which makes Lucarelli the top suspect, which is why he wants Monk to prove that he's innocent."

"Mr. Monk will never work for Salvatore Lucarelli," I said, glancing at my boss, whose ears seemed to perk up at the mention of the mobster's name.

"You don't know your boss as well as you think you do," Slade said. "Monk has worked for Lucarelli before; that's why he's asking for him again now."

I glanced again at Monk and, from the expression on his face, I knew that what Slade had said was true.

12

Mr. Monk and the Godfather

I couldn't believe that Monk had ever worked for the mob. But he had. He gave me all the details as I drove him down to the county jail in our new Lexus.

It had happened shortly before his previous assistant, Sharona Fleming, left him and I was hired. Someone walked into a barbershop that was a front for Lucarelli's gambling and protection racket and killed everybody in the place.

Lucarelli and his men wanted revenge but he didn't want to spark a mob war, so he snatched Monk off the street and pressed him into service to find out who was responsible for the massacre.

Monk took the job because he was terrified not to, and because the feds, who were staking out Lucarelli, saw this as a perfect opportunity to get a man on the inside.

The feds made Monk wear a tie with a listening device woven into it and sent him back into the heart of the San Francisco mob.

Monk caught the killer and discovered that the massacre had nothing to do with Lucarelli's money-laundering operation, but that's a long story that I'll have to tell you about another time.

Monk averted a mob war but the feds were mad at him. It wasn't because he failed to get any evidence against the mobster. What pissed them off was that Monk washed and ironed his wired tie, ruining it. If toilet seats on aircraft carriers cost four figures, just imagine what a transmitting tie must go for.

As we were nearing the jail on Seventh Street, I quickly filled Monk in on what Slade had told me. Judge Carnegie was gunned down while taking his dog on his daily morning walk. With Judge Stanton dead, Judge Carnegie was next up in the rotation to preside over Lucarelli's trial, which made the mobster the prime suspect in both killings. Now Lucarelli's trial was indefinitely delayed and the next judge in line was under police protection.

We parked the car and entered the county jail, a striking building with undulating curves of frosted glass and an enormous sheriff's badge mounted on the exterior. It looked more like a shopping mall than a jail, but once we were inside, any pretense of being something else was dropped. It looked just like you'd expect a jail to look.

We went through the various security gates, a wearisome ritual that always reminded me of that long corridor of sliding, swinging, and dropping doors that Maxwell Smart walks down at the beginning of each episode of *Get Smart.* I think they did it in the movie, too.

Salvatore Lucarelli was already waiting for us when we entered the interview room. He was a droopy-faced, balding man with a double chin. He fit my image of someone's kindly grandfather but not the most feared mob figure west of the Mississippi. There was no perceptible menace emanating from him.

He was dressed in a yellow jumpsuit, his arms and

legs shackled to a chain that was locked to a metal loop imbedded in the concrete floor of the interview room. The light cast by the coiled energy-efficient bulbs gave his skin a sickly, jaundiced tinge.

Monk and I stood across from him, a table between us in case he broke his chains, lunged at us, and tried to tear out our throats with his dentures.

"Thank you for seeing me, Mr. Monk," Lucarelli said.

"I didn't want to," Monk said. "But I was afraid of what might happen to me if I didn't."

"I would never hurt you," he said. "You have my respect."

"But you've hurt others," Monk said.

Lucarelli gave a noncommittal shrug and glanced at me. "I see you've got a pretty new assistant."

"Is that a threat?" Monk said.

"You think I'd hurt her to get at you? What good would that do me? You'd be too angry and distracted to get anything done. It's as ridiculous as the idea that I had anything to do with those judges getting killed."

"Is it?" I said. "They were both going to preside over your trial. Now no judge wants to do it. Your attorney is already arguing that the jury pool and judicial pool are hopelessly tainted and that a fair trial would be impossible. It could be months before you get a trial, if ever."

"And while all that goes on, I'm going to be in a cell not getting any younger," he said. "If I wanted to rig the trial, I wouldn't kill the judge; I'd get rid of the witnesses, or the prosecutor, or the people who are close to them. That way the trial would be over quick and I would be out."

"Maybe that's coming next," I said.

"I was just giving you a hypothetical from my years of watching *The Sopranos*," Lucarelli said. "I'm a restaurateur. All I kill are lobsters."

Monk tilted his head and regarded Lucarelli. "If you're guilty of these murders, I will prove it. And I will go to the police with what I find out no matter how much you pay Intertect."

"I know. So ask yourself this, Mr. Monk," Lucarelli said. "If I did kill those judges, why would I do something as stupid as putting you on the case?"

Judge Alan Carnegie lived in the Sunset District, which, like North Beach, has a name that belies the truth. There is no beach at North Beach anymore, and while there *is* a beach at Sunset, there's very little sunlight.

The neighborhood, bordered by the Pacific Ocean to the west, Golden Gate Park to the north, and the Twin Peaks to the east, was almost always shrouded in fog and it was no different that day.

The westernmost end of Sunset, where the judge lived, was a flat, sea-sprayed beach community composed of cafés, surf shops, bars, health food stores, bodegas, and low-slung, bleached homes of cinder block and perennially peeling wood.

The tourists all visit Haight Ashbury for a peek at the 1960s, but if you ask me, they're going to the wrong spot. The sixties really live in the Sunset District, where just about everybody seems to be wearing sandals or flip-flops and faded T-shirts or sweatshirts. But like the name of the place, looks are deceiving. Many of the beach bums lead double lives as high-paid professionals in order to afford the luxury of a laid-back lifestyle.

I parked next to the police line on one of the residential streets. We got out of the car and shouldered our way through the crowd of reporters and lookie-loos. Let me rephrase that—*I* shouldered *my* way and Monk cowered behind me in my wake, his arms tucked in close to his body so he wouldn't brush against anyone.

I lifted up the yellow police tape, expecting to hear

an officer yell at us, but no one did. Either they didn't notice us crossing the line or, like the officers at Golden Gate Park, they hadn't gotten the word about Monk.

Judge Carnegie was splayed on the sidewalk in an unnatural position, body and limbs bent at odd angles, reminding me of a broken string puppet. I guess that's what happens when you're shot six times and collapse with no concern about how you land. Of course, he was way past being concerned about anything.

He was suntanned and his hair was colored a hue of brown not found in nature. He wore a sweatshirt, denim cutoffs, and sandals. I wondered if that was what he wore under his judge's robes at the bench.

The judge had one end of a leash looped around his right wrist and it appeared, from his outstretched arm and the swath of blood on the sidewalk behind him, that his dog had dragged him for a few feet. The dog was gone.

Stottlemeyer and Disher were talking to some officers and forensic techs, so they didn't immediately notice Monk until he was already crouching beside the body.

But once the captain saw us, he marched right over, his face flushed with anger, Disher in tow.

I moved to intercept him. "It's not what you think."

"You mean you haven't violated a crime scene and that isn't Monk over there examining the corpse?"

Now I felt my hackles go up. I didn't even know I had hackles until then.

"We haven't *violated* anything, Captain. We're showing the same care and professionalism that we always have at crime scenes."

"You were official consultants then; you aren't now. You are civilians who aren't permitted to cross a police line," he said. "I've already warned you both about that. We don't need Monk's help right now, no matter how much he wants to give it."

I glanced back and saw Monk studying the trail of blood. I wanted to buy him as much time as I could.

"He's not giving away anything, not one tiny bit of information or insight," I said. "He's been hired by someone who appreciates his talents and treats him with the respect he deserves. In consideration of his years of loyal service, we're hoping you might grant him a few minutes of access to the scene as a professional courtesy."

"Don't you think you're laying it on a little thick?" Stottlemeyer said.

I shrugged. "It seems to me that you need reminding."

"Who is he working for?" he asked.

"Me," a voice said.

We turned to see Nick Slade approaching us. He wore a perfectly tailored Brioni jacket and slacks, his shirt open at the collar. He looked like money. And even if he didn't, his ride certainly did. His Bentley convertible was parked at the police line and there were two dumbstruck officers ogling it as if it were a Hawaiian Tropic bikini model.

"Why do we even bother cordoning off our crime scenes?" Stottlemeyer said, shaking his head. "You're looking good, Nick. Then again, you always do."

"You could, too, if you accepted my job offers," Slade said. "Nice tie."

Stottlemeyer lifted his yellow-white-and-blue-striped tie. "The Continental. Genuine polyester. You can buy two for ten dollars at Wal-Mart. You could probably afford four of 'em."

"I don't know why you stay on the police force."

"I like wearing a badge," he said.

"If that's all you want," Slade said, "I'll give you one."

"There's more to it than that."

"Yeah, it's the number of figures on the paycheck,"

Slade said. "It's the freedom to do your job without the politics and bureaucracy getting in the way. It's finally having all the resources you need to do it right."

"Where's the challenge in that?" Stottlemeyer said with a grin.

Disher cleared his throat. "I've never received one of your job offers."

Slade turned to him, apparently noticing him for the first time. "Do I know you?"

"You will," Disher said confidently.

"Because you're on the verge of making headlines by cracking a major case?" Slade asked, reaching out for a handshake.

"Because I'm going to send you my résumé," Disher said, gripping Slade's hand as hard as he could. I could see the effort on his face. There was none on Slade's. "Lieutenant Randall Disher, Homicide."

"Nice to meet you," Slade said, managing to sound both polite and dismissive at the same time. He glanced at Stottlemeyer and tipped his head towards Disher. "So this is your right-hand man?"

"And his left," Disher said before Stottlemeyer could answer. "Don't let my boyish good looks fool you or you'll be making the same mistake as a lot of guys on death row. I'm a grizzled, battle-scarred hard-ass."

"I didn't know that you were looking for a job," Stottlemeyer said.

"Like any man of action, I'm always open to new challenges," Disher said, releasing his grip on Slade's hand and shaking the circulation back into his own. "You get too comfortable and your edges dull. I like to keep my edges razor-sharp."

"Why don't you go sharpen them by telling those officers to stop drooling on Nick's car and to make sure no one else slips past the police line," Stottlemeyer said.

"I'll gladly whip them into shape," Disher said, and

shot Slade a look. "The rank and file don't just respect me; they fear me. You know how it is."

Disher swaggered over to the officers. I think he was trying to appear tough but instead it seemed like he was suffering from a hemorrhoid flare-up.

Slade shook his head. "Please reconsider my offer, Leland. At Intertect, you'd be working with the very best people in the investigative field."

"That's obvious," Stottlemeyer said. "You've hired Adrian Monk."

Slade looked past Stottlemeyer to Monk, who was swaying from side to side and holding his hands out in front of him. I couldn't tell if he was fighting sleep or trying to look at things from a different perspective.

"The guy is brilliant, way beyond my expectations," Slade said. "You wouldn't believe how many cases he's solved for us in just one day."

"I would," Stottlemeyer said. "So who's your client?"

Slade smiled. "Ordinarily, I'd give you a moving speech about client confidentiality, but you'll find out who it is soon enough from your sources at the county jail. It's Salvatore Lucarelli."

Stottlemeyer mulled that over for a moment. "I forgot to mention another benefit of being a cop. You don't have kiss up to mobsters for work."

"He came to me. I'm like a lawyer, Leland. I don't judge my clients. I just do the best job I can for them. He thinks he's being set up and hired me to prove it. I either can or I can't. I don't see anything immoral, unethical, or criminal in that."

"You know he's responsible. Judge Stanton and Judge Carnegie were both going to preside over Lucarelli's trial," Stottlemeyer said. "And they were both executed gangland style."

"By a woman," Slade said. "When was the last time

you heard of a mob boss hiring women to do his dirty work?"

"What makes you think it was a woman?" Stottlemeyer said.

"The same things that make you think so," Slade said. "I know everything that you know, Leland."

Slade looked over his shoulder at Monk, who circled the body, tilting and pirouetting like a ballerina on a music box.

"Maybe more," Slade said. Stottlemeyer followed his gaze. "How about some quid pro quo?"

Stottlemeyer sighed, nodded his acceptance, and we all walked over to Monk. Disher joined us, too, trying to maintain his swagger.

"Hello, Captain," Monk said. He had dark circles under his eyes and he looked even paler than usual.

"You look terrible," Stottlemeyer said. "Are you sleeping?"

"I don't think so." Monk pinched himself. "No, I'm awake. I had my doubts for a minute. But thanks for checking. What can you tell me about what happened?"

"Not much more than what you see right here," Stottlemeyer said, and nodded to Disher, who whipped out his notebook with an exaggerated flourish.

"Judge Carnegie took his dog out for a walk around eight a.m. today, as he does every morning. About eight fifteen, neighbors reported hearing gunshots. When they came out, they found the judge on the ground and the dog dragging him. They tried to get to the judge but the dog started barking and snarling and wouldn't let them near him. The first uniforms on the scene called in some officers from Animal Control, who were about to tranquilize the animal when the wife showed up. The dog calmed down and she took him away."

Stottlemeyer shook his head. "The uniforms should

have let Animal Control tranquilize the dog and prevented the wife from seeing her husband like that. Instead, they traumatized the poor woman. What the hell were they thinking?"

"They were a couple of rookies," Disher said.

"Who are going to get their heads handed to them by me as soon as we're done here," Stottlemeyer said.

"Were there any witnesses to the shooting?" Monk asked.

Disher shook his head. "But it was probably the same hooded shooter. One of the bullets went through Judge Carnegie's body and was recovered by the forensics unit. Just from eyeballing it, the ballistics expert is pretty sure the slug came from the same gun that was used to kill Judge Stanton. They'll confirm it once they get the bullet back to the lab."

Monk rolled his shoulders. "Why would the killer use the same gun?"

"Because it's his gun," Disher said.

"Her gun," Monk corrected.

"Lucarelli is sending a message," Stottlemeyer said. "He wants to be absolutely sure that we all know the killings are connected and that there will be more to come if we don't let him walk. For a man his age, the minimum prison term for his crimes might as well be a life sentence. He'll die behind bars."

"Where does Judge Carnegie live?" Monk asked.

Disher pointed over Monk's shoulder. "At the end of the street, just around the corner."

Monk glanced back at the body. So did I. And I immediately realized what the bloody swath on the sidewalk meant.

"The dog was trying to drag his master back home," I said. "My God, that's heartbreaking."

Monk looked back at Disher. "Did anyone hear anything besides the gunshots?"

"They didn't hear any screams or cars screeching away, if that's what you're asking."

Monk nodded and straightened up ever so slightly. And I knew in that instant that the mystery was solved. Don't ask me how, but I did. It wasn't just me. I glanced at Stottlemeyer and I could see that he knew it, too.

"What?" Slade asked, catching the shared look between the two of us. "What am I missing?"

"Monk knows who killed Judge Carnegie," Stottlemeyer said.

"And Judge Stanton," Monk said matter-of-factly.

Slade leaned towards Monk. "Whisper it in my ear."

"What happened to the quid pro quo?" Stottlemeyer said.

"I don't whisper in ears," Monk said.

"Why not?" Slade said.

"I might accidentally inhale some earwax," Monk said. "And die."

"You can't die from earwax," Slade said.

"I can," Monk said with a yawn.

Disher offered Monk his notebook and pen. "You could write it down."

Stottlemeyer swatted the notebook out of Disher's hand. "We want to know who did it, too."

"We would have." Disher picked up his fallen notebook. "What he wrote on one page would have left an indentation on the page underneath. I could have rubbed my pencil over it and revealed what he wrote. It's an old trick I learned on the streets."

"The Sesame Streets," Stottlemeyer said.

"I'm not ready to say who the killer is," Monk said. "There's still one more thing I need to know before I can be certain that I'm right. And the only one with the answer is Judge Carnegie's widow."

"Her husband was just gunned down," Stottlemeyer

said. "The poor woman is devastated. Couldn't you find out another way?"

"I need to talk to her," Monk said.

"Does it have to be right now?" Stottlemeyer asked. "Can't it wait until tomorrow?"

Monk shook his head. I'm not sure whether he was disagreeing with the captain or simply trying to stay awake.

Stottlemeyer groaned his assent and started trudging down the street. We all joined him.

"Sometimes I hate being a cop," he said.

"So quit and work for me," Slade said. "You, Monk, and Natalie would make a great team."

"The Odd Squad," I said.

13

Mr. Monk Is All Bite and No Bark

The row of houses on the Carnegies' street and on the next street and the one after that were virtually identical, the uniformity broken only slightly by flip-flopped floor plans or tweaks to the facades to evoke various architectural styles, like French provincial or space-age contemporary.

The homes sold for $4,000 when they were built in the 1930s and were now going for $800,000 or more if they were in good shape. The Carnegies' home was mint, literally in its color and figuratively in its condition.

There was something cartoonish about the houses and their vibrant colors. The ceramic squirrels, bunnies, deer, and garden gnomes that dotted the Carnegies' front yard landscaping only added to the storybook effect.

Stottlemeyer knocked on the front door. Almost immediately we heard barking, growling, and scratching and then the sound of claws being dragged along the floor as someone tried to restrain the dog. I hoped the Carnegies didn't have hardwood floors in their entry hall.

After a moment, the barking sounded more muffled and distant and the door was opened by a woman who'd obviously been crying. She was wearing jeans and a button-down sweater that she clutched tightly closed over her shirt. Her eyes were bloodshot from crying. Her hair was the same unnatural shade of brown as her husband's. They must have shared the same bottle of hair coloring. That's real marital intimacy.

I heard the dog barking and scratching behind some door deep inside the house and I couldn't resist glancing at the floor. The entry hall tile was covered with claw marks.

"Mrs. Carnegie," Stottlemeyer said. "I am very, very sorry to disturb you right now. I hope you can forgive me. We have one more question that can't wait."

She nodded and sniffled. "It's no problem, Captain. I want to do whatever I can to catch the bastards who took my husband from me."

"Does your dog always bark like that?" Monk asked.

"Only around strangers. He's really a sweetheart with people he's learned to trust," she said, her lower lip beginning to tremble. "Thank God he was spared. He's like our child. I don't think I could survive losing both Alan and Sweetie."

Mrs. Carnegie started to shake and cry, her shoulders heaving.

Stottlemeyer looked back at Monk. "Hurry up and ask your question."

"I just did," Monk said.

Stottlemeyer glared at him. "You had us rush over here and intrude on Mrs. Carnegie's privacy just to ask her about her dog?"

"I also thought it would be a good idea to arrest her now and secure the scene before she had a chance to get rid of any more evidence."

Mrs. Carnegie stood up straight, her eyes going wide.

Slade turned to Monk in shock. "You're saying that *she* killed the judges?"

"She's the one," Monk said.

Mrs. Carnegie started to slam the door in fury but Stottlemeyer threw his shoulder against it, preventing it from closing.

"I don't think you want to do that, Mrs. Carnegie," Stottlemeyer said, his tone of voice no longer so solicitous. "Perhaps it would be better if you stepped outside."

It wasn't really a suggestion and she knew it. She reluctantly stepped out onto the stoop.

"My husband, the love of my life, was just slaughtered outside my door," she said. "And you want me to submit myself to this abuse? Who is this horrible man?"

"Someone who has never been wrong about murder," Stottlemeyer said. "Why did she kill her husband?"

"I have no idea," Monk said.

"That's helpful," Stottlemeyer said.

"Can I go back inside now?" Mrs. Carnegie said. "Or do you want to torture me some more?"

"But I know why she killed Judge Stanton," Monk said. "She knew that her husband was the designated alternate to hear the case against Salvatore Lucarelli if anything happened to Stanton. She wanted Judge Carnegie's murder to look like a mob hit."

"You're insane," she said, then turned to Stottlemeyer. "You should be ashamed of yourself."

"I assume you have some strong evidence," Stottlemeyer said to Monk.

"You mean besides the fact that she's a woman, that her height matches the dimensions of the bicycle, and that she's wearing the Nike running shoes that match the footprint left in the dirt?"

We all gave her the once-over. Not only did I notice that everything Monk said was true, but her tears seemed to dry up and her expression of mourning had turned to one of barely contained rage.

"There are thousands of women in San Francisco who are my same height, and who own a pair of these shoes," she said. "You pathetic little man."

"That's true," Monk said. "But we also have an eyewitness."

"Who?" Disher asked.

"Sweetie," Monk said. "The neighbors reported hearing the gunshots but didn't say anything about a dog barking."

"Don't call me Sweetie," Disher said. "I'm a grizzled, battle-scarred hard-ass."

"He's referring to her dog," I said.

"If the dog always barks around people he doesn't know," Monk said, "why wasn't he barking when Judge Carnegie was confronted and shot by a stranger?"

"Because it wasn't a stranger," Stottlemeyer said, and looked at Mrs. Carnegie. "The dog wasn't trying to drag his master away after the shooting; he was trying to follow you back home."

"The dog didn't start barking until you fled and other people began to approach him," Monk said. "And the dog didn't stop barking until you returned."

She snorted derisively. "That's all you've got?"

"You're under arrest," Stottlemeyer said. "Read this woman her rights, Lieutenant."

Disher did and took out his handcuffs.

"I've been a judge's wife for twenty-three years, Captain. I know how they think," she said as Disher cuffed her hands behind her back. "This isn't evidence. It's unfounded speculation. You don't have enough to hold me for more than a few hours."

"But it's enough probable cause to get us a search warrant," Stottlemeyer said. "The bike and the hooded jacket may be gone but you haven't had the opportunity to ditch the gun yet. That should keep you in a cell while we uncover your motive."

Her wide-eyed reaction was as good as a confession. Stottlemeyer would find the gun.

Disher led her away. Slade motioned Monk and me off to one side, leaving Stottlemeyer by himself at the front door.

"You really are incredible, Mr. Monk," Slade said. "I'm going to make sure that you get all the credit you deserve for this."

"So you can whip up some publicity for yourself," I said.

"For Intertect, your employer. We are a business and publicity brings clients." Slade addressed Monk again. "There are a lot of reporters standing around the corner. The timing couldn't be better. How would you feel about joining me in an impromptu press conference to capitalize on your shining moment?"

"I'd rather not," Monk said, glancing back at Stottlemeyer, who was still standing on Mrs. Carnegie's stoop.

Slade followed his gaze. "I completely understand. I'll try not to embarrass Leland or the department too much. But they have no one to blame for this but themselves for letting you go."

I agreed with Slade on that point but there was no way he could spin this story that wouldn't end up humiliating Stottlemeyer in front of the media.

Sure, the outcome of this case proved once again how wrong and petty the captain was to fire Monk, but I still felt lousy about hurting him. Maybe our new jobs, fancy car, and comprehensive health plan had softened my anger a bit and made me more sympathetic towards the captain.

Slade hurried off after Disher and his prisoner. I'm sure that Slade wanted to make sure all three of them got in the newspaper photos and TV news footage together.

I couldn't really blame Slade for that and I owed him an apology for what I'd said. He was right. It was smart to take advantage of the opportunity and it only helped burnish Monk's reputation along with Intertect's.

Even so, I couldn't help feeling that Monk was being exploited, which was stupid, considering how generously we were both being compensated for his detecting services.

"I'm sorry, Captain," Monk said.

"You have nothing to be sorry about, Monk," he said. "Nick was right: That was some amazing detective work. We were fortunate that you showed up."

"It was just a lucky guess," Monk said.

"One that I wouldn't have made, at least not today and not for the reasons that you did," Stottlemeyer said. "It would have come after I exhausted every possible connection to Lucarelli, which might have been weeks from now. And by then, Mrs. Carnegie could have destroyed all the evidence and run off to some tropical island."

"You would have figured it out before that happened," Monk said.

"Or received an anonymous tip," Stottlemeyer said.

"Are you reconsidering letting Monk go?" I asked. "Not that he would come back if you did."

"I would," Monk said. I elbowed him hard, eliciting a pained yelp. I don't think he fully appreciated yet all the benefits of his new job. He was too sleepy.

Stottlemeyer shook his head. "I didn't have a choice then and I don't now."

"That might change after the chief sees the evening news," I said.

"There might be changes," Stottlemeyer said. "But I don't think they will involve Monk. They might involve me."

The captain walked off, his shoulders slumped.

Monk and I watched him go.

"He's a good detective," Monk said.

I nodded. "Just not a great one and he knows it."

"Maybe I should retire," Monk said.

"And do what?" I said.

"Spread the good word about Diaper Genies."

"You'd be wasting your natural talent and Stottlemeyer wouldn't want that."

"But I'd be making the world a better place."

"That's what you are doing now," I said.

"You think so?"

"You give people closure and justice," I said, and thought of my husband and the unanswered questions surrounding his death in Kosovo. "I could use some of that."

"Me, too," he said, undoubtedly thinking about the unsolved murder of his wife. "So who can we go to?"

Just as Stottlemeyer was about to turn the corner, he stopped and answered his cell phone. The call was short and we couldn't hear what was said, but his body language told us it wasn't good news. His shoulders slumped even more and he lowered his head.

Monk and I shared a look and caught up with the captain.

"What's wrong?" I asked.

"That was Carol Atwater," Stottlemeyer said. "Bill Peschel is dead."

14

Mr. Monk Cleans Up

Stottlemeyer told us that Carol left her father at home while she dropped her son off at school and took her daughter to a pediatrician's appointment. When Carol got back, she found her father floating facedown in the pool.

Monk insisted on following Stottlemeyer to Carol's house. Although he didn't know Bill Peschel at all, he felt indebted to him for bringing the miraculous Diaper Genie into his life.

When we arrived, there was a Mill Valley Police squad car, an unmarked Crown Vic, and a coroner's van parked out front. Neighbors were standing in their driveways and lawns, staring at the house and waiting for something interesting to happen.

The police photographer was just leaving as we walked up to the front door. Carol met us there, still in her wet clothes.

"I'm sorry to trouble you, Captain. I just didn't know who else to call." She gestured inside to the family room, where two uniformed Mill Valley police officers and a detective were conferring with a woman wearing a windbreaker with the word CORONER stenciled in big letters on her back. "I don't know how to talk to them or what questions I should be asking."

"You leave everything to me," he said. "You should change into some dry clothes and sit down for a few minutes. You might be in shock. Did the paramedics take a look at you before they left?"

She shook her head. "I'm just cold. I haven't had a chance to change yet."

"You can now," I said. "Do you need any help with the baby?"

"She's with the neighbors," Carol said.

Monk drifted over to the French doors and looked out into the backyard.

There was a white plastic chair in the shimmering, wet grass next to the black, wrought-iron pool fence. Two assistants lifted Peschel into the body bag. All I saw were his white tube socks before they zipped him up and lifted the body bag onto a gurney.

Carol followed our gaze. "I've left him alone before without any problems. I never imagined he'd try to go in the pool."

"It's not your fault," Stottlemeyer said.

"I looked all over the house for him before I thought to go in the backyard . . . and there he was," she said. "I tried to save him, but it took so long. I grabbed the key to the padlock, opened the gate, and dove into the pool. By the time I got to him, it was too late."

"It was probably too late before you even got back home," Stottlemeyer said. "You can't blame yourself."

I put my arm around her wet shoulders and gave her a comforting squeeze.

"You should get into some dry clothes. I'll make you something hot to drink," I said. "Would you like coffee or tea?"

"Tea," she said. "Thank you."

Carol trudged down the hall. Stottlemeyer looked at me.

"I'm glad that you came," he said. "I'm terrible at this kind of thing."

"So go do what you're good at," I said.

Stottlemeyer sighed wearily and headed for the huddle of cops, flashing them his badge as he approached. They went outside to the far corner of the patio to confer.

I headed for the kitchen and spotted a box of Lipton tea bags on the back counter, not far from Peschel's row of liquor bottles full of water.

She had one of those little faucets that give you instant boiling water, so it made my job easy. As I took a coffee cup out of the strainer and filled it with hot water, I noticed Peschel's dish towel on the counter and a glass set up on a napkin, all ready for his next customer.

That made me think of Peschel, of course, and I glanced outside.

Monk stood on the patio, where the edge met the wet, freshly cut grass, staring at the chair and the pool on the other side of the fence. There was still a puddle of water where Peschel's body had lain on the concrete.

The coroner's assistants wheeled the gurney with the body bag into the house and through the family room to the front door. I was glad Carol missed that but I was sure that the neighbors outside got a thrill when the body bag came out. People love to crane their necks to see body bags as long as it's not one of their loved ones zipped up inside of it.

I went to the refrigerator to look for honey. The doors of the appliance were covered with family photos, school art projects, grocery coupons, and her appointment calendar, all stuck in place with letters-of-the-alphabet magnets. My refrigerator was also covered with stuff, but in my case it was family photos, reminder notes for me or Julie to each other or to ourselves, and interesting newspaper clippings that I'd put up for Julie or that she put up for me.

What is it about the refrigerator that makes it the communications center and scrapbook for families? Or is it because it's a place that everyone in the household is bound to go at least once or twice during the day? Or is it just because it's a big, blank metal surface?

You can tell a lot about a family by what they stick on their refrigerator. For example, there's nothing on Monk's. It's so clean and shiny that you can use it like a mirror.

I found a bottle of honey in the fridge, put a dollop of it in the tea, then set the cup on the counter with a spoon and the sugar bowl.

Carol came down the hall in a bathrobe and slippers and took a seat on one of the bar stools. She wrapped her hands around the cup of tea, blew on it, and took a sip.

She didn't say anything and I didn't try to make conversation. What was there to talk about? Carol seemed lost in her mourning or, as Stottlemeyer suspected, she was in shock. Who could blame her?

I looked outside again and saw Monk squatting on the patio, picking up something with tweezers and putting it in the palm of his other hand.

I went outside on the pretense of seeing what Monk was up to, not that I explained myself to her. It was just the motivation behind my performance as I left the kitchen. The truth was I felt awkward standing there watching Carol drink her tea in misery and needed to escape.

I looked down at him. "What are you doing?"

"I thought I'd help Carol out by cleaning up this big mess."

All I saw were a few blades of cut grass and some white fertilizer pellets.

"If that's your idea of a big mess, then I'm never letting you in my house again."

"Do you have a Baggie?" he asked.

I reached into my purse and gave him one of the tiny plastic bags I carry with me for his used wipes or any evidence that he collects.

He emptied his hand into the bag and then stood up, nodding to himself.

"This will take some of the pressure off of her," he said, sealing the bag. "One less thing for her to worry about."

I took the Baggie from him and handed him a wipe before he could ask.

Stottlemeyer, the Mill Valley cops, and the coroner broke their huddle like a football team ready to make their play. Stottlemeyer came over to us and the others left.

"The coroner says it looks like Bill banged the back of his head on the coping when he jumped into the pool," Stottlemeyer said. "He was probably out cold when he hit the water."

"At least he didn't suffer," I said.

The captain nodded and looked back at Carol. "Maybe this is a blessing."

"How?" I asked.

"I'd rather die than lose my mind in front of my kids," Stottlemeyer said. "Bill wouldn't have wanted to end up in his daughter's kitchen, serving imaginary drinks and calling cops with tips on crimes that happened ten years ago. Maybe he had a rare moment of clarity and decided to put an end to his torment and hers while he still could."

"You're projecting. You were uncomfortable watching him replay scenes from his old life but that doesn't mean that he was suffering," I said. "He seemed happy to me."

"If I end up sitting at a card table in my son's garage believing that I'm in my office, running Homicide again, you have my permission to shoot me." Stottlemeyer looked back at Carol, sitting at the counter in the kitchen. "I'd better go talk to her. Get some rest, Monk. You look like you need it."

Monk nodded and we left through the side yard, following a path through a vegetable garden.

I was tired, too. It was a lot of death for one day and it was only the early afternoon.

The first thing I did when we got to Monk's place was to take that rolling file drawer and wheel it out the door to the Lexus.

"Where are you going with that?" he exclaimed, chasing after me to the street.

"I'm taking it home," I said.

"But the day isn't over yet."

"It is for you," I said, opening the lift-back on the SUV. "You worked all night, so you get to take the rest of the day off."

"I don't want to take the rest of the day off."

"Too bad," I said. "You're going to. You'll thank me later."

I collapsed the legs and slid the file drawer right into the car. That rolling drawer was handy. I thought about getting myself one for bringing groceries into the house. Instead of three trips to the car, I could do it in one.

"What about you?" Monk asked.

"What about me?"

"You didn't work all night," he said.

I stopped and turned to face him. "I think I deserve an afternoon off, too."

"Why?"

"On general principle," I said. "What do you care? Technically, you aren't the one paying me anymore."

He did a little double take. "I'm not?"

"Intertect is paying me," I said.

He smiled. I did, too. I think that was the first moment that he realized how great this job was. So I decided to drive the point home.

"Not only that, Mr. Monk, but they are paying for Dr. Bell, too."

"So, I could see him four days a week and it would be absolutely free."

"For you, yes. Not for Slade. But I'm sure he'd consider it a small price to pay for keeping you happy and productive."

Monk's smile got bigger. "I know how to spend the rest of the day."

I groaned. I didn't have to be a deductive genius to see what he had in mind.

"What makes you think Dr. Bell has any openings today?"

"If he doesn't, I'll just sit in his office and catch him between sessions."

"He's going to love that," I said.

"I know," Monk said.

I dropped Monk off at Dr. Bell's office, told him to call me when he was ready to be picked up, and I sped off before he could think of a reason for me to spend the afternoon with him in the waiting room.

I went home, left the file drawer in the back of the Lexus, and caught up on some very important loafing around.

You'd think I'd be inured to death after all the years I'd spent working for Monk. And I was, to a degree. I didn't turn away anymore from the victims of violent death. I could study a corpse alongside Monk, Stottlemeyer, and Disher without flinching or feeling sick. But after seeing a particularly bloody murder and a tragic drowning death I needed to decompress.

All that death was a heavy load, emotionally and visually, to carry around. It wasn't just the dead bodies that got to me; it was everything that went along with it—like meeting a mobster in jail, facing an unrepentant murderer on her doorstep, and comforting the heartbroken, guilt-stricken loved ones of the dead.

Factor in the day-to-day, minute-to-minute aggravation of smoothing things out for Monk on top of all that and you can see why I just curled up on the couch with a bag of nacho-cheese Doritos, a Diet Shasta root beer, and some unread issues of *Vanity Fair*, *The New Yorker*, and *Entertainment Weekly*.

That's the secret to keeping my svelte figure, by the way: generous amounts of junk food coupled with hours of sitting on my butt.

I engaged in that rigorous workout until Monk called around five for me to take him home.

I insisted on picking up Monk on the street because I didn't want to face Dr. Bell, who was likely to be very angry with me for dropping Monk in his waiting room and then fleeing for the day.

Monk had an actual skip to his step as he came to the car. I found that pretty amazing given the fact that he hadn't slept in a day and a half.

"How did it go with Dr. Bell?"

"I think he really enjoyed it," Monk said. "He pretended to be irritated, but it was just a show for the other patients. He didn't want them to know that I'm his favorite and that he was counting the minutes in their sessions until he could get back to me."

"You're probably right," I said.

"I usually am," he said.

15

Mr. Monk Gets an Early Start

I sat on the beach at Paradise Island, letting Daniel Craig slather suntan lotion all over my bare back. The lotion smelled like coconuts and I could feel some grains of sand gently scratching my skin as he applied the cool cream. His hands were rough, but he was using them softly, and I found the contrast intoxicatingly exciting. It was all I could do not to purr like a cat. Or maybe I did, but it was drowned out by the sound of the ringing phone.

I grabbed the phone, fully intending to throw it into the ocean, but then I opened my eyes and saw that the beautiful, white sandy beach that stretched out into eternity was actually the pillow beside my head.

"Hello?" I said, my consciousness still half in San Francisco, half on the beach with Daniel Craig.

"I'm glad you're still up," Monk said. "I was thinking about those files."

I glanced at the clock on my nightstand. It was two twenty-four a.m. I wasn't in the Bahamas anymore.

"Go to bed, Mr. Monk," I said.

"You know what would be fun? If you brought those files back to my apartment."

"You want me to drive over to your house at two thirty in the morning and deliver a bunch of case files so you can work all night again?"

"You're exaggerating," Monk said. "It's two twenty-six."

"I'm going back to the beach," I said, and hung up. I put my face in the warm spot on my pillow, closed my eyes, and tried to transport myself back to Paradise Island.

The phone rang again.

I opened my eyes, rolled over, reached behind the nightstand, and yanked the phone cord out of the wall. The phone was silenced. In my room but not the rest of the house.

A moment or two later my door flew open and Julie stood there in her nightgown, holding her portable phone.

"It's Mr. Monk," she said. "He wants me to drive to his apartment with some files."

"Tell him no and turn off your phone," I said, and put the pillow over my head.

"I'll be glad to take the files to him," she said. "If I can drive the Lexus."

I tossed the pillow aside and sat up in bed. "Do you actually think that I'm going to let a seventeen-year-old girl drive alone in the city at two thirty in the morning?"

I heard some squawking from the phone, like one of those adult voices from a Charlie Brown cartoon. Julie held the phone up to her ear, listened for a few seconds, and then covered the mouthpiece with her hand.

"Mr. Monk says you could come, too. We can make toast and have a party."

I motioned to her to bring me the phone. She handed it to me. I turned the phone off and gave it back to her.

"Good night," I said.

"How am I supposed to get back to sleep now?" she whined.

"You can count Lexuses."

I buried my face in my pillow and hoped that Daniel Craig was still waiting for me in the Bahamas.

He wasn't. By the time I got back to dreamland, Daniel was gone and the Bahamas had washed away, too. I found myself in some postapocalypse hell, living in a subterranean bunker filled with Diaper Genies, Wet Ones, and evidence Baggies. All I had to eat were Wheat Thins and Sierra Springs bottled water.

I woke up after nine, sticky with sweat, my throat dry and my right arm numb from being crooked at an odd angle under my pillow.

Ah, what a glorious morning.

I dragged myself out of bed. Julie had gotten herself to school somehow and had kindly left her half-eaten bowl of cereal, crusts of toast, and an empty coffee cup on the table for me or a member of our household staff to clean up.

I guess I deserved that for being such a bad mother.

I wasn't much of an assistant, either. I was late for work but I was in no hurry to make up for lost time. Monk had no one to blame but himself for my tardiness.

I refilled Julie's cup of coffee with what she'd left simmering in the pot, put a frosted cinnamon Pop-Tart in the toaster for my breakfast, and sat down to browse the *Chronicle*, which Julie had thoughtfully left spread out all over the table.

When it comes to reading a newspaper, I'm kind of Monkish—I like all the sections folded and in order so I can start at the front page and work my way through. I gathered up all the sections and put them back together.

The front-page section was the last one that I came to, and when I did, I got an unpleasant surprise.

The Judge Carnegie story had made the front page. This is how it began:

Police arrested Rhonda Carnegie, the wife of Judge Alan Carnegie, and charged her with the murder yesterday of her husband and the gangland-style execution of Judge Clarence Stanton in Golden Gate Park earlier this week.

Judge Carnegie was gunned down half a block from his home while walking his dog and Judge Stanton was shot multiple times the day before while jogging.

Sources within the department tell the *Chronicle* that the investigation, led by Captain Leland Stottlemeyer, was focused on reputed mob boss Salvatore Lucarelli, who was facing trial this week before Judge Stanton. After that jurist's murder, Judge Carnegie was slated to take his place at the bench. A new trial date has not been set.

The crucial break in the investigation came from famed detective Adrian Monk, who was a consultant to the police department until his contract was suddenly dropped a few days ago. Monk was immediately hired by Intertect, a San Francisco–based private detective agency.

"Mr. Monk was deeply shocked by this attack on our judiciary system and took an immediate interest in the case, but his assistance was spurned by the police," said Nicholas Slade, president and founder of Intertect. "Undeterred, and with the full support of our experienced professionals, he pursued the case and found compelling evidence that the police missed in their blind zeal to prosecute Mr. Lucarelli."

Capt. Stottlemeyer confirmed that Monk's participation in the investigation "played a decisive

role" and led to Mrs. Carnegie's arrest at her home,
a short distance from the scene of her husband's
murder a few hours earlier. She is being held without bail pending trial. Capt. Stottlemeyer refused
to comment any further or divulge any additional
details regarding the investigation or the nature of
the evidence against Mrs. Carnegie.

The captain was criticized on the opening day
of the Conference of Metropolitan Homicide Detectives this week at the Dorchester Hotel for his
division's reliance on Adrian Monk and their poor
case-closure rate if the consultant's contributions
are factored out of their annual statistics.

I couldn't read any more of the article. It was too
painful.

If that was Slade's idea of going easy on Stottlemeyer and sparing him embarrassment, I shuddered
to think what his comments would have been like if he
hadn't held back.

While I was angry with Slade for what he'd done, I
had to admire the way he spun the story to make Intertect appear efficient and community-minded and to cast
Lucarelli as a victim.

I wondered why Slade chose not to disclose that Lucarelli had hired Intertect to prove he was innocent of
the murders of the judges.

Perhaps Slade was worried that it would taint Monk's
success if people knew he was not motivated by outrage
at the heinous crime but rather that he'd been paid by
Lucarelli to clear him of the killings.

It was a testament to Stottlemeyer's devotion to
Monk, even at his own expense, that he didn't challenge
Slade's version of events. Then again, perhaps that had
less to do with sparing Monk than it did with protecting his case against Mrs. Carnegie from being muddied

by any doubt. After all, both Slade and Stottlemeyer agreed that Monk was right and neither one of them wanted Mrs. Carnegie to walk.

After reading that article, I was glad I'd forgotten to watch the news the previous night. They'd probably lambasted Captain Stottlemeyer on all the local channels.

I ate my Pop-Tart (and told myself it was healthy because it was made of flour and cinnamon, both of which are found in nature and not created in a test tube), took a quick shower, got dressed, and headed over to Monk's place.

I kept the file drawer in my car, took four bulging files from it, and carried them with me. My plan was to carefully dole the cases out to him in small batches.

So you can imagine my surprise and anger when I walked in the door around ten thirty and saw Monk at his dining room table, another rolling file drawer at his side, papers and crime scene photos spread out in front of him. Danielle was sitting at the table, too, facing her laptop computer and typing away.

Monk was wearing the same clothes he'd worn the day before. But that didn't necessarily mean he hadn't changed clothes since I'd last seen him. He bought his clothes in bulk specifically so he could wear the same thing every day if he wanted to. His clothes weren't wrinkled either but he never allowed his clothes to wrinkle.

Even so, I was convinced that he hadn't slept and hadn't changed. He was going on two days without sleep and that couldn't be good.

"Good morning, everyone," I said with intentionally false cheer.

"Good morning, Natalie," Danielle said, so perky and energetic that I wanted to smother her with one of Monk's two identical square throw pillows. But that wasn't the only motive behind my totally justifiable desire to kill her. There was the matter of that second file drawer.

"It's about time you got here," Monk said without looking up from his work. "I thought you'd gone on vacation."

"You'd know if I were on vacation, Mr. Monk, because you'd be there, too, and people would be dropping dead all around us."

Unfortunately, that wasn't a smart-ass remark. It was the truth. I'm probably the only tourist to Hawaii, Germany, and France whose vacation scrapbook includes crime scene photos. Murder follows Monk like an obsessed fan. We could take a trip to an uninhabitable ice floe in the North Pole and we'd probably stumble on the Abominable Snowman with a dagger in his back.

"Did you hear the news?" Danielle said. "The police found a gun in Mrs. Carnegie's house and ballistics positively identified it as the murder weapon. They also found the bicycle and the hooded jacket there. She took a big risk keeping all of that."

"I guess it never occurred to her that the police would suspect her so soon," I said.

"They didn't. Mr. Monk did," she said proudly. "He's solved nine cases already this morning."

"Ten," Monk said, closing a file and sliding it over to her. "The bus driver is the kidnapper. A real bus driver would have stopped at the railroad tracks and opened the door. He didn't."

"Amazing," Danielle said. "Isn't he?"

"You should see him leap tall buildings in a single bound," I said.

"Mrs. Carnegie was having an affair with a man twenty years younger than her," Danielle said. "I guess she didn't want to go through the trouble of a divorce."

"Murder does cut down on legal fees, unless you get

caught," I said, turning to Monk. "Where did you get all these files?"

"You and Julie wouldn't help, so I called Danielle and she brought them over."

"At two thirty in the morning?" I said.

"It was two thirty-five by then and she'd told us that she was available any time of the day or night."

"I meant it, too. And Mr. Slade didn't mind me waking him up, either, or going down to the office to collect some additional open cases."

I wasn't surprised, considering all the success and positive publicity Monk had brought Intertect in the last twenty-four hours. "Danielle, could I talk to you privately for a moment?"

"What about?" Monk asked.

"I'm out of tampons and I thought she might—"

Monk waved his hands frantically in the air to signal me to stop talking and then covered his ears. It was just the reaction I was expecting.

"Take it outside or I might hear something that I don't want to," he said.

I marched for the front door and Danielle followed me out. As soon as the door was closed, I got in her face, startling her.

"If you weren't a black belt I'd kick your butt right now," I said. "What were you thinking when you brought him those files?"

"I was doing my job," she said. "He asked for more cases to work on and I brought them."

"Can't you see that he hasn't slept?"

"That's because he couldn't stop thinking about the open cases," she said. "I thought if I brought them that he'd—"

"Sleep?" I interrupted her. "C'mon, Danielle, I thought you had a psychology degree. Did you really believe that once you brought him more open case files he'd go to bed? Or were you thinking about how happy Nick would be if Mr. Monk solved a dozen more cases before sunrise?"

She dropped her gaze to her feet, acknowledging her guilt, but I wasn't about to let her off the hook.

"The man is exhausted," I said. "He needs his rest. That's why I took the other file drawer home with me."

"But he called me and asked for cases to work on," she said, a defensive whine in her voice. "What was I supposed to do?"

"What is in his best interest, even if he thinks that it isn't," I said sharply. "If you are truly working for Mr. Monk, that's your priority. And right now what he needs more than anything is sleep."

"I'm sorry," she said.

"It's not me that you let down. It's him. It's too late to take these files back now; he's seen them. He's probably counted them all and won't stop thinking about them just because they aren't in his house. But no more files after this. Is that clear?"

She nodded.

"Hopefully he'll be so tired after plowing through these that he will finally get some sleep," I said, and walked back into the house.

The three of us spent the rest of the day going through the files and writing up the reports on Monk's findings. The only ones who showed any sign of fatigue were Danielle and me. Monk was on a roll, each solved case giving him momentum into the next one.

By six p.m., he'd cleared all the cases in both filing cabinets and I extracted another oath from Danielle that she wouldn't bring him any more. But he wasted no time asking.

"Where are the rest?" he asked. "Bring it on."

"There are no more cases, Mr. Monk," she said.

"Not here," he said. "You can deliver whatever case files are left at the office."

"This is it," she said. "You've cleared everything there is. You've put all our operatives out of work. We have to wait now for new business to come in."

She was so convincing I almost believed it myself. He must have believed it, or his senses were so dulled by weariness that he couldn't detect the lie, because suddenly all the fatigue he'd been outrunning with work seemed to catch up with him. His shoulders slumped and his eyes grew heavy. He dropped into his favorite easy chair.

"I'm ready for more," he said. "Bring it on."

"You'll be the first person we call," she said.

And then the damn phone rang. Monk perked up in his chair, sitting up straight, the possibility of another crime to solve giving him a jolt of energy.

I was tempted not to answer the phone but I decided the best course was to see who it was. If it was Nick Slade, or anybody else with a mystery for Monk, I intended to hang up the phone and lie to him about who'd called.

But it wasn't anyone with a case. It was Carol Atwater with an invitation to a wake.

16

Mr. Monk Wakes Up

It was unsettling to be back at Carol Atwater's house again at just about the same time of day that we'd been there before.

On our first visit, Bill Peschel was behind the kitchen counter, pretending it was a bar. On our second visit, he was dead outside and there were cops and coroners around. And now, on our third visit, Peschel was gone and someone else was at the kitchen counter, serving real wine, beer, and soft drinks to the two dozen friends and relatives.

I wondered if the counter was being used as a bar intentionally to honor Bill Peschel or if it was just an ironic coincidence. I decided on the latter. They probably used the counter as a bar every time they entertained, whether it was a cocktail party or a wake. But even so, there was something creepy about it, especially since nobody had bothered to clear away Bill's bottles of water yet.

Some people milled outside on the patio. I could see that the white chair had been moved off the wet grass and the wrought-iron pool fence was closed and locked again.

I didn't expect to see anyone I knew when I arrived with Monk besides Carol Atwater, of course, and Stottlemeyer, so I was startled when I spotted Detective Paul Braddock nursing a beer and talking with Nick Slade. Every so often, Braddock would shoot a sneer at Stottlemeyer, who was standing off to one side by himself, sipping a Diet Coke and pointedly ignoring them (which I guess meant that he wasn't actually ignoring them at all).

Monk wasn't good with crowds and small spaces. He was practically hugging himself, his head down low, as we weaved our way over to the captain.

"You must have finally had some rest, Monk," Stottlemeyer said. "You look almost like yourself again."

"I wish I could say the same for you, Captain," I said. "You look worn-down."

"I am," he said.

"Tough time at work?" I asked.

"The mayor and the chief aren't in very good moods today," Stottlemeyer said. "Haven't you watched the news?"

I shook my head. "But you closed a big double-murder case in only forty-eight hours. Doesn't that earn you any brownie points?"

"It's not the rapid investigation and solid arrest that're getting all the attention." Stottlemeyer gestured to Monk. "It's that we needed him to do it."

"I'm sorry," Monk mumbled.

"Don't be," Stottlemeyer snapped. "Never apologize for being the best at what you do, Monk. We caught the murderer, that's the important thing. Everything else is smoke."

"Smoke can kill you," Monk said.

"You think everything can kill you," Stottlemeyer said.

"It's true," Monk said. "Name one thing that isn't lethal."

"A cotton ball," I said.

"You know how many people choke to death on cotton balls every year?" Monk asked. With anyone else, I'd say it was a rhetorical question. But I'm sure he knew exactly how many, not just for the last year, but going as far back as the Roman Empire.

"Which one of these people is Phil Atwater?" I asked.

Stottlemeyer tipped his Diet Coke towards the man serving drinks at the kitchen counter. One look at Phil's poufy, blow-dried hair and Rick Springfield started singing "Jessie's Girl" in my head.

"Don't you think it's odd that Carol married a man with practically the same name as her father?" I asked, hoping to drown out the song in my head by talking. "I would never marry a man with a name close to my father's. He'd have to prove his love for me by changing his name."

"Bill is short for William and Phil is short for Phillip," Monk said. "So actually the names aren't similar at all."

"Bill and Phil sound pretty close to me," I said.

"But William and Phillip aren't," Monk said.

"But that's not what they call themselves."

"But that's what their names are," Monk said.

"I've never understood why Bill is short for William," Stottlemeyer interjected. "Where does the 'B' come from?"

"Why is Bob short for Robert?" I said. "Where does that 'B' come from?"

"Misspellings that were left uncorrected and, as a result, went on to contaminate the entire English language," Monk said. "Let that be a warning to us all on the importance of proofreading."

No one could accuse us of not engaging in highly intellectual conversations.

Carol Atwater approached us. "Thank you all for coming."

"Your father indirectly changed my life forever," Monk said.

"He did?" Carol asked. "How?"

"By accompanying the captain here, I was introduced to the Diaper Genie and its potential to save the world," Monk said. "I'll be sure that your father is mentioned during the Nobel ceremony."

She stared at him in bewilderment. "You mean like the Nobel Prize?"

"Don't ask," I said. "How are you doing?"

"Okay, I guess," she said. "We cremated Dad this morning and scattered his ashes in front of his old bar like he wanted. It's a Jamba Juice now, but that doesn't matter, does it?"

"I hope you cleaned it up afterwards," Monk said. "You aren't supposed to spread dead people in front of restaurants."

I nudged him hard and Stottlemeyer spoke up quickly to cover Monk's insensitivity.

"That spot will always be Bill's Tavern to me," Stottlemeyer said. "To all of us."

I looked over at Braddock and Slade, both of whom were watching us. "They knew your father, too?"

"Dad called them a couple of times since he moved in, with some hot tips from the nineteen nineties," she said. "Nick has been here twice before. Detective Braddock came for the first time the same day that you three were here. He's in town for a convention."

"The three of us were on the force at the same time.

Bill gave us each a lot of good leads on crimes that happened or were in the works," Stottlemeyer said. "I don't know how he decided which one of us to grace with a particular bit of gossip. If he played favorites, I never noticed or cared. His bar was in the heart of the Tenderloin, his customers lived in the shadows, and they talked a lot when they were drunk. He always knew the word on the street."

"Didn't the street know he was passing it along to you?" I said.

"We didn't advertise it and I doubt he did, either. I liked Bill, but he played both sides of the fence. He was every bit as dirty as—" He suddenly remembered who was standing there and lowered his head with embarrassment. "What I mean is—"

"I know what you meant, Captain," she said, but without any resentment in her voice. "One of the reasons Dad ratted on his friends and customers and told you the scuttlebutt that he heard was so you'd look the other way on his little schemes and scams. I loved my father, warts and all. And he certainly had plenty of warts."

Monk cringed. "And you let him stand in your kitchen where your family's food is prepared? Where your guests are eating and drinking now? You're going to have to gut that kitchen down to the studs."

Carol stared coldly at Monk. "Excuse me, I should probably see how the other guests are doing."

She gave Stottlemeyer a kiss on the cheek, cast one more cold glance at Monk, and moved on.

"You're a sensitive guy, Monk," Stottlemeyer said.

"That's why I didn't tell her that she and her family and everyone here who has consumed anything served from that wart-infested hellhole will need to be decontaminated by a haz-mat team," Monk said. "I'll call her tomorrow, when it won't be as traumatic. Someone should also call the health department about that Jamba

Juice. People have probably been tracking warty Bill Pe-schel in and out of the place all day."

Nick broke away from Braddock to talk with Carol, and Braddock sauntered over to us.

"Oh joy," Stottlemeyer said as he saw Braddock approaching.

"Maybe he's just coming over to share his condolences," I said.

"I'm sure he is," Stottlemeyer said. "For my career."

"Hey, Monk, I'm surprised to see you here," Braddock said. "I didn't know you knew old Billy-boy back in the day."

"I didn't," Monk said. "I met him for the first time a few days ago. He was the captain's friend."

Braddock nodded. "That makes sense. You don't need snitches, do you, Monk? You can close a case without help, unlike Leland here. He needs all the help he can get."

"You're right, Paul. I do. I solicit the unique skills and special relationships of the people around me to get the job done."

"To make up for your own weaknesses," Braddock said. "It's sad."

"I guess that's why I'm a Homicide captain in the big city of San Francisco and you're giving parking tickets in the tiny little desert town of Banning."

Braddock's face turned bright red. His rage must have been pretty close to the surface to start with.

"The way I hear it, you aren't going to have that job much longer."

"Maybe so," Stottlemeyer said. "But it's still a job that you'll never get."

"The only difference between you and me is him," Braddock said, jabbing a finger in Monk's direction. "Without your little Rainman, you're nothing."

"Which still is more of a cop than you'll ever be. I

make my cases using evidence, not beatings," Stottlemeyer said, watching as Braddock's hand clenched into
a fist, crushing the empty can he was holding. "Trying to
wring a confession out of that beer can?"

Braddock swung his fist at Stottlemeyer, who deftly
dodged it with his left arm, splashing the people nearby
with Diet Coke, and punched him in the nose with his
right.

The detective staggered back, bumping into two
mourners and causing an immediate stir in the room.
Everyone was watching now. Nick seemed embarrassed
but Carol was mortified.

Furious and bloodied, Braddock swung again, but
Stottlemeyer easily ducked under it and punched the detective hard in the stomach, doubling him over.

Stottlemeyer followed up with a right uppercut to the
chin that sent Braddock staggering backwards out the
open French doors to the backyard, where he lost his
footing and slid on his butt across the wet grass as if it
were a Slip 'n Slide.

The captain was going out for more but Slade grabbed
him from behind and held him back.

"Leland," Nick said. "That's enough. You're at a
wake, for God's sake."

That seemed to snap Stottlemeyer out of it. Phil Atwater and a couple of other men helped Braddock to
his feet.

Braddock was a dazed mess. There was blood spatter
on his white shirt from his smashed nose and the back of
his pants were all wet and grass-stained.

I looked over at Monk, who stepped past Stottlemeyer
and Slade onto the patio. He had his head cocked at an
angle, observing the situation as if he'd never seen anything like it.

"Haven't you ever seen someone get punched before?" I asked as I joined him. "If Stottlemeyer hadn't socked him, I might have."

"There are grass stains on his pants," Monk said.

"That's what happens when you slide on wet grass."

"Or walk on it with your socks," Monk said. "The lawn is so green and lush because it's watered every day at the same time. It was wet yesterday, too, but Bill Peschel's socks weren't stained. They were bright white."

He was right. I remembered seeing Peschel's sock-covered feet just before they zipped up his body bag.

"Maybe the chlorinated water leached out the stains," Nick said.

Spoken like a man who had never done a load of children's laundry. But Carol had and, judging by the horrified expression creeping onto her face, the implication of Monk's observation was beginning to sink in.

It certainly had for me and Stottlemeyer. We both had kids. Grass stains don't wash out easily, if they ever wash out at all. So the fact that Bill's socks weren't stained could mean only one thing: He didn't walk across the grass.

The captain shrugged his arms free from Slade's loosened grasp and stepped forward.

Monk picked up a white plastic chair, set it on the grass near the fence, and waved me over.

"Stand on this," he said.

"Why don't you?"

"I'm afraid of heights."

I sighed, grabbed the top of the fence for support, and stepped onto the chair. It wobbled and sank under my weight into the sodden lawn with a moist, squishy sound.

"You don't weigh half as much as Bill Peschel did," Monk said. "But the chair he stood on wasn't sunk into the lawn. It was right on top."

"Maybe the chair was moved by one of the coroners, cops, or the police photographer," Stottlemeyer said.

"Then there should be four holes made by the chair in the grass somewhere along the pool fence."

Monk bent over and walked slowly around the entire perimeter of the pool.

He walked very, very, very slowly.

So slowly that I'm pretty sure he was counting the blades of grass as he went.

Everyone was silent, watching Monk. Even Braddock was transfixed, holding a towel to his bloody nose.

After what felt like hours of frustration and suspense, Monk returned to me, tipped his head from side to side, rolled his shoulders, and then addressed the crowd.

"Bill Peschel didn't step on a chair, climb over the fence, and jump into the pool," Monk said. "He was murdered."

17

Mr. Monk Asks Around

Before long the guests were gone and the crowd at Carol Atwater's house was made up of cops and crime scene investigators from the Mill Valley Police Department. Even Carol and her family had left, preferring to spend the night in a hotel. I wondered if they'd ever come back to this house now.

Stottlemeyer and Slade stuck around—the captain to protect Carol's interests and Slade to publicize his own.

Slade was careful to remind Monk that he worked for Intertect and that any further observations he wanted to share had to go through him first.

"I don't know what forensic evidence they hope to find," Slade said, watching the forensic technicians doing their thing. "The scene has been hopelessly compromised and contaminated. The yard has been watered, which is bound to have washed away trace evidence, and everything has been trampled and touched by dozens of people since Peschel's death."

"You mean his murder," Monk said.

"They're just following procedure," Stottlemeyer

said. "They know as well as you and I do how futile it is."

"It's my fault the evidence is lost or ruined," Monk said. "I saw all the things that were out of place yesterday and didn't put it together. What was the matter with me?"

"You were tired," I said, shooting a nasty glare at Slade, who didn't seem to pick up on it.

"But it was all right in front of my face," Monk said.

"And mine and theirs," Stottlemeyer said, nodding towards the Mill Valley police. "At least I'm accustomed to missing the clues that you see. They're not. They really feel like jerks."

"Then it's the perfect time to let them know that Monk's consulting services are available through Intertect," Slade said, and excused himself from us to try to snag himself a new client.

"Who could have wanted Bill Peschel dead?" Monk asked.

"Anyone who got sent to prison because of one of the tips that he gave the police," I said.

"Why wait until now?" Stottlemeyer asked. "Peschel retired and moved to Florida ten years ago."

"Maybe the killer just got released from prison," I said. "Or maybe it took the killer this long to figure out that it was Peschel who ratted him out. Or maybe he only recently learned that Peschel had moved back to the Bay Area. Maybe it's all of those things put together."

"That's a lot of maybes," Stottlemeyer said.

"I thought maybes were your specialty," I said.

"My specialty doesn't matter," Stottlemeyer said. "This is a Mill Valley homicide. I don't have jurisdiction here."

Slade came back over to us. "I was just told that the Mill Valley Police Department has a policy of not hiring people to do the job that they are paid to do. They don't have money to burn like the San Francisco police do. That's a direct quote."

"Tough break for you," Stottlemeyer said.

"They'll come around after a few weeks of getting nowhere," Slade said.

"After a few weeks, it will be too late," Monk said. "The trail will be cold."

"You've solved a bunch of cases for me already that were colder than a few weeks," Slade said.

"This is different," Monk said.

"Yeah, the Mill Valley police know that somebody would have gotten away with murder if it weren't for you," Slade said. "You've embarrassed them. They aren't going to be able to stick this case in a drawer if they get nowhere with it. They'll have to come back to us. The public will pressure them into it."

"How's the public going to know anything about it?" Stottlemeyer asked.

"There were a lot of people here today," Slade said. "Word will get around. And I'll be sending out a press release this afternoon. See you later."

Slade walked away.

Stottlemeyer sighed and looked at us. "I'd better get back to the office, assuming that I still have one."

"Why are you being so pessimistic? The murders of Judges Stanton and Carnegie were solved. It's old news," I said. "There will be other headlines today. Your bosses can't be as angry with you as they were yesterday."

"I just punched a cop at a wake," Stottlemeyer said.

"He had it coming," I said.

"True, but I don't think the chief is going to see it that way."

"Who says he's ever going to know?"

"Braddock will make sure that he does," Stottlemeyer said. "Every cop at the convention is going to ask him how his nose got busted and he'll tell them, though he'll frame the story so that he looks terrific and I come across as a raging psychopath."

"With his charming personality, it's probably not the first time someone has slugged him," I said.

Stottlemeyer shook his head. "Braddock is used to giving beatings, not taking them. He's always been protected by the authority of his badge. Most people are afraid to hit him back. He's not used to a fight that isn't rigged in his favor before he even throws a punch. He isn't going to take this well."

"It's not Braddock that I'm concerned about," Monk said. "What are we going to do about Bill Peschel's murder?"

"Bill lived and worked in San Francisco most of his life. Odds are that whatever happened here began across the bay on my turf," Stottlemeyer said. "The homicide case may be out of my jurisdiction but I'm going to do some asking around anyway."

"Me too," Monk said.

Stottlemeyer nodded and walked away. As soon as he was gone, I gave Monk a look.

"Who are you going to ask?"

"Danielle," Monk said.

"But no one has hired you to investigate this murder," I said.

"I've hired me," Monk said.

As I drove us back to San Francisco, Monk called Danielle Hossack and asked her to dig up all the information that she could about Bill Peschel, his daughter, and her husband. She promised to get Monk a preliminary report tomorrow.

"I understand why you want background on Bill Peschel," I said. "But why on the others?"

"You mentioned to me that Peschel made a lot of money from the sale of his bar and some stocks."

"Carol said he was an early investor in InTouch-Space-dot-com, which is the biggest social networking site on earth."

Monk looked at me blankly, so I explained what I was talking about.

"It's an online community where millions of people share information about themselves, their interests, and their hobbies, make new friends, renew relationships with old ones, and play all kinds of games."

Monk still looked at me blankly.

"Let me put it another way," I said. "InTouchSpace allows you to socialize with others without ever leaving your house or actually meeting another human being in the flesh. You might actually like it. Julie and I use it. So does Ambrose. He's very active on it."

"My brother is talking to strangers with his computer?"

"He's agoraphobic," I said. "How else is he going to interact with people?"

"Why would he want to?"

"Because he's a human being," I said. "And human beings need relationships."

"Not if they want to stay healthy," Monk said. "Relationships aren't sanitary."

"They are on a computer," I said.

"Haven't you ever heard of computer viruses?"

I could see that this was yet another argument I wasn't going to win. Besides, we were getting so far away from the subject of Bill Peschel's murder that I'd almost forgotten the point I'd originally wanted to make.

"Do you really think that Carol Atwater murdered her father?"

Monk shrugged. "Maybe in addition to his stocks, Bill also had a hefty insurance policy. We only have her word about what happened that morning. What if it's all a lie? It wouldn't be the first time that greed led to murder."

"I have a hard time believing that she cracked her father on the head, pushed him into the pool, and then staged the accident with her daughter in the house."

"It's easy enough to check out her story. But I have other reasons for learning more about her and her husband. The murder may have had nothing to do with Peschel's past. It might have been related to something that Carol and Phil are or were involved with. It might have been a warning of some kind. Or maybe Peschel interrupted a burglary."

"In other words, you have no idea what you are looking for."

"I'm looking for a murderer," he said.

Until Danielle got back to us, we had nothing to go on in the Peschel investigation. And since we'd worked through all the open cases at Intertect—well, at least as far as Monk knew—there was nothing else for us to do.

Monk came to this conclusion even faster than I did and asked me to take him to Dr. Bell's office so he could try to squeeze in some sessions between other patients.

Once again, I dropped Monk off and made a speedy getaway.

I used the time to run some errands for Monk— buying groceries, picking up his dry cleaning, and taking it all back to his place and putting it away. It was actually a pleasure to do those chores without him at my side, turning what should be a painless two-hour experience into a six-hour ordeal.

He called me at six to come get him. When I drove up to the Victorian house where Dr. Bell lived and worked, I found Monk and the doctor sitting on the front stoop together.

I felt my stomach tighten. I knew I was about to get in big trouble, but I put on a smile and pretended that I was oblivious to any wrongdoing.

Monk started for the car but Dr. Bell stopped him.

"Adrian, I just realized there are only three sharpened pencils on my desk."

"And you left the office? What were you thinking?"

"I must have been preoccupied," he said. "I was paying such rapt attention to your troubles that everything else became insignificant."

"Of course, that's only natural. Stay here, I'll handle it," Monk said, and rushed back inside as if there were a grease fire on the stove.

Dr. Bell came up to the passenger side of the car and leaned in the open window to talk to me. He was nearly bald, with a close-cropped gray mustache and beard. His loose black turtleneck sweater and blue jeans made him seem far more casual than I knew him to be.

"Would you like to tell me what's going on, Natalie?"

"I'm doing fine, thanks."

"I'm not," Dr. Bell said. "Twice now I've had Adrian in my waiting room for hours at a time trying to squeeze in five-minute therapy sessions between my other patients or to sit in on their appointments."

"I guess it means that he really likes you," I said. "That's good, isn't it? I'm sure you were worried about whether he'd learn to trust you the way he did Dr. Kroger. Well, now you know that he does. Congratulations!"

Dr. Bell smiled. "I am his psychiatrist, not his babysitter. You can't drop him off here every time you want some free time."

"This isn't about me," I said. "It's about Mr. Monk. He needs you and his new medical plan will cover the extra sessions."

"It's not about the money. It's about the comfort and privacy of my other patients," Dr. Bell said. "If Adrian has free time, perhaps he can find a hobby or his new employer can assign him some additional cases to keep him busy."

"You don't understand," I said. "Mr. Monk will work himself to death."

"That's a preferable fate to my patients murdering him in my waiting room," Dr. Bell said. "Or if I do it myself."

Monk bounded out of the door. "It's all taken care of, Dr. Bell. Crisis averted."

"Thank you, Adrian," Dr. Bell said. "It's a big relief."

"So, same time tomorrow?"

"I don't think so," Dr. Bell said.

"Why not?"

"You're going to be very busy," Dr. Bell said, directing his words more to me than to Monk.

"How do you know?"

"Call it a hunch," Dr. Bell said.

18

Mr. Monk and Disher's Big Case

As it turned out, Dr. Bell's hunch was right. I arrived at Monk's apartment the next morning to find him already hard at work at his kitchen table, a rolling cart of files at his side.

More cases from Intertect.

Black belt or not, I was going to kick Danielle's tight little butt into the street.

"Where is she?" I demanded.

"Who?" Monk asked.

"Danielle Hossack."

"I have no idea," Monk said. "But I hope that wherever she is she's getting me the information that I asked for."

"Then if she isn't here, who brought you all those files?"

"A detective from Intertect came to my door first thing this morning," Monk said. "All that publicity must have brought in a slew of new cases. It's a good thing we don't have anything to go on with the Peschel case yet because I'm swamped. I can get these cases out of the way first."

I turned and headed back to the door.

"Where are you going?" he asked.

"Down to Intertect to see if I can give Danielle a hand."

I was thinking of giving it to her the same way that Stottlemeyer gave it to Braddock.

"That's a good idea," Monk said. "I'm so glad to see you two are working so well together."

I kept on walking so he couldn't see my red-faced anger. I broke a few speed laws heading downtown and was worked up into a fine rage by the time I got to Monk's office at Intertect.

Danielle was sitting at her desk, typing away on her computer. I stabbed a finger in her direction.

"Come with me," I said, marching past her into Monk's office. As soon as she was inside, I slammed the door behind her.

"What's wrong?" she asked oh so innocently.

"You are," I said. "You're fired."

Her eyes went wide. "Why?"

"I told you not to send any more files to Mr. Monk and you did it anyway," I said. "You're looking out for Intertect, not for Mr. Monk. That's unacceptable."

"I don't know what you're talking about."

"Another one of those rolling file drawers was delivered to his apartment this morning. It didn't roll to his place by itself."

"I didn't send them," she said angrily, but I could tell that it wasn't directed at me. "I wouldn't do that to him or to you."

"If you didn't, then who did?"

Her face tightened and she glanced towards the door. "There is only one person with the authority to send files to anyone."

The way she said it left little doubt who she was talking about. I knew I owed her an apology, but I didn't want to do anything that would slow my momentum or cool my anger.

I threw open the door, marched down the hall, and blew past Slade's buxom secretary, opening the door to his corner office and entering uninvited. His secretary tried to chase after me, but she was too top-heavy to keep up.

Slade was hunched over a putter, knocking golf balls into what looked like a silver dustpan, which was engraved with the words, INTOUCHSPACE INVITATIONAL GOLF TOURNAMENT. His office was larger than Monk's apartment. There were lots of pictures on the walls of him with his arm around celebrities, most of them women.

"Are you insensitive, greedy, or just plain stupid?" I said.

"I can be all of the above," Slade said. "I suppose it depends on the situation and how much alcohol is being served."

Slade waved his secretary away and she closed the door behind me.

"You've heard of killing the goose that laid the golden egg? Well, that's exactly what you are doing with Mr. Monk," I said. "You've giving him way too much work to do."

"And I'm paying him handsomely for it. Not only that, he's closing the cases as fast as I can give them to him. He enjoys it."

"Kids like ice cream, but that doesn't mean you let them gorge themselves on the stuff," I said. "He can't keep up this pace."

"I haven't heard any complaints from him."

"You're hearing it from me," I said. "As of now, he's taking a break."

"He's only worked four days and he already wants a vacation? That's got to be a record."

"So is the number of cases he's solved for you this

week," I said. "This is nonnegotiable. If you don't like it, fire him."

"Maybe I'll just fire you," he said.

"Mr. Monk will go with me," I said.

"Why? He doesn't have to rely on you anymore," Slade said. "I can give him all the assistants that he wants."

"So fire me and see what happens," I said.

He looked at me for a long moment, then broke into a smile. "Let's not overreact, Ms. Teeger. Monk has certainly earned a breather. We can revisit this discussion next week."

"No, we won't," I said. "All his cases will go through me from now on and I will divvy them out to him as I see fit."

"You're very protective of Mr. Monk," Slade said.

"If you're smart, you will be, too. He's going to be worth a lot of money to Intertect if you treat him right. I suggest you start now."

I turned on my heel and walked out. Danielle was waiting outside the door along with Slade's startled secretary. I blew right past them and headed back towards Monk's office. Danielle hurried behind me, catching up with me once I got inside. She closed the door behind her as I sagged into the seat behind Monk's desk.

I started to shake. I think it was from all that excess adrenaline in my veins.

"I owe you an apology," I said.

"No worries," she said. "You were terrific."

"What do you mean?"

"I heard what you said to Nick. The whole office did."

"I was that loud?"

"You were practically roaring. Mr. Monk is very lucky to have you in his corner."

"He might not think so when he finds out what I've done."

"It's what you do that allows him to succeed," Danielle said. "He's the world's best detective because you are his assistant."

"If you're kissing up for a raise, you're doing it to the wrong person. Technically, you work for the guy I just yelled at."

She smiled. "I think I have as much to learn from you as I do from Mr. Monk."

"Speaking of learning," I said, eager to change the subject, "what information do you have on the Peschels that I can take back with me for Mr. Monk?"

"I'm still working on the background reports. However, the Mill Valley police managed to find some traces of blood and skin on the edge of the kitchen counter that they've matched to Bill Peschel," she said. "The coroner took a second look at Peschel's head wound and now believes he sustained it in the kitchen and not the pool."

"Brilliant deduction on her part," I said.

"But necessary," she said. "Now it's confirmed that Peschel's death wasn't an accident."

"It was the moment Mr. Monk said it was murder," I said. "That's another thing you'll learn. When it comes to murder, he's never wrong."

What you're about to read now, and in a few places later on in this story, happened to Lieutenant Randy Disher when I wasn't around. I'm not a mind reader, so I can't tell you firsthand what was going on. But I've heard enough about it from him and from the other people involved that I think I can give you a good picture of what occurred.

When Disher dreamed of being a cop, filling out

mountains of paperwork wasn't part of the fantasy. But that was how he spent most of his time when he should have been on the streets, hunting down leads, taking on the syndicate, and speeding through San Francisco in a green '68 Mustang like Steve McQueen in *Bullitt*.

That was what he was born to do, not paperwork. That was why he became a cop. And that was why his nickname was Bullitt. He gave it to himself on his first day at the police academy but, for reasons he could never figure out, it didn't stick.

Neither did Dirty Randy.

But he persevered. Over the years, he'd drop the nickname into conversation when it felt right and whenever a new detective transferred into Homicide, he'd introduce himself like this:

"Welcome to Homicide, hombre. I'm Lieutenant Randy Disher, but everybody calls me Bullitt."

He did it again a few days ago when Detective Jack Lansdale transferred in. But this time he tried to manipulate the situation some more to improve his chances.

"What do they call you?" Disher asked.

"Jack," he said.

"I mean, what's your nickname?"

"I don't have one."

"Tell you what: you think of one and that's what I'll call you," Disher said. "Pretty soon everybody will pick up on it. How about the Jackal?"

Moonface would have been more appropriate, Disher thought. Judging by Lansdale's face, he'd picked at every zit he'd ever had as a kid. He must have had a lot of zits.

"Jack is fine," Lansdale said.

"But it could be short for Jackal," Disher said. "I hear you're like a wild dog when you get on a case."

Disher gave him a big wink. He hadn't heard anything about Lansdale, though he was pretty sure that his own exploits were legend by now.

"No, I'm not," Jack said. "I pride myself on being slow and methodical."

"Then it's an ironic nickname, which is even better, though they call me Bullitt because they mean it."

"Mean what?"

"That I'm cool, I'm tough, and the ladies dig me, like McQueen in the movie," Disher said. He couldn't afford a Mustang, but he drove a Ford Focus, which at least was from the same company. "I'll call you Jackal and you call me Bullitt, not just when we are talking to each other, but whenever we talk about each other to other people."

Disher had thought it could really work this time, but then Monk showed up with that Diaper Genie for him. Lansdale hadn't looked at him the same way since.

Captain Stottlemeyer called out for him from inside his office.

Disher hated it when the captain did that, summoning him like a slave.

Why couldn't Stottlemeyer get up, walk to his door, and ask him to come in? Or pick up the phone and call his extension? That would be the respectful thing to do.

But no, the captain had to bark from his desk like an irritated pit bull.

Stottlemeyer had been in a sour mood from the instant the new operating budget landed on his desk last week. And his mood had gotten progressively worse since his appearance onstage with Monk at the national homicide detectives' conference, which, much to Disher's dismay, he hadn't been invited to. (Disher didn't care about attending their panel; he just wanted to hang out with other homicide cops, talk shop, and get his Bullitt persona out there to the rest of the country.)

Just when Disher thought that Stottlemeyer couldn't get any gloomier or more short-tempered, Nicholas Slade grabbed all the glory for Rhonda Carnegie's arrest on the judge murders and humiliated the department.

Now Stottlemeyer was practically foaming at the mouth day and night.

Disher heard that Stottlemeyer was so unhinged that he'd slugged a cop at a funeral yesterday.

Not wanting to be the victim of the captain's next violent outburst, Disher grabbed his notebook and hurried into Stottlemeyer's office, but not before shooting a glance at Lansdale, who sat at the next desk.

"High-level strategic conference," he said. "Need-to-know only."

Disher closed the door behind him and approached the captain's desk. "What's up, sir?"

Stottlemeyer rubbed his eyes and sighed. "A homicide has just come in. Investigating this one is going to be like dancing in a minefield."

"Fine by me," Disher said in his best Eastwoodian snarl. "Let's dance."

Stottlemeyer looked up at him with a weary gaze. "I'm serious, Randy, this case could be a career killer if you're not careful."

Disher felt a tingle of nervous excitement in his stomach. Did he hear what he thought he'd just heard? Did the captain recuse himself from the case?

"Where are you going to be?" Disher asked.

"Right here, riding this desk. You're going to be on your own on this one, reporting directly to the deputy chief."

"You're telling me to go over your head?"

"Isn't that what I just said?"

This didn't make any sense to Disher. It was one thing for the captain to let him take the lead on a case, but quite another to tell him not to report to him at all.

Then he realized what the captain meant when he said the case could be a career killer if he mishandled it.

This wasn't just another homicide investigation.

This was a field test of Disher's ability to lead.

Running this investigation would be a real-world demonstration of his abilities, a chance to prove himself directly to the powers-that-be.

Well, it was about time.

"Why are you taking yourself out of the loop?" Disher asked.

"I have a conflict of interest," Stottlemeyer said.

Disher nodded. "I understand. You can't be objective when it comes to me. You're already biased in my favor. The brass wants to see me in action and come to their own conclusions about my command and leadership skills."

"What are you talking about?"

"This field test," Disher said. "I'm ready for it. The tougher the better. That's why they call me Bullitt."

"Who does?"

"Them," Disher said, waving his hand in the air as if clearing smoke. "Those in the they. Not all of the they, but some of them. Those theys do."

Stottlemeyer sighed. "It's not an official test, though I suppose that it could end up being one."

"Then why are you cutting yourself out?"

"Because I know the victim," he replied.

"How do you know him?"

"I broke his nose yesterday." Stottlemeyer reached into a drawer and tossed a file across the desk to Disher. "The victim is Detective Paul Braddock, Banning Police Department. His body was found in his hotel room by a maid at the Dorchester this morning."

Disher picked up the file. "What's this?"

"A file that I kept on Braddock," Stottlemeyer said. "He used to be a detective here until I forced him out."

"I didn't know you did time in Internal Affairs."

"I didn't," Stottlemeyer said. "This was a personal project. Ten years ago, I told him he could quit or I could give that file to IA. He quit."

"Why did you do that?"

"Because he was a dirty cop who liked to beat people," Stottlemeyer said. "And I wanted to spare the department the embarrassment."

"This is ancient history," Disher said, holding up the file. "What does it have to do with his murder?"

"Maybe nothing," Stottlemeyer said. "But if you're not careful, the past has a way of coming back to haunt you. Or kill you."

"I'm on it," Disher said, and left the captain's office, the file tucked under his arm. He pointed at Lansdale and headed out of the squad room. "You're with me, Jackal."

"It's Jack," Lansdale said, getting up and taking his coat from the back of his chair.

"It's whatever I say it is, Detective. We've got a murder to solve," Disher said. "Watch and learn. The clock is ticking and the hands are dripping blood."

19

Mr. Monk and Bullitt

While Lansdale drove their Crown Vic, Disher reviewed the file on Braddock that Stottlemeyer gave him. Stottlemeyer had meticulously detailed dozens of instances of abuse and gotten statements from several of Braddock's victims.

But Disher was having trouble concentrating on the reports. Reading in the car made him nauseous, which was one distraction, and he couldn't stop thinking about what this investigation could mean for him, which was another.

This case was more than a chance to impress the deputy chief. It was also a once-in-a-lifetime opportunity to shine on a national stage. Cops from all over the country were at the conference and they would be watching his progress with keen interest. A success could raise his profile considerably. But if he mucked it up, Bullitt would be riding a motor scooter instead of a Mustang, marking the tires of parked cars with a meter maid's chalk stick.

Disher suddenly felt the three egg-and-cheese Mc-Muffins he had for breakfast climbing up his throat with a hot vengeance. He yelled for Lansdale to pull over, opened the passenger door to the car before they even came to a stop, and vomited in the street, right in front of a Japanese tour group standing on the curb.

He wiped his mouth with a Dunkin' Donuts napkin he found in the map pocket of the door and smiled at the revolted tourists.

"Sorry about that," he said. *"Mune on sawaru na. Shinu kakugo shiro."*

The Japanese tourists glowered at him and marched away in a huff.

Disher closed the door and turned to Lansdale. "What is their problem?"

"I don't know, maybe it has something to do with you puking on their shoes."

"I missed their shoes by a good two inches," Disher said. "Besides, I showed them the courtesy of apologizing in English and Japanese."

"No, you didn't," Lansdale said.

"Mune on sawaru na, shinu kakugo shiro means, 'Please forgive me for the inconvenience, I'm truly sorry.'"

"It means, 'Stop groping my breasts and prepare to die,'" Lansdale said.

"I think you're mistaken," Disher said.

"My wife is Japanese," Lansdale said.

"Oh, so I guess you've heard that a lot," Disher said, and slapped the dash. "Let's go, Jackal, we've got some bad guys to catch."

Lansdale drove them up another block to the hotel and parked right in front. Disher put on a pair of sunglasses for the Caruso effect before getting out and hurrying inside.

Sure enough, all eyes were on him as he headed across the lobby towards the elevators, so everybody saw him when he tripped over the suitcase and slid on his stomach across the slick, marble floor.

Lansdale helped Disher to his feet.

"Who put that suitcase down in front of me?" Disher said. "I want him arrested for assaulting an officer."

"It was there when we came in. You headed straight for it, Bullitt. You might want to take off your sunglasses indoors, the lighting is pretty dim in here."

"Then tell them to turn up the lights; we're running a murder investigation here," Disher said. "Clues hide in the dark. And it's 'Bullitt, *sir*,' to you."

"Yes, sir," Lansdale said. "Bullitt, sir."

Disher looked around, pretending to be scanning for clues, when he was really checking to see if anyone was laughing at him. If they were, they were hiding it well. That was when he spotted the surveillance cameras in the corners of the ceiling.

"I want the surveillance tapes on all floors, elevators, and stairwells for the last twenty-four hours and a complete list of guests who are staying in the hotel."

"Will do," Lansdale said.

They got into the elevator and rode it up to the seventh floor in silence. Disher pocketed his sunglasses. When the doors opened, they were greeted by a uniformed officer, who glanced at the badges clipped to their belts before letting them exit the elevator. The entire floor was being treated as a crime scene, which would have been Disher's first move if it hadn't been done already.

Disher approached the open door to Braddock's hotel room and looked inside. The room was cramped with forensic techs who were taking pictures, bagging things, and brushing every surface for prints.

"Take five, boys, we need the room," Disher said. "Everyone goes but the ME."

He stepped aside as the techs filed out of the room, leaving behind only Dr. Daniel Hetzer, who crouched beside Braddock's body, which was facedown on the floor beside the king-sized bed.

Dr. Hetzer maintained two days' worth of stubble on his pale, fleshy cheeks to compensate for the lack of hair on his head. He used to be a two-pack-a-day smoker until he gave up cigarettes for alcohol instead. But he still smelled of cigarette smoke.

Disher looked around the room. The bed was made, but the comforter was wrinkled and pillows were bunched up against the headboard as a backrest. The TV remote was on the floor beside the bed. Braddock was watching TV when his killer arrived, which meant the killer wasn't lying in wait for him, which meant the killer was invited in, which meant it was someone Braddock knew.

The dining table was tipped over. There was a broken bottle of scotch and the shards of two broken glasses on the floor. Disher was surprised the doctor wasn't lapping up the puddle like a thirsty dog.

"Cause of death?" Disher asked.

"Strangulation," Hetzer said. "But he took a beating sometime before that. His nose is broken and there's a bruise on his chest."

He turned the body over so Disher and Lansdale could see Braddock's broken nose, which was Stottlemeyer's handiwork, and the red ligature marks around his neck, which were somebody else's.

"You might want to check between Braddock's teeth for traces of the comforter," Disher told Dr. Hetzer.

"You think that Braddock liked to chew his bedsheets?" Lansdale said.

"I think Braddock knocked his killer back into the table as he was being strangled. Then the killer pushed Braddock facedown into the bed, put all his weight on Braddock's back, and added smothering to his murderous repertoire."

Dr. Hetzer nodded. "Judging by the position of the body, I'd say you're probably right."

"I didn't get this badge out of a box of Cap'n Crunch, Doc," Disher said. "When was he killed?"

"I'm guessing midnight," Hetzer said, "Give or take an hour or two."

"Can't you be more specific?"

"I wish I could, but the AC was turned on full blast. It was like a meat locker when we got here."

"Someone was trying to make it difficult for us to pin down exactly when the murder occurred," Disher said. "We're dealing with a pro. What was Braddock strangled with?"

"I'd say a belt, a rolled-up towel, or the sash of a bathrobe."

Disher turned to Lansdale. "Make sure the forensic boys bag anything in this room that could have been used to strangle somebody. And talk to the people in the adjoining rooms, upstairs and downstairs, too. Maybe they heard something. I also want those glass shards tested for prints ASAP. I want to know who he was drinking with."

"What are you going to be doing?" Lansdale asked.

"The heavy thinking," Disher said. "You bring me the pieces and I'll put the puzzle together."

Monk spent the day at his apartment working through the files that Nick Slade had sent over that morning. I tried to help as best I could, but since I'm not a detective genius, it basically meant being a sounding board as he sorted through the clues and then being a stenographer as he laid out the solutions to the mysteries.

Danielle came by late that afternoon with a file under her arm. When I saw the file, I involuntarily tensed up. But it wasn't another case to add to the pile Monk was dealing with. It was her research into Bill Peschel, his daughter, Carol, and her husband, Phil.

Monk set aside his remaining cases for the moment to listen to what Danielle had dug up.

"Your instincts were right, Mr. Monk," she said. "Carol and her husband are living a lie. They aren't a prosperous, upper-middle-class family."

"They're communist sleeper agents who've infiltrated American society," Monk said.

Danielle and I stared at him.

"You are aware that we are in the twenty-first century," I said. "And that the Berlin Wall fell, the Soviet Union collapsed, and the Cold War is over?"

"Yes," Monk said.

"That's not it," I said.

"How do you know?" he said.

"Because the Berlin Wall fell, the Soviet Union collapsed, and the Cold War is over."

"Okay," Monk said. "They're wanted fugitives."

Danielle and I stared at him.

"They're brother and sister," Monk said.

Danielle and I stared at him.

"They're illegal aliens," Monk said.

"Have you been possessed by Randy Disher?" I asked.

"Why do you say that?" Monk replied.

"They're broke," Danielle said. "Their personal bank accounts are nearly depleted and they've reached the spending limit on their credit cards."

"That's not nearly as interesting a lie to be living as the others," Monk said.

"We'll have to tell them to work on that," I said.

"Phil lost his job as a sales rep for a pool equipment company four months ago," Danielle said. "He leaves the house each morning in a jacket and tie but spends his day sitting in an easy chair at a Barnes and Noble in San Rafael doing crossword puzzles."

"How do you know all this?" I asked.

"We traced his credit card usage," she said. "I also put him under surveillance."

"You can do that?" Monk said.

"I can't but you can," Danielle said. "I hope you don't think that I abused your authority."

"I didn't know I had any authority," Monk said. "What else can I do with it?"

"Let's concentrate on the case," I said. I didn't want Monk thinking too hard about the resources that were available to him or he'd assign Intertect's operatives to watch the streets for people spitting out their gum on the sidewalks. "Does Carol know that he's out of work?"

"The bank accounts and credit cards are all under his name, so the statements go to him," Danielle said. "So it's possible that she doesn't. But I do know that they've been living on the money her father has been giving them from his savings and stocks."

"What are they worth?" I asked.

"The combined value is nearly one million dollars," she said. "Now that Peschel is dead, they can add the one-point-five-million-dollar life insurance payoff to the pot."

"Not if her husband killed him," Monk said.

"Phil certainly had a strong financial motive for murder," Danielle said.

I nodded in agreement. "And he knew better than anybody exactly when Carol and the kids were going to be out of the house that morning."

"So would anyone who looked at her refrigerator," Monk said.

I was surprised that Monk had noticed her calendar on the refrigerator, but I shouldn't have been. He notices everything, even when it appears he isn't paying any attention at all.

"I wouldn't rule Carol out as a suspect just yet," Monk said. "She might have known that her husband was out of work. The two of them could have planned the murder together."

"But they were already living off her dad's money," I said. "What did they have to gain from killing him?"

"Taking care of him was a burden," Monk said. "And there was the danger posed by his warts."

"What warts?" Danielle asked.

"Carol told us at the wake that he was covered with them," Monk said.

"She wasn't being literal," I said. "'Warts and all' is an expression."

"That means he's covered in grotesque, blistering tumors created by a highly contagious virus."

"It means she loved him despite the fact that he wasn't a perfect person," I said, then turned to Danielle. "Maybe you could elaborate on that."

She explained that Peschel dropped out of high school and drifted up and down the state, working as a manual laborer in agriculture and construction for a few years, before landing back in San Francisco, where he did all kinds of odd jobs, like taxi driver, short-order cook, ditchdigger, and, finally, bartender at a Tenderloin dive called Lucky Duke's.

Along the way, Peschel built up a police record of minor offenses, like assault, petty theft, and drunk-and-disorderly conduct. He also did some "debt collection" for Bobby Fisset, a big racketeer in the city during the late fifties, early sixties.

In 1967, Peschel met Clara, a salesgirl at Capwell's department store, and got her pregnant. They were married a few months before she started showing.

"How did you find out all of this?" Monk interrupted.

"For starters, the police maintained a confidential file on him."

"If it was confidential," I asked, "how did you see it?"

"Nick has sources in the SFPD," Danielle said. "I also looked at all relevant federal, state, county, and local records and, posing as an obituary writer for the *Chronicle*, I interviewed Carol Atwater for details on his early life."

Monk nodded, impressed.

I hoped he wasn't drawing any comparisons between her efforts and mine on his behalf. I'd never done any research like that for him. For one thing, I wouldn't know how to begin. For another, she had resources I couldn't hope to match.

Even so, I felt a pang of insecurity and a cramp of jealousy. I tend to internalize my anxieties.

Danielle continued briefing us on what she'd learned: Lucky Duke's luck ran out in 1970 and he was stricken with throat cancer. Peschel took over running the bar. And when Duke died nine months later, Peschel borrowed money from Fisset to buy the business from Duke's widow and rename it Bill's Tavern.

To pay off the debt, Peschel let Fisset use a back room at the bar to run a private poker club.

After Fisset was gunned down outside of Alioto's restaurant on Fisherman's Wharf in 1973, Peschel secretly gave the police tips that helped nab the shooter and avert a mob war.

"By working in the Tenderloin for years and associating with Fisset, Peschel established his street cred with the lowlifes and criminals," Danielle said. "They saw him as one of them."

"He was," Monk said. "And warty, too."

"By helping the police catch Fisset's killers and prevent a lot of bloodshed, he earned the trust of the police, who showed their gratitude by making him a paid informant and turning a blind eye to his various nickel-and-dime illegal activities to make ends meet."

Something didn't make sense to me. "If the tavern was such a dive, and Peschel was scratching and scraping for money his whole life, how was he able to sell his business for enough money to retire with his wife to Florida?"

"He sold the tavern for thirty-five thousand dollars," Danielle said. "He became rich off of his InTouchSpace-dot-com stock and the sale of his Florida condo."

"How did he luck into buying shares of InTouchSpace before it went big?"

"Word on the street, I guess," she said.

"He was on the wrong street for that word," Monk said, shrugging his shoulders. "Something doesn't fit."

"So what's next?" I asked.

"We talk to the suspects," Monk said. "But we don't touch them under any circumstances."

"Why not?" Danielle asked.

"Warts could run in the family," he replied.

20

Mr. Monk and the Ties That Bind

The surveillance footage from the Dorchester Hotel was delivered by Lansdale to Disher's desk on several CDs. The lobby, all the entrances and exits, the stairwells, and the elevators were covered by cameras. The various floors themselves were not.

"What kind of half-assed security system is that?" Disher said.

"I asked them the same thing," Lansdale said. "Their reply was that they are a hotel, not a Vegas casino, and this isn't a totalitarian state."

"What is that supposed to mean?"

"They're cheap and irresponsible," Lansdale said. "But nobody could have gotten in or out of the hotel without being caught on camera."

"Unless they climbed up the face of the building and entered through Braddock's window."

"Do you really think that's possible?"

"Never rule out any possibility, even if it's impossible," Disher said. "The impossible is only impossible until it becomes possible. Why aren't you writing that down?"

"Because it doesn't make any sense."

"It would if you had my years of experience on the mean streets. I'm giving you pearls of wisdom here. You'll want to remember them." Disher handed half of the CDs to Lansdale. "You look at these, I'll go through the rest."

Lansdale retreated to his desk and Disher stuck a CD into his computer.

For the next hour, Disher scanned through footage of the loading dock and the stairwell, but didn't see any activity. There were no deliveries and nobody used the staircase.

When he was finished with those CDs, he started going through footage from the lobby. He was twenty minutes into that when he saw someone come in at ten p.m., go up the grand staircase to the conference area, and then disappear.

Disher glanced around to see if anyone was watching him. Lansdale was slouched in his seat, staring at his screen, going through elevator footage and taking notes. Disher turned back to his screen and fast-forwarded until he saw the same man come down the staircase and leave about thirty minutes later.

"Hey, Jackal, do we have any surveillance footage of the conference floors?"

Lansdale shook his head. "Nothing on the second and third floors, except the stairwells."

"Anything unusual show up on the elevator footage?"

"Yeah, I was just about to tell you about it," Lansdale said. "Around ten fifteen one of those guys in the beef-eater costumes got on at the second floor and went up to the seventh, got off, then came down again about twenty minutes later."

"Can you see his face?"

"Nope," Lansdale said.

This wasn't good, Disher thought. Not at all.

He got up and knocked on the captain's door. Stottle-meyer waved him in from behind his desk.

Disher stepped in and closed the door behind him.

"How's the investigation going?" Stottlemeyer asked, looking up from his work.

"Is there anything you want to tell me, Captain?"

"About what?"

"About you and Braddock?"

"It's all in the file," Stottlemeyer said. "Except the part about me punching him yesterday at Bill Peschel's wake, but I assume you've heard all about that."

"You also didn't mention that you were at the Dorchester Hotel last night."

Stottlemeyer sighed wearily. "I didn't think it was relevant."

"What were you doing there?"

"I got a call around nine thirty last night from a guy who said he was a cop attending the conference. He said he had evidence that Braddock was taking bribes from a gang that's running meth labs out of mobile homes in the desert. He asked me to meet him in one of the small conference rooms at the hotel."

"Who was the cop?"

"He wouldn't tell me until we met face-to-face, which didn't happen," Stottlemeyer said. "I got there at ten, waited around for twenty minutes, and when he didn't show, I left."

"And you didn't think that was relevant to the investigation?" Disher asked, failing to hide his irritation with his boss.

"I was one of hundreds of cops and tourists in the hotel last night. I was only there for a half hour and then I left. I didn't see what it had to do with your investigation." Stottlemeyer narrowed his eyes at Disher. "But since you think it's relevant, I'm guessing that Braddock's time of death was ten-ish."

"It could have been," Disher said. "The killer jacked up the air-conditioning in Braddock's room to make it harder for us to pinpoint the exact time of death."

Stottlemeyer stroked his mustache, a nervous habit he had while he was thinking. "Do you suppose that the call I got might have been a ruse to get me to the Dorchester at the same time that Braddock was being killed?"

"I don't think so. Like you said, there were lots of other people there at the same time, including some of the best homicide detectives in the nation," Disher said, heading for the door. "I wouldn't worry about it, sir."

Disher walked out of the office. But he could feel Stottlemeyer's gaze on his back like a heat lamp.

I picked up Monk at nine on the dot and we drove over the Golden Gate Bridge to Marin County.

The lanes going into San Francisco from Marin County were clogged with the last of the rush-hour commuters, Starbucks coffee in their dashboard cup holders, Bluetooth devices in their ears, and NPR playing on their radios.

How do I know what station they were listening to on their radios? Because I know Marin County residents are well educated, own at least one Bob Dylan or Van Morrison album, and are notoriously liberal for people with so much money.

And because I like to embrace clichés that have some truth to them and I enjoy making broad generalizations that support my biases. If you haven't learned that about me by now, you haven't been reading very closely.

The Barnes & Noble smelled more like a coffee-house than a bookstore. The tables of their café were full of young, well-dressed people hunched over their MacBooks, idly picking at pastries and sipping their hot drinks, trying to look busy and deep in deep thoughts.

Phil Atwater wasn't among the self-consciously studious in the café, probably because the menu was too expensive for a man whose unemployment checks had just run out. He was getting his gourmet coffee from McDonald's and slipping a Starbucks cardboard heat sleeve around the cup that didn't entirely hide the Golden Arches. We found him drinking his coffee in an easy chair at the farthest corner of the store, where he was reading a book entitled *The Thirty Steps to Becoming a Millionaire in Thirty Days*.

"Is one of the steps murdering your father-in-law?" Monk asked.

Phil looked up at us, dropped the book, and started to get up.

"Mr. Monk, Ms. Teeger, fancy bumping into you here. I just stopped in to browse a bit before work. I'd rather spend my time here than stuck in traffic. But I'd better get going—"

"You can sit down, Phil," I interrupted. "We know you were fired from your job months ago."

"I wasn't fired, I was downsized," he said, sitting down again. "There's a difference. It had nothing to do with my job performance."

"Does your wife know?" Monk asked. I noticed Phil had ignored Monk's first, provocative question.

"I can't bring myself to tell her. It's humiliating."

"So you have been hiding out here," I said.

"I've been using this as my base of operations, reading the want ads and applying for jobs. I've had a few interviews, but nothing has come of it. There's not a big demand for guys like me."

"What do you have to lose by telling your wife the truth now?" I asked.

"Her respect," Phil replied. "I still have my pride."

"Or you don't want her to find out your darker secret," Monk said. He drifted over to a cardboard display riser of *Murder, She Wrote* paperbacks that were stacked cover-out, four or five books to a pocket shelf.

"Like what?" Phil asked.

"That you murdered your father-in-law so you could get his inheritance," Monk said, adding and subtracting paperbacks from one shelf to another so there were an equal number in each stack.

"I'm unemployed," Phil said. "That doesn't make me a killer."

"You knew when your wife was leaving the house with the kids," I said. "So you went back home, hit Peschel over the head, and tossed him in the pool, then tried to make it look like he jumped in himself in a fog of dementia."

"Fog of dementia?" Phil chuckled ruefully. "You make it sound so mild, almost poetic. You try living with a delusional, gutter-mouthed old coot who thinks he's still tending bar in a Tenderloin dump filled with hookers and drunks. I'd sit across from him and he wouldn't know if I was one of his scumbag boozers, or someone shopping for a killer, or a cop he could sell them all out to."

"So you killed him to put him out of his misery and yours," I said.

"If I killed him, which I didn't, what makes you think I'd admit it to you now?"

"Because if you did murder him, I'll find out anyway," Monk said, still shifting books around. "I was hoping you'd save me the trouble. I have a lot of cases to deal with as it is."

"Sorry to disappoint you, but the only thing I'm guilty of is pride and cowardice."

"And shoplifting," Monk said.

"That's not true," Phil said.

"Then why did you peel the price tag off that book and remove the magnetic theft strip from the spine?"

"I didn't," he said.

Monk gestured to the floor with the *Murder, She Wrote* paperback that was in his hand. "You tried to kick them under your seat but the sticker stuck to your shoe."

Phil looked down. Sure enough, the price sticker was stuck to the heel of his scuffed leather dress shoe.

"So what? The guy who wrote this book has already made his million bucks," Phil said. "He doesn't need twenty more from me."

"That's how a life of crime begins," Monk said. "Today it's a book, tomorrow it's murdering your father-in-law."

"Didn't you already accuse me of doing that?"

"So now after stealing a life, you think you are free to steal anything," Monk said. "It's the same idea, only in reverse."

"You're wrong about me," Phil said.

"If you're not going to confess," Monk said, "maybe you could at least answer a question for me. Where did Peschel get the tip about InTouchSpace stock?"

"It must have been from his real estate agent," Phil said.

"Why do you say that?" I asked.

"Because his tavern was bought by Dalberg Enterprises when they purchased the building it was in," Phil said. "That's Steve Wurzel's real estate investment company."

"Who is Steve Wurzel?" Monk asked.

That was like asking who Bill Gates was, though I'm not certain that Monk knew the answer to that, either. It illustrates one of the great contradictions in Monk's character. He knows so much about so many things and yet he knows so little about so much. He could tell you the history of dental fillings but probably couldn't name three songs performed by the Beatles.

"He was the creator of InTouchSpace," I said.

"Why would he want to buy Bill Peschel's tavern? Was it a prime piece of real estate?"

Phil shook his head. "The storefront was boarded up and empty for a decade until the Jamba Juice moved in last year. It's taken that long for the neighborhood to gentrify."

"Based on what you've told me about the success of InTouchSpace," Monk said, "I suppose Wurzel had the deep pockets to wait ten years for his investment to pay off."

"He didn't," I said. "His estate did. Wurzel is dead."

"When did he die?" Monk asked.

And in the instant before I answered his question, I felt a sensation that was both mental and physical, of things seeming to snap into place. It was a feeling I'm sure Monk would have understood. Except for me the end result wasn't startling clarity, it was greater confusion.

"Ten years ago," I said.

Monk cocked his head and, without saying a word, headed towards the cash registers, the paperback in his hand. He was finished with Phil.

I thanked Phil for his help, told him not to make any travel plans (since that's what cops always tell suspects), and hurried after Monk, who was standing in the checkout line.

"Do you think it's a coincidence that Peschel's good fortune and Wurzel's death both happened ten years ago?"

"I don't know," Monk said. "A lot of things happened ten years ago."

His wife Trudy's unsolved murder, for one thing. I

could have kicked myself for not anticipating that my question would bring up those painful memories.

"Are you hoping for a little inspiration on the case from Jessica Fletcher?" I asked, trying to distract him from his dark thoughts.

"Who is she?"

"A mystery writer who solves murders," I said, motioning to the *Murder, She Wrote* novel in his hand. "The heroine of the book you want to read."

"I'm not going to read it," Monk said.

"Then why are you buying it?"

"To even up the display. Now there are four books cover-out in each pocket shelf."

"You're buying a book you don't want just so the stacks on the shelves are even?"

"It's a small sacrifice to make so the world will be a better place."

There was a file from Forensics waiting on Disher's desk when he came in that morning. Disher waved hello to Stottlemeyer, who acknowledged him with a nod from inside his office, then sat down and opened the file, which was full of crime scene photos and lab reports.

Disher started to read through it all, starting with the autopsy report.

The medical examiner confirmed that Braddock was strangled to death. As Disher predicted, there were threads from the comforter in Braddock's mouth and nose.

The forensic report was next.

The CSI boys were able to lift a strand of polyester from Braddock's neck and, based on the colors and composition of the fabric, they were able to trace it back to a yellow-white-and-blue-striped tie made specifically for Wal-Mart called the Continental. The bad news was that the tie was sold by the thousands at their stores worldwide.

Disher glanced at the picture of the tie and felt a chill run right up his back.

He'd seen the tie before.

But that didn't mean anything, he told himself. Lots of people wore that same tie. He was overreacting.

Disher shifted his attention to the fingerprint report.

There were hundreds of partial prints recovered, which was typical of hotel rooms. Most of the prints were too obscured by other prints to be readable. Even so, they were able to match up the prints to about thirty people, half of whom were hotel staff. One was Braddock himself.

But it was the prints that were recovered from the shards of the broken drinking glass that were the most telling and disturbing.

Another chill crept up Disher's spine and raised goose bumps all over his body.

This time, he couldn't explain away the connection.

He knew what he had to do. It made him feel nauseous and it had nothing to do with the egg-and-cheese croissant he'd scarfed down for breakfast.

Disher slid the photo of the tie from the file, wrote an address on the back, then got up slowly. Trying to appear totally at ease, he sauntered self-consciously over to Lansdale's desk and leaned down, his back to Stottlemeyer's office.

"I want you to go to the address on the back of this photo with the crime scene techs and wait for me to call you with a search warrant," Disher whispered to Lansdale. "Don't mess the place up. Be thorough but subtle. Search inside and out."

"What am I looking for?"

Disher tapped the photo. "This tie and anything else that you think might be related to Paul Braddock's murder."

"Who lives there?" Lansdale asked.

"Captain Stottlemeyer," Disher said.

Lansdale involuntarily glanced towards the captain's office but Disher had intentionally used his body to block his view.

"Just act natural," Disher said. "I don't want the captain to know about this until the deed is done."

"You think the captain murdered Braddock? Are you out of your mind?"

"God, I hope so," Disher said.

He didn't see the need to tell Lansdale yet about how Braddock had thoroughly humiliated Stottlemeyer in front of his peers.

Or that Stottlemeyer had beaten the crap out of Braddock at somebody's wake.

Or that Stottlemeyer was at the hotel at the time of the murder and was wearing a tie exactly like the one that was used to strangle Paul Braddock.

Or that Stottlemeyer's fingerprints were on the broken glass in Braddock's room.

Instead, Disher sent Lansdale off to search Captain Stottlemeyer's apartment and then went to the men's room to throw up before he called the deputy chief.

21

Mr. Monk and the Betrayal

The mysterious fate of Silicon Valley entrepreneur and visionary Steve Wurzel was widely known in San Francisco and probably across the nation. But I couldn't blame Monk for not knowing about it, since it happened around the time of Trudy's murder and his own complete mental breakdown.

So on our way back over the Golden Gate Bridge, I told Monk the story.

Wurzel set off early one foggy morning on his motorcycle to travel the winding coastal highway from his home in San Francisco to his weekend getaway in Mendocino, a picturesque village on the cliffs above the pounding waves of the Pacific.

He never arrived.

Much of the coastal route is a dangerous, twisting, two-lane highway running along the edge of jagged cliffs with nothing but a few planks of rotted wood between you and a spiraling plunge to the rocky surf below.

And where the road deviates away from the cliff's edge, it snakes into dense forests and across bridges over deep gorges.

It's an exhilarating and very scary drive, a road that offers spectacular views and the potential for spectacular deaths.

The Highway Patrol, the Mendocino County Sheriff, and the U.S. Coast Guard mounted a massive search along the coast, on land and at sea, but no sign of Wurzel or his motorcycle was found. After a few days, the official search was suspended.

Wurzel's wife, Linda, and their Silicon Valley friends weren't ready to give up. They mounted an ambitious, expensive, and exhaustive search effort of their own, but also failed to find him.

All of this happened only a few weeks before In-TouchSpace received a massive infusion of venture capital funds and exploded on the Internet, becoming a global social phenomenon and making all of the early investors, including many who helped finance the search for Wurzel, unbelievably rich.

After Wurzel was declared dead, several women came forward claiming a share of his billion-dollar estate on the grounds that they were his lovers and that he'd fathered children with them. But without DNA to confirm paternity, the cases were thrown out.

What, if anything, any of that had to do with the murder of a senile old bartender was beyond my powers of reasoning and deduction. And, apparently, it was beyond Monk's as well. Because after I was finished telling him the story, he didn't make any teasing statements hinting that he'd solved the murder. Instead, he asked me to take him home so he could get back to work on the remaining cases that Slade had given him.

"What about the Peschel case?" I asked.

"We'll have to wait and see what the captain has turned up," Monk said. "Perhaps someone was released from prison who had a grudge. But I wouldn't rule out Carol or her husband yet."

"Don't you wonder why Wurzel bought Peschel's tavern?"

"I suppose Wurzel was betting on the neighborhood becoming more desirable in the future and the property increasing significantly in value."

"It just seems odd," I said.

"The only connection between the two of them is that Wurzel bought Peschel's business and Peschel invested in InTouchSpace at about the same time. What is odd about that?"

It was as if we'd switched roles.

Usually, he was the one saying that something was odd and I was the one questioning it. The frustrating thing was that I couldn't even say exactly what was odd about this, except that thinking about it gave me a tickle in my chest.

"They're both dead," I said. "Wurzel disappeared under mysterious circumstances and Peschel was murdered."

"Ten years apart," Monk said. "There's nothing odd about that."

"Both of their last names end with the letters 'e-l,'" I said.

Monk gave me a look.

"Okay, that was stupid. But if there's nothing odd, why did you cock your head when I told you at the bookstore that Wurzel died ten years ago?"

"What are you talking about?"

"You cocked your head, like a chicken," I said, demonstrating by cocking my own. "You do that whenever you hear something that doesn't fit or that makes something fit that didn't fit before."

"You mentioned death, and whenever I hear about a death in the context of a murder investigation, my interest is piqued."

"There you go," I said. "You admit it: You're piqued."

"The pique passed," Monk said. "My head is swimming with murders and deaths over the last few days. I am having trouble keeping them all straight."

"I'm telling you, Mr. Monk, there's something ticklish about this."

"Ticklish?"

"I feel a tickle, right in the middle of my chest."

"Maybe you are having a heart attack," Monk said.

"I am not having a heart attack."

"Do you feel any shooting pains in your left arm?"

"No, but I'm beginning to feel one in my head," I said.

"We should stop by a hospital."

"I'm fine."

"You have heart palpitations and a throbbing headache," Monk said. "That's not fine. It's fatal."

"Something's bugging me, that's all," I said.

"Heart palpitations and a throbbing headache. It could be the onset of a massive stroke."

"I think it's my subconscious," I said. Perhaps after all the years of working for Monk, and all the murders that he'd solved with me tagging along, I was finally developing some detective instincts of my own.

But what good would they do me if I had no idea what my instincts were trying to tell me?

"We should stop and see Dr. Bell," Monk said. "He can help you with that. Maybe he can help me, too, as long as we're there."

"I have a better idea," I said.

"What could be better than seeing Dr. Bell? It's on the way. You'll thank me later."

I flipped open my cell phone and, breaking the law requiring motorists to use hands-free units while driving, I called Danielle. I asked her to give us a rundown on Dalberg Enterprises and to find out where we could bump into Linda Wurzel.

"Why would we want to meet her?" Monk asked after I finished the call.

"I don't," I said. "You do."

While Lansdale and the forensics unit searched Captain Stottlemeyer's apartment, Lieutenant Randy Disher sat at his desk, racked with guilt.

He knew he was doing what he had to do, but he couldn't help feeling that he was betraying his commanding officer, his mentor, and his friend.

Disher tried to distract himself from his despicable behavior by going through the statements taken from the hotel guests who were on Braddock's floor the night of the murder.

A detective from Wichita stayed in the room next to Braddock's. He said that someone knocked on Braddock's door around ten p.m. and, shortly thereafter, he heard a thump and the sound of a glass breaking, but nothing that alarmed him or made him think there was trouble.

The detective's statement would go a long way towards convincing a jury that Braddock was killed in his seventh-floor hotel room between ten and ten thirty p.m., which, unfortunately, was the same time that Captain Stottlemeyer said that he was sitting by himself in a conference room on the second floor.

Supposedly.

Disher scolded himself for thinking that way, for yet another betrayal of his friend, in thought if not in deed.

But Disher had no choice. He had to follow the evidence where it led him. And as the captain said, this case could make or break his career. He couldn't afford any mistakes.

Disher had called the deputy chief, half hoping that his boss would countermand his decision to search the captain's apartment. But, to Disher's dismay, the deputy chief agreed with Disher's actions and congratulated him on not letting his loyalty cloud his judgment.

It didn't make Disher feel any better.

His last hope was that Lansdale's search would come up empty. But that hope was dashed the moment Lansdale walked in and Disher saw the evidence bag in his hand.

Stottlemeyer's tie was in it.

Disher bolted from his seat and quickly led Lansdale back into the corridor.

"What are you thinking, waving the evidence bag around the squad room?" Disher said. "Do you want everyone to know what we're doing?"

"They will pretty soon anyway," Lansdale said. "We found the tie buried in the captain's trash can outside. Forensics says the tie is a positive match with the fiber recovered from Braddock and that there's blood on it."

Disher snatched the bag from Lansdale and looked at the tie inside.

There was no denying it. It matched the description of the tie that Braddock was strangled with. And he knew in his gut that a DNA test would match the blood on the tie with Braddock, too.

If the suspect were anybody else but Stottlemeyer, Disher wouldn't be hesitating over what to do next. It was a no-brainer. The case was closed. They had their killer.

"I know you two are close," Lansdale said. "If you can't do what has to be done, I can."

Disher glared at Lansdale, reached into his pocket, and pulled out his billfold. "Go to lunch at Sorrento's and take the rest of the squad with you. And the clerical staff, too. I want everybody out. It's on me."

He handed some cash to Lansdale. They shared a look. Lansdale gave Disher his money back.

"No, it's on me," Lansdale said. He walked past Disher into the squad room.

Disher hid the evidence bag behind his back and a few moments later Lansdale came out, leading a dozen other people towards the stairs.

One of the detectives called out to Disher, "Lansdale's taking us all to Sorrento's to celebrate his first week in Homicide. Are you joining us?"

"I'll catch up," Disher said.

When they were gone, Disher took a deep breath and went back into the squad room. The only one left inside was Stottlemeyer, who was in his office. He waved Disher inside.

"What's the special occasion?" Stottlemeyer asked as Disher entered, his hands behind his back.

"The end of Lansdale's first week in Homicide," Disher said.

"There must be more to it than that for him to be taking everybody out to celebrate," Stottlemeyer said. "Did you close the Braddock case already?"

Disher nodded. "Yes, sir."

"That's great news, Randy," Stottlemeyer said, rising from his seat. "So why are you looking so glum?"

"I still have to make the arrest," Disher said.

"That's the best part," Stottlemeyer said.

"Not this time," Disher said, and showed Stottlemeyer the evidence bag that was behind his back. "This is the murder weapon."

"That looks like my tie," Stottlemeyer said, walking around the desk to get a closer look at it.

"It is," Disher said.

"I don't think I like where this conversation is going."

"I know that I don't," Disher said.

Stottlemeyer met his gaze, then looked past Disher to the empty squad room. He put it together and winced from the emotional sting.

"You think that I murdered Braddock?"

"You hated him, sir. The file you gave me documents that."

"He was a dirty cop, Randy. I hate any cop who abuses people, manufactures evidence, or is on the take."

"But this dirty cop humiliated you in front of hundreds of cops from across America," Disher said. "You were outraged. Everybody knows it. You even attacked Braddock at a wake. You had to be restrained."

Stottlemeyer took a deep breath and held up his hands in front of his chest in submission. "I admit I lost control, but there's a big difference between slugging a guy in the mouth and murder."

"He was strangled with a tie like this on the same night that you were in the hotel. We found it in your trash. There's blood on it that we both know will turn out to be his."

"It is," Stottlemeyer said. "I got it on my tie at the wake, which is why I threw it out when I got home. I'm an experienced homicide detective. If I wanted to dispose of a murder weapon, do you think I'd just drop it in my trash can?"

"Maybe you weren't thinking rationally," Disher said. "Anger does that to a person."

"I'm rational now, and looking at your case objectively as your commanding officer, I'm telling you that you don't have the evidence to make this charge stick. All you have is my tie and I've explained how I got blood on it. And, to my embarrassment, I've got lots of witnesses who can confirm that story," Stottlemeyer said. "Yes, I was in the hotel that night but I didn't leave the second-floor conference room there and I'll bet that the security camera footage backs me up on that."

"The footage shows when you arrived and when you left the hotel. There are no cameras on the second floor, but there are in the elevator."

"And did you see me on it? No. Did you see me in the stairwells? No."

"At ten fifteen, someone in a beefeater outfit that obscured his face got into the elevator on the second floor and took it up to the seventh," Disher said. "We believe the killer took off the uniform, stashed it in a utility closet, then went to Braddock's room and killed him. He then put the costume back on and returned to the second floor."

"It could have been any one of the hundreds of people in the hotel that night," Stottlemeyer said. "You have no evidence that puts me in Braddock's room."

"There was a broken glass on the floor. Your fingerprints were on it," Disher said.

"Oh," Stottlemeyer said.

"The theory is you told him that you came to apologize, you had a drink with him, and when his back was turned, you slipped your tie around his throat and strangled him. The table was tipped over in the struggle and the glass broke. You forgot about it."

Stottlemeyer rubbed his mustache. "It's obvious what's happening here. Someone is setting me up."

"That's not for me to decide," Disher said. "My job is to follow the evidence."

"Forget the evidence for a minute. You know me, Randy."

"Not lately, Captain. Over the last couple of weeks, you've been a different person."

"One stupid enough to murder a cop with his own tie and leave behind a glass with his fingerprints on it?"

"You also fired Monk."

"What does that have to do with anything?"

"The deputy chief thinks it was so Monk wouldn't be around to investigate Braddock's murder."

"If I intended to murder Braddock, don't you think I would come up with a better plan than this?"

"I'm sorry, Captain," Disher said, his voice cracking, his hands shaking. "I'm placing you under arrest for the murder of Paul Braddock."

"You're making a mistake, Randy."

"I certainly hope so," Disher said, and gave Stottlemeyer his handcuffs. "Could you put these on, please?"

"Why don't you?"

"Because I'm going to throw up." Disher hurried to the garbage can beside the desk and gagged into it. Between heaves, he tried to read the captain his rights.

"It's okay," Stottlemeyer said, cuffing his own hands behind his back. "I know them."

22

Mr. Monk Goes to Jail

Monk worked on his remaining Intertect cases at his dining table while I tried to hone my detecting instincts by reading the *Murder, She Wrote* novel he bought in Mill Valley.

I can't say that I learned much about investigative procedure but I discovered that you should stay far away from Cabot Cove. That tiny New England village is deadlier than Beirut, South Central Los Angeles, and the darkest back alley in Juarez combined. Cabot Cove probably has the highest per capita murder rate of anyplace on earth. Even though every killer eventually gets caught by Jessica Fletcher, I still wouldn't feel safe there. I'm surprised the old biddy walks around town unarmed.

Jessica was about to prove that her second cousin twice removed was innocent of murder when Monk's phone rang. I answered it.

"I need to see Monk right away," Captain Stottlemeyer said. "Meet me in the interview room at the Seventh Street lockup."

He hung up before I could ask him for more details. I

assumed he'd made a breakthrough on the Peschel case and so did Monk.

On the way there, Monk and I tried to guess what was in store for us. We decided that the captain had either arrested someone for the crime or had found someone behind bars who had vital information on the killing. What other reason could there be for meeting at the jail? Monk suggested that it might even be a grateful Salvatore Lucarelli, offering to trade information in return for a reduced sentence.

So we went into the jail with a certain level of excitement, believing that we were in for something good. We were led to the same interview room where we'd met with Lucarelli a few days before, so I was prepared to see him there again.

I guess that's why when I saw the man in the yellow jumpsuit, in that first split second I thought it was Lucarelli. Or perhaps my mind didn't want to believe what my eyes were telling me.

It was Captain Stottlemeyer sitting there this time. Only he wasn't in chains.

Monk let out a little gasp. "Leland? What happened?"

I rarely heard Monk refer to the captain by his first name. But this wasn't a normal situation.

"I've been arrested for murder," Stottlemeyer said.

"Who did you kill?" Monk asked.

"Nobody," Stottlemeyer said. "How could you think I've murdered anyone?"

"Because you're in jail for murder," Monk said.

"That doesn't mean I'm guilty."

"The police don't arrest innocent people," Monk said. "They are very good at what they do."

"Ordinarily, I would appreciate that vote of confidence, but since I'm sitting here for a crime I didn't commit, you'll have to forgive me if I don't agree with you."

"Who was murdered?" I asked.

"Paul Braddock," Stottlemeyer said.

"How?" Monk asked.

"He was strangled in his hotel room," Stottlemeyer said.

"When?" Monk asked.

"The night of the wake."

"When you beat him up," Monk said.

"Yes," Stottlemeyer said.

"After he humiliated you in front of hundreds of homicide detectives," I said.

"Yes," Stottlemeyer said.

"So all the police have against you is one of the strongest motives for murder that I've ever heard in all my years of investigating homicides," Monk said. "It's not so bad."

He wasn't being sarcastic. He didn't know how to be. I think he was trying—in his own sweet, unconvincing way—to be reassuring. He failed miserably.

Stottlemeyer cleared his throat. "And I was in the hotel at the time of the murder."

Monk nodded. "Is that all?"

"And he was strangled with a tie identical to the one I was wearing."

Monk nodded again. "That's it?"

"And they found my fingerprints on a broken glass in Braddock's room."

Monk nodded some more. "Anything else?"

"They found my tie, stained with Braddock's blood, in my garbage can."

Monk hadn't stopped nodding. "Any more?"

"And I fired you shortly before Braddock's murder, which meant that the one detective in San Francisco with an unbroken record for solving homicides wasn't around to investigate this case."

Monk kept right on nodding. He was nodding so much

I was afraid he'd give himself a concussion, so I grabbed his head to stop him. He kept trying to nod anyway. I held his head tight.

"You can stop nodding, Mr. Monk, the captain is finished listing all the evidence against him," I said, glancing at Stottlemeyer. "Aren't you?"

Now Stottlemeyer nodded.

Monk took a deep breath and let it out slowly, signaling to me that he was calm. He wasn't fighting against my grip any longer. I let go of his head and he held it steady.

"So," Monk said. "Why did you kill him?"

"I didn't," Stottlemeyer said. "That's why I called you. I'm being framed and you're the only one who can prove it."

"Isn't Randy working his butt off to clear your name?" I asked.

"Who do you think put together the case against me?" Stottlemeyer said. "He thinks I'm guilty."

"How could he?" I said.

"Only because the captain had an incredibly strong motive and all the evidence pointed to him," Monk said. "Other than that, Lieutenant Disher has nothing."

"That's comforting," Stottlemeyer said. "So, will you help me or not?"

"Of course I will," Monk said.

"Me, too," I said.

Stottlemeyer smiled. "Then I know this is all going to work out fine."

"I hope he gets himself a good lawyer," Monk said as we left the jail and headed for the Lexus, which was parked at a meter a short way up Seventh Street.

"Do you think he's going to need one?"

"A good lawyer might be able to plea-bargain him down to a sentence that's less than life in prison." Monk tapped each meter that we passed. It was a habit of his that I had never understood.

"That won't be necessary, because this case will never get that far," I said. "You'll prove him innocent long before a trial."

"What makes you think I'm going to do that?"

"Because you just said you would," I said.

"I said I would help him," Monk said. "We'll start interviewing criminal defense attorneys today."

"What about investigating the murder and proving him innocent instead?"

"Are you kidding?" Monk said. "He did it."

"How can you say that?"

"Oh, I don't know. Maybe it's because *he did it*."

"You know Captain Stottlemeyer better than that," I said. "He couldn't murder anyone."

"Until now. Did you hear all the evidence against him?"

"I wouldn't care if they'd caught Stottlemeyer in the act, cinching the tie around Braddock's throat."

"Did they?" Monk asked.

"No, they didn't," I said through gritted teeth, withstanding the urge to slap him silly.

"Are you sure? We should double-check, because that's the only thing they haven't got against him."

"If Leland Stottlemeyer says he's innocent, then he is. You should believe that, too."

I drove us straight to police headquarters so we could have a talk with that scoundrel Randy Disher.

We found him carrying a box into the captain's office, which had been completely stripped bare of all of Stottlemeyer's files and personal belongings.

Disher set the box on the empty desk and faced us grimly. "I heard that the captain had called you. I figured it was better that you heard the bad news directly from him rather than me."

"I ought to slap you," I said.

"That would be assaulting a police officer," Monk said. "It's a criminal offense."

"Perfect, then I should do it," I said. "Lieutenant Disher seems to enjoy arresting his friends."

"It's not Lieutenant anymore," Disher mumbled. "It's Acting Captain Disher."

That was when I noticed that the box he'd brought in was full of stuff from his desk. I felt my face get hot.

"So that's what this is all about. You sold out the captain for a promotion," I said. "I see it didn't take you very long to haul away his stuff and move yourself in."

"It's a temporary assignment and I had no idea the deputy chief was going to do it," Disher said. "And it was Internal Affairs that cleaned out his office, not me."

"They didn't do a very good job," Monk said. "There's still dust on the shelves. If you give me Lysol, a rag, and some rubber gloves, I'll take care of it."

I pointed my finger at Monk.

"If you even try, I will break your arm like a chopstick." Monk flinched and I turned to Disher. "Why did Internal Affairs take the captain's things?"

"It is standard operating procedure in situations like this," Disher said. "They are looking for evidence of other crimes he might have committed."

"*Other* crimes?" The next thing I knew I was swinging at Disher's face.

Disher didn't raise a hand to defend himself or move out of the way. But before the flat of my hand could connect with his boyish cheek, Monk grabbed my arm and pinned it behind me.

"What's the matter with you?" Monk said. He seemed truly distraught.

"It's okay, Monk. Let her slap me. I deserve it for what I've done."

"He's right," I said to Monk. "Let go of me."

"Lieutenant Disher was only doing his job," Monk said.

"Acting Captain Disher," he corrected.

I tried to slap Disher with my free hand, but with Monk clutching my other arm, I was off balance and the blow fell short of the mark. Disher would have had to lean towards me for the slap to connect. I guess he didn't want to be punished as much as he claimed or he would have.

"I know that I betrayed the captain," Disher said. "But I was only following the evidence where it led. I had no choice but to arrest him. My only hope, and his, is that you can prove that he's innocent."

"You should be doing that," I seethed. It's amazing that I wasn't foaming at the mouth.

"I'll help you any way that I can, but it will have to be unofficially," Disher said. "I am going to leave now and get myself a cup of coffee. While I am gone, you are absolutely forbidden to read the file in the box on the desk, because it contains all of the forensic reports, witness statements, and crime scene photos on the Braddock investigation. Is that clear?"

He gave us a big, exaggerated wink.

"Yes," Monk said.

Disher nodded, closed the blinds on all of the captain's office windows, and walked out, closing the door behind him. We were alone and out of sight. Monk let go of me and I jerked away from him.

"Are you having female problems?" he asked.

I glared at him in fury. "Did you actually just ask me if I have my period?"

"Ssssh," Monk said, waving his hands frantically. "There's no reason to start talking like a sailor."

"I've got to meet this wretched sailor that you

keep talking about," I said. "No, Mr. Monk, I am not menstruating."

"Ssssh," Monk said, waving his arms again. "First you're violent, now you're a gutter mouth. What is wrong with you?"

"A good friend of mine was just arrested for a murder he didn't commit—*that* is what is wrong with me and it should be wrong with you, too."

I reached into the box and pulled out the Braddock file. Monk tried to grab it from me but I yanked the file away.

"Are you crazy? Acting Captain Disher said we are *absolutely forbidden* to read that file."

"Which was his way of saying he wanted us to read it," I said, laying the crime scene photos out on the empty desk.

"*Absolutely forbidden* means the opposite," Monk said, gathering each photo up, one by one.

"But he meant the opposite of the opposite," I said, laying out the forensic report and the photos of the evidence. "It was his way of saying we weren't allowed to read the file but he was letting us read it anyway."

"If that's what he wanted to say, why didn't he say that instead of *absolutely forbidden*?" Monk said, picking up the forensic report and photos.

"He was protecting his butt," I said, laying out the witness statements. "He was saying that if we get caught reading it, we are on our own."

"He was saying all that when he said we were *absolutely forbidden* to open the file."

"Yes," I said, dropping the empty file on the desk. "That's why he gave us the big wink."

"He probably had dust in his eye." Monk shoved all the papers and photos back into the file and returned it to the box. "*Absolutely forbidden* means *absolutely forbidden*."

Whether it did or not, I knew that Monk had seen every photo in the file and, whether he wanted to or not, had unconsciously noted every significant detail in them. He couldn't help himself.

"If you say so," I said. "How do you feel about visiting the crime scene?"

"Ambivalent," he said.

23

Mr. Monk and the Odd Floor

I went to the front desk of the Dorchester and asked the clerk if I could rent a room. I didn't think that they would let us just look around simply because we were private eyes, and I'm lousy when it comes to bribing people. Besides, I had Slade's magic credit card.

"Of course," the clerk said. He was so youthful, clean-cut, and gleamingly straight-toothed that he could have worked at Disneyland. "How long will you be staying?"

I glanced over my shoulder at Monk, who was busy arranging the suitcases at the porter's stand by size, then returned my gaze to the clerk.

"One night," I said. "I'd like room seven thirteen."

The clerk cleared his throat with discomfort. "Perhaps you'd like a different room."

"Is it occupied?"

"No," he said, clearing his throat again.

"Then what's the problem?"

"It's just that the gentleman who was staying there most recently suffered a tragedy."

"That's a shame for him but what does that have to do with me?"

"I wouldn't want to sleep in a room where someone died," the clerk said.

"No one's asking you to," I said. "I've got a companion already."

I tipped my head towards Monk, who was still busy lining up the suitcases.

The man flushed with embarrassment. "I wasn't suggesting—I mean, I was just trying to be helpful."

"By offering yourself to me?"

"No, no, you've got it all wrong—" he stammered.

"We're in a hurry," I interrupted, handing him my Intertect credit card with a smile. "Could you make it snappy, Romeo?"

He quickly checked us in and handed me an electronic key card.

"Have a pleasant stay," he said.

"I will." I winked and took the card from him. It was fun flustering him. It was nice to know I could still fluster somebody.

I went over to Monk, who was admiring the row of suitcases, perfectly staggered from the smallest to the largest like the signal-strength icon on a cell phone.

"We're in," I said. "The room is on the seventh floor."

I figured the uneven floor number was enough bad news for the moment—there was no reason to tell Monk yet that we were going to an odd room, too.

"You didn't say anything about going to the seventh floor," Monk said.

"That's where his room is," I said.

"He should have been on the fourth or sixth," Monk said. "Or some other even-numbered floor."

"But he wasn't," I said.

"No wonder he's dead," Monk said. "They shouldn't even put rooms on those floors. It's irresponsible, dangerous, immoral, and unnatural."

"What should they do, just leave the odd-numbered floors empty?"

"Yes, for the sake of humanity," Monk said. "It must have been unbearable for Braddock. Maybe he killed himself."

"You think Braddock strangled himself with a tie because he couldn't endure another night on an odd-numbered floor?"

"It's the most logical alternative," Monk said. "The captain should use that argument as the cornerstone of his defense strategy."

I couldn't take any more of his insanity and marched to the elevator. "I'll meet you up there."

I knew that he'd be taking the stairs. He was too claustrophobic to ride an elevator. But if I wasn't there to meet him on the seventh floor, to physically drag him out of the stairwell if necessary, he might not make it to the room at all.

I got in the elevator, rode it to the seventh floor, and went to room 713. A maid was cleaning the room across the hall, the door propped open with her cart of cleaning supplies, linens, toiletries, and clean glasses.

I opened the door to room 713 and went inside.

There was nothing in the room to indicate that a murder had taken place there a few nights ago. The table was upright, the glasses were replaced, and the bed was made. It was all crisp and clean and smelled of disinfectant.

But I knew better.

A few months ago at a crime scene in another hotel room, Disher demonstrated to me how to use a device that shines a special light to illuminate all the bodily fluid stains that are otherwise invisible to the naked eye. He swept the light over the scene and revealed that everything in the room had been, at one time or another, splattered with bodily fluids—the bedspread, the headboard, the walls, the ceilings, the tabletops, the countertops, the lamps, even the TV remote control.

I couldn't figure out how some of the stains got where they were. The remote control alone had looked as if it had been dipped in blood or drool or God knows what. It was disgusting to see, even for someone without Monk's germophobia. Now I couldn't enter a hotel room without imagining all the bodily fluids that I knew were all over the place but that I couldn't actually see.

That was probably how Monk saw everything in this world. His eyes were like that special light.

So were mine as I walked into Braddock's hotel room. I looked at the bedspread and in my mind I saw the drool that must have spilled out of Braddock's gaping mouth as he struggled for air that would never come.

I wasn't sure what bringing Monk to Braddock's room would accomplish, but it seemed to me that visiting the crime scene, even after it had been cleaned up, was still the logical first step in a homicide investigation.

I left the room and went to the stairwell, getting to the door just as Monk huffed and puffed his way up the final few steps.

"You ought to try the elevator sometime," I said. "It's not that bad."

"If you enjoy the experience of being buried alive in a coffin that moves," Monk said, catching his breath.

"It's not like being buried alive."

"I've been buried alive. Twice. Once in a coffin and once in a car. Have you?"

"No," I said. I vividly remembered those harrowing experiences. On both occasions, he'd come very close to suffocating to death.

"Then I think I know a little bit more about what being buried alive feels like than you do."

He had me there.

I led him down the hall to the room. He stopped to inspect the maid's cart and I used the opportunity to open the door, hoping he wouldn't notice the room number.

The maid looked up at him from inside the other room, where she was stripping a bed.

"You are doing God's work," Monk said to her. "I salute you for your bravery, courage, and sacrifice."

She looked baffled. He turned to face me and stopped cold.

"That's room seven thirteen," Monk said, defeating my pathetic attempt at misdirection.

"Yes, it is. It's where the murder occurred."

"I'm not surprised," Monk said. "The room is cursed."

"You have to come inside," I said.

"I can see just fine from here," he said, standing at the threshold.

"Braddock was on the floor, between the bed and the window," I said. "You can't see the floor from where you are standing."

"I don't need to." He leaned inside once, angling himself so he could see into the bathroom to his left.

Monk turned and looked back through the open door of the room across the hall. He cocked his head and rolled his shoulders.

Something was bugging him. Well, lots of things were bugging him, like being on an odd-numbered floor in front of an odd-numbered room with patterned, floral wallpaper that probably didn't match up correctly. What I meant was that something was bugging him even more than all the other things that bug him at any given moment.

He examined the glasses on the maid's cart. They each had tiny paper lids on top to indicate that they were clean.

Monk picked one of the glasses up and held it to the light.

"What is it?" I asked, still holding the door open.

"Water spots." He took the lid off and put the glass with the dirty dishes that were in a tub on a lower shelf of the cart. He deposited the lid in the cart's trash bag.

"That's it? Water spots?"

Monk went into the room across the hall and quickly peered into the bathroom and then came back to me. The maid watched us warily as she finished making the bed.

"I'm a horrible person," Monk said. "Despicable, lower than low."

"Why do you say that?"

"Because I didn't believe Captain Stottlemeyer," Monk said.

"And you do now?"

Monk nodded. "He's innocent. The evidence is clear."

"You found evidence without even stepping into the room where the murder occurred?"

"Each hotel room has four glasses," Monk said. "Two in the bathroom and two on the desk on either side of the ice bucket. All four glasses are identical. But according to the crime scene photos, there were five glasses in Braddock's room when he was killed. The fifth one was broken on the floor and had the captain's fingerprints on it."

"The glass was planted," I said.

"I think it was the water glass the captain was drinking from when we spoke here at the conference," Monk said. "But I can't prove it. So the captain is no better off now than he was before."

"Yes, he is," I said.

"I don't see how."

"You're on the case now, Mr. Monk."

"But I don't know where to go or what to do next to prove that the captain is innocent."

"You'll think of something," I said. "I have faith. So does Captain Stottlemeyer."

I was so thankful that Monk had accepted the captain's innocence that I walked down the stairwell with him instead of taking the elevator.

When we emerged in the lobby, the first thing I saw was Nicholas Slade striding in and, from the look on his face, I didn't think it was a coincidence that he was there.

He marched straight towards us.

"We need to talk," he said.

Whenever someone says, "We need to talk," what they really mean is that they want to tear your head off about something. So you have two choices: You can either brace yourself for a verbal beating or run for the nearest exit.

My instinct, no doubt tied to childhood, when my dad used those same words (though he'd add "young lady" at the end) when he caught me doing something bad, was to run. But I fought back the urge.

"How did you know we were here?" I asked.

"I'm a great detective," he said.

"Mr. Monk is a great detective," I said. "You are a very good one."

It's probably not too smart to insult your boss with a backhanded compliment when he's already mad at you, but when I'm forced into a corner, cockiness is how I deal with my worry or fear. I was afraid I was about to see my wonderful health plan and my company car evaporate before I really got a chance to use them.

"I heard what happened to Leland and that you were down there to see him. If I were trying to prove him innocent, the crime scene is the first place I'd go," Slade said. Score one for me and my detecting instincts. "And you used our corporate card to rent the room."

"You track our credit card usage in real time?" I said. "That seems a little Orwellian to me."

"Technically, it's not your privacy I'd be intruding on, since it's my credit card you were using. But I didn't have to go to the trouble. Intertect handles the security for the hotel. I got a call that you were here."

"Oh," I said.

"Oh," he repeated. "If you'd called me before you came down here, you could have saved the company two hundred and fifty dollars."

"Is that what you're mad about?" I asked. "The money?"

"I'm not mad," Slade said. "I'm confused and I'm disappointed. First you tell me that Mr. Monk needs a rest—"

"I don't need a rest," Monk interrupted.

"—which I gave him, then I find out that you used that free time to investigate Bill Peschel's death."

"Murder," Monk said.

"Nobody has hired us on that case," Slade said. "Your fee is three hundred dollars an hour and until someone signs a contract with me and hands us a check for a retainer, you are not to spend a single moment of your time, or anybody else's in my employ, on that case."

"I make three hundred dollars an hour?" Monk said.

"Now Leland has asked for your help and you agreed to give it without consulting me first," Slade said. "Have you forgotten who you are working for, Mr. Monk?"

"I have to help my friend," Monk said.

"He is my friend, too," Slade said.

"The captain is innocent, he needs Mr. Monk's help, and he can't possibly afford to pay your rates," I said.

"Leland doesn't have to," Slade said. "We'll help him for nothing. It will be our pro bono case for the year. Consider yourselves assigned to the case. All the resources of Intertect are at your disposal. But you have to promise me that you will stop investigating Peschel's death."

"Murder," Monk said.

"It's not our problem," Slade said.

"Wasn't he your friend, too?" I asked.

"Not like Leland, not even close," Slade said. "Unless the Atwaters hire us, or the Mill Valley police do, or anybody else who'd like to pay our regular fees, we are not getting involved in that investigation."

"I wasn't doing much on it," Monk said. "Nothing at all, really."

"You went out to question Phil Atwater," Slade said. "That's investigation."

Slade may have discovered we were working on the Peschel case because of the surveillance Danielle had ordered and maybe because she checked the Atwaters' credit card activity. But the only way Slade could have known we met with Phil was if Danielle had told him. She'd betrayed us.

"By working on the case for free," Slade continued, "you are actually working against Intertect. You are removing the incentive for anyone to hire us to do the work. It's self-destructive. It's like phoning in anonymous tips to the police after they fired you."

"You knew about that?" Monk said.

"I'm a great detective." Slade glanced at me. "Correction, a good detective."

"I don't know why they bother telling people it's an anonymous tip line when it's not anonymous at all," Monk said. "I'm going to write a very stern letter to the chief of police about this."

"They aren't going to be too happy with you when they get it," I said.

"Don't worry," Monk said. "I'll send it anonymously."

24

Mr. Monk Feels the Pressure

Captain Stottlemeyer sat across from us in the interview room at the jail as Monk told him his theory about the glass. He looked as jaundiced as Lucarelli did when he sat in that same chair.

Perhaps it was the yellow glow of those energy-efficient lightbulbs combined with the yellow jumpsuit that created that effect. Or perhaps it was a physical symptom of incarceration in a windowless cell and hours of contemplating your impending lifelong imprisonment.

"My ex-wife won't let my kids come see me, so the only information they are getting about all this is what they read online or see on the news," Stottlemeyer said. "But you know what the worst part of this is?"

"The three Velcro strips on your jumpsuit," Monk said. "It's a blatant violation of the Geneva convention."

"Velcro strips didn't exist when they convened the Geneva convention," I said.

"Giving a man only three Velcro strips is cruel and inhuman punishment," Monk said. "Where the hell is that fourth strip? It's pure, unrelenting psychological torture. I don't know how you can stand it, Captain."

"What's worse is that Salvatore Lucarelli is in the cell across from mine," Stottlemeyer said. "I have to look at that smug smile on his face."

"Do you think he's behind this?" I asked.

"It could be anybody. You make a lot of enemies in my job. Lucarelli is just one of them."

"I'm sorry," Monk said.

"What are you sorry about?" Stottlemeyer asked.

"This," he said. "It's all my fault."

You can always count on Monk to make any situation about himself. It's not that Monk is selfish, it's just that he needs to believe that the whole world revolves around him. It's the only way he can reasonably exert complete control over it.

"How is it your fault?" Stottlemeyer said.

"If I'd been more vigilant, I might have seen this coming," Monk said.

"How? Are you psychic?"

"No," Monk said.

"Then how could you have seen it coming?"

"A frame is built," Monk said. "The construction was happening all around us."

"It doesn't mean that it happened in front of our eyes," Stottlemeyer said.

"It had to," Monk said. "Someone saw the opportunity to frame you and took it. Whoever it was knew you had a motive to kill Braddock."

"That was obvious to anyone who was at the conference, which is why they swiped the glass afterwards and held on to it," Stottlemeyer said. "But I have a hard time imagining that another cop did this."

"Who else could it be?" I asked.

"There's a large service staff at the hotel," Stottlemeyer said. "One of them could have been an ex-con or related to someone Braddock put away."

"Braddock isn't the one sitting in jail," I said.

"I'm thinking that maybe this isn't about me," Stottlemeyer said. "I'm just the fall guy. I don't think it's a coincidence that Peschel and Braddock were murdered within forty-eight hours of each other. Braddock got tips from Peschel, too."

"You think the killer was someone Braddock put away based on a tip from Peschel," I said.

Stottlemeyer nodded. "And knowing Braddock, he probably gave the guy a good beating first."

"Where do we even begin to look?" I asked.

"You'd have to go over Braddock's arrests in the last year or two that he was with the San Francisco police," Stottlemeyer said. "You won't find Bill's name anywhere, since he never testified, but there might be a reference in the files saying that Braddock acted on a tip from a confidential informant."

"That could take weeks," I said. "And that's assuming we could even get access to those files."

"Nick can. He's got all kind of sources in the department who talk to him when they shouldn't," Stottlemeyer said. "He's also in a perfect position to scrutinize the background of every member of the Dorchester staff, if he's willing to do it."

"He will," I said.

"But what can I do?" Monk asked.

"What you do best," Stottlemeyer said.

"Which is what?"

"Be yourself," Stottlemeyer said. "If the clues are out there, you'll see them, if you haven't already."

"If I've seen the clues," Monk said, "why don't I have the solution?"

"I don't understand the way you think, Monk. It gives me a headache to even try. But I know you see and hear more than you think you do," Stottlemeyer said. "My guess is that all those details are swirling around in your head like a million pixels waiting to combine into a picture."

Maybe a few of them were in my head, too, which was why I got that ticklish feeling about the ten years between Steve Wurzel's disappearance and Peschel's death.

"I hope you're right," Monk said.

"I'm not hoping," Stottlemeyer said. "I'm counting on it."

"I wish you wouldn't," Monk said. "I don't work well under pressure."

"Think of the pressure I'm under," Stottlemeyer said. "I'm wearing a jumpsuit with three Velcro strips."

Monk rose from his chair. "You're right. What was I thinking? No suffering of mine can compare to the living hell that you are enduring. Your misery is my misery until this ordeal is over."

"That's the spirit," Stottlemeyer said.

I called Danielle on our way out of the jail and asked her to get some operatives to take a look at any old cases that might have involved Peschel.

She had some information to give us on the Wurzels but I told her to give us the briefing at Monk's apartment. I wanted to give her hell but not over the phone and definitely not at Intertect.

As soon as we got back, Monk hurried to the bathroom to give his hands a quick rinse. Danielle showed up about twenty-five minutes later, so I figured we had at least five more minutes to ourselves before he was finished washing his hands.

That was more than enough time for me to cut off her head and hand it to her, figuratively speaking, of course.

"We need to talk," I said, echoing both Slade and

my father. I thought about adding "young lady," but it would have made me feel even older in comparison to her. "I thought we had an understanding."

"I haven't sent any more files over," she said, stiffening up defensively. She was bracing for an attack and she was going to get one.

"I'm talking about trust," I said. "When we first met, you told me that you worked for Mr. Monk first, Nick second, and that we never had to worry about your loyalty."

"That's right," she said. "I meant it, too."

"It's not enough to say it, Danielle. You have to actually follow through."

"I have," she said.

"We ran into Nick at the Dorchester Hotel. He knew that Mr. Monk and I met with Phil Atwater in Mill Valley," I said. "I can think of only one way he could have known about that."

She loosened up, seemingly relieved, which was not the reaction I was expecting. "That's because you don't know about the tracker."

"What are you talking about?"

"Each car in the Intertect fleet is equipped with a GPS locator unit," she said. "It's just like the ones that trucking companies install on their big rigs so they can keep track of their freight at all times."

It gave me the creeps. "Intertect keeps its operatives under surveillance?"

She shook her head. "Every operative knows that there is a locator on their cars. Nick says it's for our own safety and security. We're in a dangerous line of work. If we get into trouble, Intertect can always send backup to our last-known location or, if we disappear from the grid, they can even backtrack where we've been for the last few weeks and retrace our steps."

"Are our phones tapped, too?"

"Of course not," she said. "Watching you isn't the point. It's about keeping our people safe."

"Uh-huh," I said. "Does Intertect log your keystrokes on your computer?"

"Yes," she said. "But it's not what you think."

"What I think is that I am never using a computer or a phone at Intertect."

"The company takes these measures for your protection and to guarantee that if you are killed in the course of your work, your investigation doesn't die with you."

"That's cold," I said.

"That's pragmatic," she said.

"So Nick knows where we've been and any research work that you've done for us."

"I don't know if he does or not, but if he wanted to, the information is readily available to him from his computer. Is there any reason you wouldn't want him to know what we've been doing?"

"I cherish my privacy and Mr. Monk's."

"Welcome to corporate America in the digital age," she said. "Intertect isn't any different from any other big company as far as keeping tabs on the activity of its employees."

"Do you have a personal computer that wasn't supplied by Intertect?"

"Yes," she replied. "My laptop."

"From now on, I want you to use only that for any work you do for Mr. Monk," I said. "If we want Nick to know what we are doing, we'll tell him."

I wasn't willing to give up my nice Lexus just because it spied on me. But now I knew how all those female Russian spies and SPECTRE agents felt when they slept with James Bond.

"Trust works both ways," Danielle said. "I need to

know you're going to give me the benefit of the doubt instead of immediately assuming that I've betrayed you in some way."

"You're right," I said. "I'm sorry. You've done great work. Mr. Monk is very impressed with you."

"What about you?"

"You make me feel old and inadequate." I said it without even thinking and shocked myself with the truth of it.

"You're joking," she said.

"I wish I were," I said.

"I meant what I told you at Intertect," Danielle said. "You and Mr. Monk are a team. You don't realize just how experienced an investigator you really are. You could hold your own with any of our operatives."

That was when Monk walked into the room. "There's nothing quite as refreshing as washing your hands, brushing your teeth, irrigating your nasal passages, cleaning inside your ears, and flushing your eyes. I'm ready to take on the world."

It seemed to me that Monk took on the world every time he walked out his front door. The world usually won.

"I have the information that you asked for on Linda Wurzel," Danielle said, handing me a photograph.

"What about Dalberg Enterprises?" I asked, glancing at the picture.

Wurzel was tall and thin and wearing a blue pantsuit Hillary Clinton would have loved and a necklace of big pearls that reminded me of Wilma Flintstone's bling. Her unnaturally alert eyes, sharp jawline, sculpted nose, fish lips, bronze tan, and drum-tight brow suggested to me she'd had more than a few intimate encounters in a tanning bed with Mr. Botox, Mr. Collagen, and Mr. Scalpel.

"Linda Wurzel *is* Dalberg Enterprises," Danielle said.

"Dalberg is her maiden name. She was in real estate before she met her husband and his wealth allowed her to considerably enlarge her property portfolio."

"So she's the one who bought Peschel's building," I said. "Not her husband."

"Yes," Danielle said. "Though I don't know how involved her husband was after their marriage in her real estate speculation. He might have provided more than just money. Since her husband's death, she sits on the board of InTouchSpace and devotes the rest of her attention, and a considerable chunk of her wealth, to various philanthropic and arts organizations."

"Where can we find her?" I asked.

"Mr. Slade made us promise to stay out of the Peschel investigation," Monk said.

"He *asked* us to," I said. "We didn't promise. And this isn't about the Peschel case, this is about Braddock's murder."

"I don't see the connection," Monk said.

"They are both dead, Captain Stottlemeyer is in jail, and I had a tickle." I turned to Danielle. "So, where is Linda Wurzel?"

"She has an office downtown and an estate in Sea Cliff," Danielle said. "And three days a week she has a standing appointment at JoAnne's. She has one today."

"Is that her psychiatrist?" Monk asked.

"Her beautician," Danielle said. "JoAnne has a very exclusive salon in Chinatown."

"That's the last neighborhood I'd expect someone in her social class to go for manicure and a facial." Chinatown was a historic neighborhood and popular tourist attraction, filled with tacky gift shops and great restaurants, but it wasn't exactly known for trend-setting style. At least I thought it wasn't.

"JoAnne's is *the* place to go for the latest beauty treatments," Danielle said. "All the socialites, heiresses, and debutantes go there, as well as every actress and model north of LA, south of Seattle, and west of Santa Fe."

"It's that good?" I asked.

"That's what all the magazines say," Danielle replied. "I wish I could afford it. Geisha facials start at two hundred and fifty dollars and garra rufa pedicures can cost as much as two hundred."

Thank God for Slade's credit card.

"I suddenly feel the need to beautify myself," I said. "How about you, Mr. Monk?"

"I just washed my hands, brushed my teeth, irrigated my nasal passages, cleaned my ears, and flushed my eyes," Monk said. "I don't see how you could improve on that without being hosed down and decontaminated by a certified hazardous materials team."

"You're about to find out," I said.

25

Mr. Monk and the Geisha Facial

Whenever friends of mine from out of town come to visit, they always want me to take them to Fisherman's Wharf and Chinatown.

Fisherman's Wharf has lost all of its authentic charm and become a low-end shopping center with a Fisherman's Wharf theme. But I take my friends there anyway and reward myself for my sacrifice with a loaf of fresh, hot sourdough bread at Boudin, which is no longer the simple bakery that it once was, either. Taking its cue from the rest of the neighborhood, Boudin has become a massive attraction, complete with tour, two restaurants, and a gift shop.

It's depressing.

But Chinatown is still pretty much the real thing, a distinct city within a city. I don't wait until out-of-town friends show up to go there. It's one of my favorite places.

There are lots of ways into Chinatown, but tourists always want to go through the pagoda-style, three-arched gate on Grant Avenue and Bush Street that's adorned with ornamental dragons, carps, and lions. It's a manufactured photo op built in 1970 and draws a clear line between the Union Square shopping district and the main street of Chinatown.

I avoid the gate for exactly that reason and I usually wander in from the opposite end of Grant Avenue.

Visually, Chinatown is nothing like China. It's an American backdrop dressed up with Chinese stuff, sort of the urban equivalent of decorating a Ramada Inn banquet room with surfboards, piles of sand, suntan lotion, and seashells for a party with a beach theme. Red lanterns are strewn across streets with names like Stockton and Sacramento. Pagoda cornices, green tiles, and colorful Chinese signage are affixed to the kind of standard Edwardian stone and concrete buildings found on any Main Street in America.

But even so, it's the real deal. There are twenty thousand Chinese people living in the neighborhood, so you'll find some uniquely Chinese touches that will transport you, if not to China, at least to somewhere away from the familiar.

There are pagoda-styled streetlights supported by twin golden dragons whose tails twine around the poles. You won't find that in your housing tract. In the windows of meat markets and grocery stories, you'll see turtles, ducks, squid, pigs, and eels ready for the dinner table. You won't find that at your neighborhood Safeway.

When you walk the streets you'll hear a cacophony of Chinese, from people talking and yelling, movie clips playing loudly in DVD shops, and music blaring from the stores, apartments, and car radios.

And you'll smell incense mingling with the luscious aroma of Chinese food being fried, grilled, boiled, and steamed in the countless bakeries, restaurants, and tearooms.

Chinatown is a complete sensory experience.

I like letting myself be pushed by the flow of tourists

down Grant Avenue because it takes me past the scores of gift shops that are spilling out onto the sidewalks with things like silk ties, back scratchers, prayer wheels, Buddha statues, chopsticks, porcelain figurines, teapots, T-shirts, pottery, sandals, wind chimes, pot holders, mahjongg sets, bells, Hello Kitty pillows and bootleg Versace bags.

Monk hates Chinatown, of course, for all the reasons I love it. He becomes overwhelmed by the disorganization, the disarray, and the lack of symmetry. For him, it's anarchy.

So rather than inflict Grant Avenue on him, I parked on the western periphery of Chinatown and we walked down one of the less busy and ornamented streets to JoAnne's, an unassuming storefront tucked between a dim sum restaurant and a laundry.

The simple sign on the salon read, JOANNE'S, beneath what I assumed was the same thing written in much larger Chinese script. Elaborate drapes, decorated with pagodas, waterfalls, dragons, and carp, were closed over the windows, so it wasn't possible to peek inside. But from the outside, the salon didn't look to me like the epicenter of chic for skin and nail treatments.

I opened the door and we stepped inside.

Based on the facade, inside I expected to see a drab neighborhood nail salon full of wizened old Chinese women sitting in torn vinyl chairs.

I was half-right.

The old Chinese women were there, but so were women of all ages, sizes, races, and ethnicities. They all wore white terry-cloth robes and sat in retro-futuristic chairs made of black leather and chrome. Their faces were being slathered with white cream and their fingernails were being buffed like sports cars by beautiful, slender young Chinese stylists with incredibly smooth skin, identical short haircuts, and one-piece white uniforms that resembled a lab coat on top and a miniskirt on the bottom.

The stylists looked so much alike that they might have been androids manufactured from a single mold.

The place resembled a nightclub more than a salon. The floors were black marble, the walls were gleaming white, and the curved-edge counters were stainless steel and it was all bathed in an otherworldly blue glow from ambient LED lighting.

"I like it here," Monk said.

I wasn't surprised. The stylists all looked alike and the customers, with the white face cream and matching robes, did, too. The interior was shiny and clean and the ambient light was the same blue as toilet bowl cleaner.

I spotted Linda Wurzel in the back of the salon. She didn't have cream on her face or I might not have recognized her from a distance. She was wearing a robe and sitting in a chair in front of an ankle-high aquarium on the floor. It wasn't until we got closer that I realized that her feet were actually *in* the aquarium and that there were several other women nearby sitting with their feet in individual fish tanks, too.

Dozens of tiny brown fish swarmed around her feet as if they were devouring them.

"Excuse me, Mrs. Wurzel?"

She looked up at me with those unnaturally alert eyes. "Yes?"

"I'm sorry to disturb you. I'm Natalie Teeger and this is Adrian Monk."

She glanced at Monk, whose gaze was fixed on her feet.

"The famous detective? The one who solved the murder of those two judges?"

"That's him," I said.

"You work with Nick Slade," she said.

"You know him?"

"I've bumped into him at the InTouchSpace Invitational Golf Tournament," she said. "He was one of our many early investors. What can I do for you?"

"You could take your feet out of that aquarium," Monk said.

"It's not an aquarium," she said. "I'm getting a pedicure. The fish are eating the dead skin on my feet."

"Piranha!" Monk yelled.

He grabbed her legs under the knees and yanked her feet out of the water.

Her chair tipped over backwards but I caught it before she fell.

Linda Wurzel yelped in surprise and slapped his hands, drawing stares from everyone in the room.

"Let go of me," she said.

Monk did. "Are you insane? You're lucky you still have feet."

"I appreciate your concern for me, Mr. Monk, but they aren't piranha; they are garra rufa, which means 'doctor fish,'" she said. "They're harmless carp."

"They aren't harmless if they are gnawing on your flesh," Monk said. I have to admit I was with Monk on this one.

"They're only eating the dead skin," she said, and dipped her feet back in, causing Monk to gasp. I wasn't too comfortable with it, either. "It's a painless and totally natural pedicure that has been around for centuries."

"So has the bubonic plague but we don't use it as a weight-loss treatment," Monk said.

Wurzel laughed. "This is a far more hygienic pedicure than anything traditional salons do. But I'm sure you didn't come here to save me from some hungry carp."

Monk eyed the fish warily, as if waiting for them to show their true, vicious nature. I had a hard time tearing my eyes away from them myself.

"We're investigating the murder of a police officer named Paul Braddock," I said.

"What does that have to do with me?" Wurzel asked.

"We think his murder might have something to do with the killing of Bill Peschel."

She shook her head. "I still don't see how I can help. I don't know either one of them."

"You bought Peschel's tavern in the Tenderloin ten years ago," I said. "There's a Jamba Juice there now."

"Oh, yes, I remember the building," she said. "You'll have to forgive me; I own so many properties."

"Why did you buy that one?" Monk asked without taking his eyes off of the fish.

"I buy properties throughout San Francisco in areas that I think will eventually become prime residential and shopping districts," she said. "So far, I've been right more times than I've been wrong."

"Did your husband ever visit Peschel's tavern or have any kind of relationship with him?" I said.

"Of course not," she said. "Why would you think so?"

"Because Peschel's early investment in InTouch-Space made him very well-off."

"That's true of hundreds of other people," she said.

"And you bought his building," I said.

"I don't see what you're getting at," she said.

Frankly, neither did I. But I had that ticklish feeling in my chest again and I didn't know why.

A Chinese woman approached holding a bowl of white cream. She looked like a slightly older version of the Chinese androids we saw when we came in. She must have been the original model.

"Hello, I am JoAnne," she said. "Welcome to my salon."

I was right.

"May I?" JoAnne asked Wurzel.

"Please do," Wurzel replied. JoAnne started to apply

the cream to her face. "Have you ever had a geisha facial, Miss Teeger?"

"It's a little out of my price range."

"It's heaven," she said.

"You'll be there soon if you keep letting creatures feed on you," Monk said.

"There's nothing dangerous about it," JoAnne said. "It's certified by the health department. It's totally natural."

"So is letting vultures and maggots pick at your flesh," Monk said. "Is that your next beauty treatment?"

I gestured to the white cream. "Why is this called a geisha facial?"

"Because Kabuki actors and geishas would use the cream to remove their makeup and replenish their skin," JoAnne said. "The Chinese have also used it for centuries. I'm using my great-great-great-grandmother's mixture."

"What's in this that isn't in my jar of Noxzema?"

"Milled nightingale guanine mixed with rice bran," JoAnne said.

Monk looked up. "You must be mistaken. Guanine is—"

"Bird poop," she interrupted. "This is made from nightingale droppings."

Monk froze and his face went almost as white as Mrs. Wurzel's.

"You're putting avian excrement on this woman?" He looked at Wurzel. "And you're letting her?"

"It feels wonderful," Wurzel said.

"The guanine has been sterilized with ultraviolet light to kill the bacteria," JoAnne said. "It cleans and revitalizes your skin better than anything else."

"You're cleaning people's skin with excrement instead of soap," Monk said.

"I wouldn't put it quite like that," JoAnne said. "But yes, I suppose you're right."

Monk turned his head and looked at all the other women in the salon with the cream on their faces. He swallowed hard.

"Excuse me, I need to leave," he said slowly, measuring his words. "Natalie, could I borrow your cell phone, please?"

I handed him my phone and he immediately started dialing as he walked away. He was probably making an emergency call to Dr. Bell. All in all, I thought he was showing admirable restraint. I was prepared for him to tackle JoAnne and wrestle the cream from her grasp.

JoAnne and Mrs. Wurzel watched him go. They didn't realize they'd gotten off lucky.

"What's his problem?" Wurzel asked.

"He can't accept that putting bird poop on your face is good for you. It offends his sensibilities," I said. "I have to admit I'm skeptical, too."

"I'm glad I didn't tell him about our kitty litter exfoliation treatment or our Egyptian cleanse," JoAnne said.

I could guess what the kitty litter exfoliation was but not the Egyptian option.

"What's an Egyptian cleanse? Camel pee?"

JoAnne laughed and so did Mrs. Wurzel. It was nice to know that I hadn't offended them.

"Cow bile, ostrich eggs, and resin," Joanne said.

"I think I'll stick with Noxzema," I said, and turned to Mrs. Wurzel. "If anything occurs to you about Bill Peschel or Paul Braddock, please give us a call at Intertect."

I didn't have a card to give her but I figured Intertect was in the book.

"I will," she said.

I walked outside and found Monk standing across the street. I assumed that he wanted to put some distance between himself, the poop facials, and the flesh-eating carp.

Monk said good-bye to whomever he was talking to and handed me the phone.

"That's a chamber of horrors."

"I wouldn't pay two hundred bucks to have bird crap smeared on my face," I said. "But maybe it works. Women wouldn't be coming from all over to have it done if it didn't."

"JoAnne must be using some form of mind control on them," Monk said.

"It's not mind control. It's insecurity and futility. They just want to look young and pretty as long as they can and keep the pimples and wrinkles away forever. I'm the same way. I think it's hardwired into us."

"Those women are in mortal danger," Monk said. "It took all of my willpower not to do something about it on the spot."

"Why didn't you?"

"Because it's a dangerous, volatile situation. JoAnne and her evil minions are practically holding loaded guns to the heads of those women. I didn't want to cause a panic. So I played it cool."

"I'm glad that you did, Mr. Monk. I think that taking a relaxed, low-key approach was exactly the right thing to do."

"I'm leaving it to the professionals," he said.

"What professionals?"

That's when I heard the sirens. Within moments, fire trucks pulled up in front of us and firefighters in hazardous materials suits charged into the salon.

"You called a haz-mat team?" It was a rhetorical question, of course, since the team was right there.

"And plenty of backup," he said.

"Backup?" I asked. "What kind of backup?"

No sooner were the words out of my mouth than two black, windowless vans screeched to a stop behind the fire trucks, the back doors flew open, and dozens of men in full paramilitary gear and carrying automatic weapons spilled out and stormed into the building.

"Who are they?"

"Homeland Security," Monk said.

Linda Wurzel and the other customers were hustled outside at gunpoint in their bathrobes and white face masks. That would have been embarrassing enough, but then the satellite broadcast vans from the local TV stations began to arrive.

I hustled Monk away before Wurzel or any of the reporters or cops spotted him.

"Why are we leaving?" Monk said. "I want that Red Chinese poop terrorist to know who took her down."

"I don't think that Nick Slade would appreciate the publicity," I said.

"Why not?" Monk said. "Who knows how many people we've saved today."

"Because the women might not see it that way and could sue for intentional and malicious infliction of emotional distress," I said, thinking in particular of Mrs. Wurzel and her deep pockets. "Intertect could be tied up in litigation for the next ten years."

Monk froze. I turned to yank him along when I saw that sparkle in his eyes, that goofy grin on his face, and that telltale rolling of his shoulders.

He'd solved the mystery.

26

Mr. Monk and the Tickle

"You know, don't you?" I said as we headed back to the Lexus.

"Know what?" he asked.

"Who killed Bill Peschel and Paul Braddock and framed Captain Stottlemeyer for murder."

"You don't need me to tell you," Monk said. "You figured everything out this morning."

"I haven't figured out anything," I said.

"You had a tickle."

"I don't know what the tickle meant."

"Yes, you do," Monk said. "That's why you insisted that we meet Linda Wurzel. She is the key to everything."

"She's the killer?"

"No, but she's pure evil."

We reached the car. I unlocked the doors and we got inside. But we weren't going anywhere until he explained himself.

"I really hope you're not just saying that because she has poop facials and fish pedicures."

"That's a big, big, big part of it," Monk said. "Because usually when you meet someone who cleans themselves with excrement and bathes with flesh-eating fish, it means that you're in hell and that person is *Satan*."

"As convincing an argument as that is, do you have anything more to go on?"

"What more could anyone possibly need?"

"Oh, I don't know," I said. "Evidence, maybe?"

"That's all I have. Everything else that I know can't be proven. She's the only person who can clear the captain of murder. There's only one problem."

"What's that?"

"She'll never do it," he said.

I rubbed my forehead. I could feel a Monkache coming on. "But *you* know Captain Stottlemeyer is innocent."

"Yes," he said.

"And *you* know who killed Bill Peschel and Paul Braddock and why."

"Yes," Monk said. "And I know who killed Steve Wurzel."

"He was murdered?"

"Of course he was," Monk said. "But you already knew that."

"I did?"

"Peschel sold his business and retired ten years ago, right after Steve Wurzel disappeared on his way to Mendocino," Monk said. "There was a connection."

I felt the tickle coming back in my chest as strong as my beating heart.

"What was it?"

"You knew what it was. Linda Wurzel," Monk said. "Satan's concubine. But that's not all that happened ten years ago."

The tickle was those three words. *Ten years ago*.

Suddenly I experienced the same strange mental and physical sensation that I had after meeting Phil Atwater. I could almost feel the synapses in my brain firing, forging new connections, drawing together disparate facts and memories to create one cohesive understanding.

And, for a moment, I knew what it was to be Adrian Monk, to experience a world where everything is even, symmetrical, and fits perfectly into its natural place.

It was beauty and it was bliss.

In that moment of clarity, I realized why I almost figured out the mystery before he did. It was because I knew some facts that Monk didn't until he met Linda Wurzel. Now that he had those facts, too, the answer came to him almost immediately.

"Nick Slade left the San Francisco Police Department ten years ago," I said. "And he opened up Intertect using money he received from his InTouchSpace investment."

Monk learned days ago that Slade left the police force ten years back but until he met Linda Wurzel, he didn't know that the detective opened Intertect with money that he'd earned from his early InTouchSpace investment.

But I did.

On the day Slade hired us, Danielle told me that he'd used his investment revenue as the capital to start his business and later I saw the InTouchSpace Invitational putter in his office. I just never put the two facts together. Monk would have in an instant if he'd been there or if I'd only been smart enough to tell him what I knew.

But now that Monk had all the facts, he'd come to the inescapable conclusion that I'd just reached myself.

"Nick Slade killed Steve Wurzel, Bill Peschel, and Paul Braddock," I said. "What I don't know is why."

"Yes, you do," Monk said. "Bill Peschel told us and probably Braddock, too. That's why Slade had to kill them both and frame Stottlemeyer for the crime."

Monk didn't have to be so damn oblique. He could have come right out and told me whodunit and why. But he never did. My theory was that he liked to savor his summation and enjoy the way everything fit together.

Only this time, I got the sense that he was doing it for an entirely different reason.

Monk was doing it *for me*.

Somehow he knew I was capable of solving this murder on my own and that was what he was making me do. He was guiding me the way a good, understanding teacher would with a promising student.

It may have been the kindest, most sensitive thing he had ever done for me.

I rolled down the window for some air and went through a mental checklist of what I knew about Peschel. He ran a sleazy tavern in the Tenderloin. He made a few extra bucks as a police informant, selling tips on crimes to Stottlemeyer, Slade, and Braddock. Ten years ago, he sold his place to Linda Wurzel and retired, living the high life on his InTouchSpace investment ever since.

When we met Peschel, he was living in his daughter's house and suffering from dementia. He thought that it was ten years ago, the kitchen was his tavern, and that Stottlemeyer and Monk had come to see him for information.

Of course, all the tips he had to sell us were a decade old. There was something about a jewelry heist and something else about a woman who—

Aha!

"Linda Wurzel went to Peschel's tavern to find someone she could hire to kill her husband," I said. "Peschel gave the tip to Slade, who was still a cop back then. Slade pretended to be a hit man and met with her."

"But instead of arresting her, which was his sworn duty, Slade decided the deal was too good to pass up," Monk said. "He ran Steve Wurzel off a cliff somewhere between here and Mendocino."

"Do you think Peschel helped him?"

Monk shrugged. "Whether he did or not, they both got paid. Linda bought Peschel's bar and gave them both InTouchSpace stock."

"She got stinking rich, Peschel retired, and Slade got his detective agency," I said. "Everybody was happy."

"Until Peschel became senile and started calling his old cop buddies with ten-year-old tips," Monk said. "Slade couldn't take the chance that Stottlemeyer or Braddock would start thinking about what Peschel had told them and put it all together."

"Slade had to clean up the mess and silence all three of them," I said, knowing that Monk would appreciate the metaphor. "Taking care of Peschel was the easy part. But what about Stottlemeyer and Braddock? How was he going to do that?"

"That must have been worrying him until saw us at the conference," Monk said. "Watching Braddock humiliate the captain in front of everybody was a godsend for him. So he stole the captain's glass to use later."

"Things got even better for Slade when Stottlemeyer fired you and then took a swing at Braddock at the wake," I said. "He probably couldn't believe how lucky he was."

"Then he hired me," Monk said.

"He purposely kept you so busy that you couldn't think straight."

"But you could," Monk said. "You saw all the clues."

"I felt them more than saw them," I said, touching my chest.

"That's even more important. It's instinct and a natural sense of order," Monk said. "That's how you solved three murders."

"I didn't," I said. "You did."

"You did before I did," Monk said.

"But I didn't know I did it until you did it," I said.

"You had to do it before I knew I did it so I didn't actually do it even though you let me do it just now."

"You still did it," he said. "And you did it first."

"But I couldn't do it," I said. "So you solved it."

Monk shook his head. "*We* solved it."

I gave him a big kiss on the cheek and my eyes filled with tears.

"What's wrong?" he asked. Tears scared him almost as much as germs. Maybe more. He knew how to deal with germs.

"Nothing," I said, handing him a disinfectant wipe from my purse. "These are happy tears. I know exactly who I am."

"You're Natalie Teeger," Monk said.

"Adrian Monk's assistant," I said, wiping his cheek where I'd kissed him.

"And this was a mystery to you before?"

"In a way it was," I said. "But not anymore."

"I'm glad we solved one mystery today," he said.

"Are you forgetting about the one we were just talking about?" I put the used wipe in a tiny plastic bag and stuffed it in my purse. News choppers were flying overhead.

"I'm afraid that's all it is, just talk," Monk said. "We can't prove any of it."

He was right. The only ones who knew the truth were Linda Wurzel and Nick Slade and they certainly weren't going to confess. Even worse, now they would know that we were onto them.

"Nick is going to know that we talked to Wurzel," I said. "If she doesn't call and tell him, he'll figure it out himself from tracking our car."

"We're under surveillance?"

I told him about the tracking device on the Intertect cars, the keystroke monitoring of their computers, and my suspicion that even the phones at the company were bugged.

"Slade is obsessed with keeping track of his operatives," I said.

"Especially us." Monk glanced up at the news choppers. There were three of them hovering over Chinatown now. "I just hope the car isn't bugged, too. You need to call Julie and ask her to meet us at my apartment right away."

"Why?"

"We're going to switch cars with her and let her drive this one all over the Bay Area," Monk said.

"She's going to love that," I said. "That's all she's wanted since I got the car."

"Call Danielle on her cell phone and tell her to meet us there, too, but in her own car."

Monk obviously didn't want Slade to be able to track our movements anymore.

"What do you have in mind?"

"Linda Wurzel will be tied up with the authorities and the media for at least another hour and then she'll want to go home. That gives us barely enough time to get organized."

"For what?"

"Around-the-clock surveillance," Monk said. "We aren't letting Linda Wurzel out of our sight."

"For how long?"

"Until hell freezes over," Monk said. "And we'll know when that happens because she'll be covered in ice."

27

Mr. Monk and the Abandoned Warehouse

It was getting dark when we swapped cars with Julie outside of Monk's apartment. She couldn't wait to pick up her friends and put some miles on the Lexus cruising around San Francisco, which was just fine with Monk and less fine with me.

I didn't think she'd be in any danger from Nick Slade. I was more concerned about the trouble that she and her friends might get into on their own.

As soon as Julie left, Danielle pulled up behind us in her Mini Cooper convertible and we met on the sidewalk for a quick briefing.

I didn't want to tell her the whole story yet, and Monk agreed with me, so we left out the part about Nick Slade being a triple murderer.

All she needed to know was that we were keeping an eye on Linda Wurzel.

Danielle probably suspected that there was more going on than we were letting on, but she didn't press the point. She pulled out a map of Sea Cliff, an exclusive, very wealthy neighborhood that was tucked between the Presidio and Lincoln Park and boasted breathtaking views of the Pacific, the Golden Gate Bridge, the Marin headlands, and, on clear days, Mount Tamalpais.

Linda Wurzel lived on a curving street. If we parked a car at either end, we could keep her house in sight and follow her no matter which direction she took when she left.

By keeping in touch via cell phone, we could then tail her wherever she went, switching off who was behind her so she wouldn't notice that she was being followed.

That was how the professionals did it and, for the first time, I actually felt like one.

"What are we following her for?" Danielle said.

"We'll know when we see it," Monk said.

He ran into his apartment to get Wheat Thins, water, and extra wipes and then we sped off to Wurzel's estate.

Two stone pillars on the western and eastern corners of Twenty-fifth Avenue and El Camino Del Mar marked the entrance to Sea Cliff so that everyone knew that this was a neighborhood set apart from the rest of the city.

Nobody needed a couple of pillars to know that. The smell of money was enough.

The immaculately maintained Mediterranean mansions of Sea Cliff were surrounded by gardens of sculpted shrubs and beautiful pines set against sweeping bay views.

We parked on the west end of the street, Danielle took the east.

I rolled down the window a crack so I could enjoy the brisk sea breeze and hear the waves crashing against the cliffs below.

Wurzel's house was huge and stately, surrounded by a tall wrought-iron fence with security cameras discreetly placed in key positions along the perimeter. The bushes on the property were pruned to look like swirling torna-does of green and her trees were shaped like enormous balls. A polished cobblestone driveway curved past the front door on its way to the garage to the western side, presumably so a chauffeur could drop Wurzel off before parking the car.

We timed things just right. A few moments after we parked, Wurzel passed us in a two-toned, silver-and-gray Maybach that made an S-class Mercedes look like a Toyota Corolla.

The gates of her mansion swung open and she drove into her compound, parked at her front steps, and hustled into the house.

She'd driven herself to and from Chinatown. What was the point of having such a huge car if you weren't going to enjoy the luxury of riding in the reclining, heated, double-quilted, nubuck leather backseat, the *Wall Street Journal* spread out on your gold-trimmed cherrywood desk while CNN played on one of the four flat-screen TVs?

That was why I didn't get the same setup in my Buick.

For the first four hours that we sat there, I passed the time trying to think of ways that we could prove that Nick Slade was guilty of murdering Peschel or Braddock.

I came up with a few ways but then I shot them down myself without even telling Monk about them.

My first thought was that maybe someone had seen his Bentley parked in Peschel's neighborhood the morning of the murder.

But even if we could establish that the Bentley was his, that wouldn't prove he had killed Peschel, only that he had visited with him, which he'd done a few times before.

And what if Slade hadn't taken his distinctive Bentley to Peschel's but chose to be discreet by using one of the cars from his fleet instead? Wouldn't his tracking system have a record of where he went?

Then again, the record wouldn't prove he was in the car, or that he'd killed Peschel. And that was assuming Slade hadn't erased the record so the car's travel history couldn't be dug up.

I was getting nowhere proving that Slade killed Peschel, so I shifted my thinking to the Braddock case.

Obviously Slade was the guy in the elevator in the beefeater suit. If there was footage of Stottlemeyer entering and leaving the hotel, wouldn't there be tape of Slade, too?

Then again, so what if there was?

Even if he was there at the time of the murder, that wouldn't prove he'd killed Braddock, only that he was in the hotel. And he could claim he was there for a number of legitimate reasons—to have a drink, to visit friends, or to check up on his operatives, who were, after all, responsible for security at the Dorchester.

And since Intertect controlled the surveillance system, Slade probably had the ability to erase himself from the video if he wanted to.

Monk was right: Stottlemeyer was screwed. And I wasn't sure what sitting on Linda Wurzel would do to change that. But maybe I was just tired and grumpy. I also regretted not using the bathroom while we were at Monk's apartment.

I called Danielle to check in on her. She was listening to an unabridged audiobook of *Anna Karenina*, sipping green tea, eating trail mix, and generally having a grand time on her first stakeout.

I had the *Murder, She Wrote* book in my purse, but I couldn't read it because turning on the interior light would alert Wurzel and her neighbors that we were sitting out there. There had already been a couple of private security patrols but we'd ducked down each time they'd passed.

So I napped.

It seemed like I'd closed my eyes for only a second when Monk nudged me awake. It was after midnight and Wurzel was leaving her house in the Maybach and heading in Danielle's direction.

I gave her a call, alerted her that Wurzel was coming, and started the car.

I have to admit it was exciting. I'd never tailed anyone like this before. And Danielle sounded thrilled, too. We stayed in constant contact by phone so that we could take turns driving behind or in front of Wurzel.

She led us east across the city to Mission Bay and the long-abandoned, decaying Bethlehem Steel warehouses, foundries, and machine shops on the piers.

It wasn't exactly a cheery place.

The huge buildings were decomposing like corpses, the weathered brick chipping away, the windows shattered, the corrugating metal peeling off in rusted, rotting strips.

If you've ever watched a cop show, then you know only bad things happen when you visit abandoned warehouses at night.

The last time I'd been here it was to see the body of a murdered cop who'd made the mistake of meeting the wrong person in the darkness of this decaying industrial wasteland.

Once it was clear where Wurzel was going, we hung a few blocks back, our headlights turned off, watching as her car disappeared into one of the hangar-sized buildings.

I turned to Monk. "Now what?"

"We follow her," Monk said.

I didn't like that idea much at all. "Shouldn't we call the police?"

"Why?"

"Because this could be dangerous," I said.

"But no crime has been committed," Monk said.

"There have been three murders," I said. "I'd rather there weren't three more."

"Call Danielle and tell her we're sneaking into the warehouse and to join us inside," he said. "Let's see who Linda is meeting with so late at night in such a desolate place."

I called Danielle, then the two of us went on foot to the warehouse, Monk trying hard not to brush against anything dirty or step in anything that might stain his shoes.

There was a sign outside of the warehouse. It featured an architect's colorful drawing of a quaint Mediterranean village, complete with a marina and gardens, under a headline that read, A NEW RETAIL AND RESIDENTIAL DEVELOPMENT COMING SOON FROM DALBERG ENTERPRISES.

This is going to sound stupid, but after I saw that sign, I felt safer, as if I were shielded from harm by the powers of gentrification.

There was a door ajar at the back of the warehouse and we crept inside.

The space was lit by the glare of high-beams from Wurzel's Maybach and Slade's Bentley, which were parked in the center of the massive machine shop. Wurzel and Slade stood face-to-face in front of the cars, lit like two singers on a stage. But I doubted that they'd come to sing and dance.

I could hear their voices but I couldn't make out what was being said. She sounded angry, though.

We cautiously and quietly weaved around piles of broken bricks, twisted pipes, and piles of rusting machines that could have been the skeletons of huge metal beasts.

Wurzel and Slade were only a few yards in front of us. I muted the ringer on my cell, so no incoming calls would inadvertently reveal our location, and hit speed dial.

"It happened so long ago I actually stopped worrying that anyone would find out," she said. "What went wrong?"

"We were victims of the vagaries of old age," Slade said. "But I took care of it."

"If you did, they wouldn't have come to me," she said. "How did they connect me to any of it?"

"It doesn't matter," Slade said.

"Of course it does," she said. "You made this mess. I expect you to clean it up."

"I intend to, Linda." Slade pulled out a gun from inside his jacket. He took a silencer from a pocket and screwed it onto the end of the gun. "You're going to sleep with the fishes tonight."

She started to back up. "You're not seriously considering shooting me."

"Only if you don't dive off the pier into the bay on your own," he said. "Don't worry, being in the water will do wonders for your complexion. The fish will eat all of your dead skin. You can have an open casket at your funeral."

He aimed the gun at her. We weren't armed. There was nothing we could do to stop this.

Monk stepped out of hiding. "It's over, Slade."

I stepped out beside him.

Slade seemed more amused than startled by our sudden appearance.

He kept the gun on Linda Wurzel, who stood frozen in place, her mouth hanging open in shock.

"So I guess that's not you driving my Lexus all over Berkeley," Slade said. "I underestimated you both."

For a moment, I forgot all about Slade, the gun, and the deadly situation we were in.

What was Julie doing out after midnight in Berkeley? Who was she with? I was tempted to call her right then and give her hell.

"I knew that she would call you in a panic but I didn't expect you to kill her," Monk said.

"I'm on a spree," Slade said jovially. No one seemed to find it very funny except him.

"It's over," Monk said. "Put down the gun."

"Not until I've shot her and the two of you," Slade said.

"I don't think so," I said, raising my voice so it echoed through the warehouse. "We called the police. Any minute now this pier will be crawling with cops."

I hoped that Danielle was hiding in the darkness somewhere out there and made the call or we were dead.

"I don't believe you," Slade said. "But even if you're telling the truth, we'll be done in just a few moments. Tell me, Monk, what was my undoing?"

"You killed Steve Wurzel instead of arresting Linda Wurzel," Monk said.

"I mean besides that," Slade said.

"You didn't make any mistakes," Monk said. "You covered your tracks flawlessly."

"And yet, here you are," Slade said.

"Because we believe Stottlemeyer is innocent. Nobody else thinks so. You were the only one who knew Stottlemeyer, Peschel, and Braddock and attended the conference. And you shared something else with Peschel: an investment in InTouchSpace stock that changed your lives ten years ago."

"But where's the evidence?"

"There isn't any," Monk said. "Unless she talks, or you do."

Slade smiled. "That was my thinking, too."

"So there's no reason to kill me," Wurzel said. "It would be suicidal for me to talk."

"I'm playing it safe," Slade said. "You might make another stupid mistake like you did tonight or go as nutty as Peschel did someday."

"She already has," Monk said. "You should see what she puts on her face."

"Shut up, you fool," Wurzel said. "You're not helping any of us."

I had to agree but I kept my mouth shut. The more they talked the more likely it was that the police would show up before we got killed.

"Don't be angry at Monk," Slade said. "I've already made up my mind."

He lifted his gun and aimed at Wurzel's head. Her time, and ours, had just run out.

That was when Danielle leapt from atop a pile of bricks with a banshee scream, flying through the air like an arrow, her legs extended in front of her.

She slammed into Slade before he could react, knocking the gun from his hand as he fell, his errant shot blasting one of the tires on Wurzel's car.

Slade popped up on his feet almost immediately and so did Danielle. The two of them danced across the floor in a violent ballet of karate kicks, spins, and chops.

Wurzel, Monk, and I searched for the gun. I found it at the same moment Wurzel did. I elbowed her out of the way and snatched up the gun just as Slade trapped Danielle in a choke hold and turned to face us.

Danielle gurgled, her face bright red, her eyes bulging out. She couldn't breathe.

"Drop the gun or I will break her neck," Slade said.

I took aim. "You do and I'll blow your head off. I'll do it anyway if you don't let her go in the next ten seconds."

Wurzel stood to my far left, clutching herself and shaking. I didn't know whether it was from fear or fury or both.

"You don't have any firearms training," Slade said. "You're probably a lousy shot."

Danielle looked as if she were close to passing out.

A few more seconds and it wouldn't matter whether I shot him or not.

"My husband was a navy fighter pilot," I said, trying to keep my voice and my hand steady. I told myself that I was Dirty Harry in a bra. "Do you really want to gamble that he didn't teach me how to shoot?"

"I did a thorough check on you," he said.

"Then you know I met Mr. Monk after I killed an intruder in my home with my bare hands," I said. "Whether I'm a lousy shot or not, this has got to be easier than that was."

"Actually, you used a pair of scissors," Monk said.

"That were in my bare hands," I said.

"It's not the same thing," Monk said.

"The *point* is that I'm capable of killing, and giving me a gun makes it easy." I turned back to Slade. "Shall we see if I'm right?"

"You might hit Danielle instead," Slade said.

She gurgled some more, becoming deadweight in Slade's arms.

"If I'm lucky, the bullet will go through her and into you," I said. "If not, I'll shoot again."

"Maybe you should reconsider," Monk said to me.

"Maybe *he* should," I said.

Slade studied me like a poker player trying to detect a bluff. The pot at stake was Danielle's life and his freedom. If he judged wrong, he could die.

He released Danielle and raised his hands, palms out.

She dropped to her knees, clutching her throat and gasping for breath. I hoped she didn't hate me too much.

Monk sagged with relief.

I wasn't ready to relax yet. I kept the gun trained on Slade. I could hear sirens outside, drawing closer. This would all be over soon.

"Step away from her, Nick," I said.

He did.

"Are you okay?" I asked Danielle. She staggered to her feet and nodded to me, going to Monk's side. A more sensitive man than Monk would have tried to comfort her in some way.

"Now what?" Slade asked casually.

"We wait for the police to arrive and arrest you," Monk said.

The sirens were louder now, maybe only a couple of blocks away.

"On what charge?" Slade said. I found his calmness unnerving. Didn't he know that he was finished?

"Three counts of murder and one of attempted murder," Monk said. "For starters."

"I don't know what you're talking about," Slade said. "I came here to protect Linda while she surveyed her property. This is a dangerous place to be at night."

"You just tried to kill her," Monk said.

"Says who?" Slade replied.

"All of us," Monk said.

"Not her," Slade said, tipping his head towards Wurzel. "She's not going to press charges or back up your crazy accusations. To do that, she'd have to confess to hiring me to murder her husband and she's not going to do that. Are you, Linda, dear?"

The truth of his words sank into her skin like needles. Mine, too.

Wurzel shook her head slowly. "You're a bastard, Nick."

"Maybe so, but you're stuck with me," Slade said.

"Until he kills you," I said.

Wurzel knew I was right. Her face was as white as a freshly applied geisha facial. But she had no choice. She had to play along with him tonight and worry later about the danger he posed to her. She had enough money to hire a dozen bodyguards to protect her or a hit man to take Slade down.

He had to know that, too.

"I've had a change of heart," Slade said. "But whether I have or not, neither one of us wants to go to prison and if we both keep our mouths shut, we never will."

I only had to look at Monk to know that Slade was right. Monk was crestfallen, his shoulders slumped, his head lowered. This was going to be the first time that he'd been beaten by a murderer cleverer than he was.

I couldn't bear to see Monk suffer for another second.

"You're both going to prison tonight," I said.

Slade shook his head as if he were deeply disappointed in me. "You haven't been listening, Natalie."

"Yes, I have." I reached into my pocket with my free hand and pulled out my cell phone. "And so has my voice mail."

That was the speed-dial number I hit when we came into the warehouse.

Slade's cocky smile evaporated.

Monk looked at me with astonishment. "Really?"

"Really," I said.

"And so has the nine-one-one operator," Danielle said in a raspy voice, picking up her cell phone from the pile of bricks where she'd left it. "I kept the line open while I kicked your ass."

Wurzel leaned against her Maybach for support and began to cry. Soon she'd be living in a cell half the size of her car and a lot less sumptuous.

Monk straightened up and nodded to himself, obviously pleased and proud of his two assistants. The case was solved. The bad guys were going to pay for their crimes. Balance had been restored.

For him, it was as close to perfect as things could ever get.

Behind us, three black-and-white police cars roared into the warehouse.

I glanced at Slade, who glared at me with such murderous intent that I was tempted to shoot him just to be safe.

"You're fired," he said.

28

Mr. Monk Changes the World

I hated to lose the Lexus, the expense account, and the health plan, but at least we were still alive.

While the police handcuffed Slade and Wurzel, and Monk was briefing Disher, I called Julie and told her to get her fanny back home and warned her that I probably wouldn't be back until morning.

"Who's the lucky guy?" she asked.

"Lieutenant Disher," I said.

"You've got to be kidding," she said with true horror in her voice.

"It's not what you think. He's going to be taking my statement," I said. "We caught a murderer tonight."

"Cool," she said.

I wished her sweet dreams and hung up. I didn't tell her that I'd nearly been killed and I never would. There are some things she doesn't need to know.

I slipped my phone in my purse and saw that the back door of the Maybach was open. Danielle sat in the backseat of Wurzel's car, watching me and sipping a bottle of water.

"Comfy?" I asked.

"I figure this is as close as I will ever get to a car like this, so I should take advantage of the opportunity," she said. "And the minifridge. She's got Godiva chocolate, grapes, and six different kinds of cheese in there."

"You saved our lives tonight," I said. "Thank you."

She dismissed the notion with a wave of her hand. "You returned the favor."

"About that," I said, hesitating. "You know that was all just talk, right? I mean, I wouldn't have done anything to hurt you."

"That's not what Nick thought. I could feel his heart pounding against my back."

"I don't know if I would have taken the shot or not," I said.

"I do," Danielle said.

That gave her an edge on me. I still wasn't sure what I would have done.

"What are you going to do now?"

"Look for a job," she said. "Maybe one in a less dangerous line of work."

"But you're good at this," I said.

"I'm not sure that I want to be," she said. "I'm going to take some time off and think about it."

Monk and Disher came over to us.

"Congratulations," Disher said. "You did some amazing detective work. Monk has filled me in on everything. But I'll still need you to come downtown and give me your official statements."

"Can you make the charges stick?" I asked.

"The nine-one-one recording and the voice mail are as good as signed confessions," Disher said. "Slade and Wurzel know it, too. They're already competing to see who can roll over on the other one first in exchange for a lesser sentence."

"When will the captain be released?" Monk asked.

"As soon as the DA can wake up a judge," Disher

said. "But in the meantime, he's relaxing in the officers' break room with some coffee and doughnuts."

"So for the time being you're still Acting Captain Disher," I said.

"Yes, I am." He smiled at Danielle and offered his hand. "We haven't been introduced. As Natalie said, I'm Acting Captain Disher. But everybody calls me Bullitt."

"They do?" Monk asked.

"Yes, they do," Disher stated.

"I don't," Monk said.

"That's because you're out of the loop," Disher said. "I'm in the loop. You could say the loop loops around me."

She shook Disher's hand. "Why do they call you that?"

He puffed out his chest a bit and hiked up his pants. "It's obvious once you see me in action on the streets. I'm basically fearless."

"Excuse me, Bullitt," I said. "Where do you think Stottlemeyer will go once he's released?"

"He'll probably swing by the station to thank you before he goes home," Disher said, turning back to Danielle. "After your statement, how would you like a tour of police headquarters?"

"You could start by showing her your acting captain's office," I said. "I'm sure she'd like that."

"Oh my God." Disher suddenly froze. "All my stuff is still in there."

He spun around and ran back to his car.

"What's his problem?" Danielle asked.

I shrugged. "You never know with Bullitt."

It was nearly sunrise by the time we finished up with our statements. Danielle went home but we hung around so we could see Stottlemeyer when he came back.

Monk used the time to wash the windows, dust the

shelves, and mop the floors in Stottlemeyer's office. He offered to let me help him but I declined. I knew how much he enjoyed doing it on his own without having to worry about me doing it wrong.

Yes, there is a right way and a wrong way to mop. It involves a highly elaborate technique, which, if not done exactly right, could cause a plague and the demise of entire civilizations.

Rather than risk that, I got myself a cup of coffee, sat at Lansdale's desk, and watched Monk work and Disher fill out his reports. I didn't even realize that Stottlemeyer had come in, and neither did they, until he was standing right in front of me. He was back in his rumpled clothes, and looked bone-tired, but there was a smile on his face.

"'If I'm lucky, the bullet will go through her and into you,'" Stottlemeyer said. "We're going to have to start calling you Dirty Natalie."

Disher grimaced. It would kill him if that nickname caught on. I was tempted to encourage it just to get back at him for arresting Captain Stottlemeyer.

"How did you know I said that?" I asked the captain.

"They've been playing excerpts of your 911 tape all over the building," Stottlemeyer said. "You're one tough broad."

"This is news to you?" I said.

"Nope," he said. "I've been on the receiving end before."

Monk came out of the captain's office, his hands still in rubber gloves.

"Welcome back, Leland," he said. "Your office is clean and disinfected. You don't want to know what it was like before."

Stottlemeyer grabbed Monk, pulled him into a bear

hug, and clapped him on the back. "I knew I could count on you, Monk. Thank you."

"It's what I do," Monk said, his body stiff, his arms flush against his sides.

"Better than anybody," Stottlemeyer said, clapping him hard on the back again before letting him go. "And no matter what anybody says, that doesn't bother me one bit, especially right now."

He looked past Monk to Disher, who stood there nervously, unable to meet Stottlemeyer's eye.

The captain sighed and held out his hand to Disher. "I've got no hard feelings, Randy. You were just doing your job and doing it well."

Disher grabbed the captain's outstretched hand and pulled him into a big hug.

"Thank you," Disher said. "I'm so glad it's all over."

"Me, too," the captain said.

But Disher wouldn't let go. "It was a living hell for me."

"Yeah, you had it rough," Stottlemeyer said, trying to pull free. But Disher held tight. "I need to go now."

Monk and I headed for the door. Stottlemeyer turned to look at us pleadingly.

"I could use some help here," he said.

"We're helped out," I said, and opened the door for Monk.

"It's the burden of the badge," Disher said. "It has no soul. But I've got a soul."

"I know you do," Stottlemeyer said, patting Disher on the back. "I know."

I closed the door behind us.

Julie was waiting up for me when I got home shortly after sunrise. She was sitting on the couch, facing the door, her arms folded under her chest.

"You didn't have to wait up for me," I said.

As I got closer, I could see that her eyes were red and her cheeks were tear-streaked.

I sat down beside her, put my arm around her shoulders, and drew her to me. "What's wrong, honey?"

"There was a message waiting on our voice mail," she said. "I listened to it."

I closed my eyes and kissed the top of her head. "I'm sorry."

"You could have been killed, Mom."

"I wasn't," I said.

"What were you thinking, going into an abandoned warehouse in the middle of the night?"

"I was doing my job," I said.

"Going after murderers," she said.

"I think maybe it's what I'm good at," I said.

"You are," Julie said.

"You think so?"

"'I'm capable of killing, and giving me a gun makes it easy,'" she said, quoting me verbatim.

I winced. "That wasn't what I was referring to."

"Dad was a great fighter pilot but that didn't stop him from being shot down. I don't want to lose you, too."

"Maybe I should quit and do something safer."

"You could get killed crossing the street. This job makes you happy," she said. "Happier than I have ever seen you doing anything else. But you have to promise me that you will be more careful."

"Hey, I'm the one who is supposed to do the worrying in this relationship."

"That changed when people started pointing guns at you," she said. "Do you promise?"

"I promise," I said.

It had been so long since I'd held my daughter. Once she became a teenager, the last thing she wanted was her mother's affection. She didn't want to feel like a baby. But she didn't care now and I was thankful for it.

We held each other, safe and loved, until we both fell asleep.

I took the next day off to catch up on my sleep and decompress from all the excitement. The arrests and Stottlemeyer's release happened too late to make the morning paper and I didn't turn on the TV.

I spent the day puttering around the house and taking it easy. I finished the *Murder, She Wrote* book, though. I don't know how that old lady can handle it. I was a good thirty years younger than her and solving murders and facing down killers wiped me out.

The Wurzel case was front-page news the next morning. The story laid out exactly what Slade and Wurzel had done, and how it led to the murders of Peschel and Braddock, but otherwise it was thin on details of how the case was cracked. Monk was mentioned only in passing and I wasn't referred to at all (which was no surprise, since nobody from the media had tried to call me the previous day). The implication was that the police had doggedly pursued the case, spurred by their belief that Captain Stottlemeyer had to be innocent.

I didn't care that the story was inaccurate. I wasn't looking for publicity or recognition. It was enough for me that we'd come out of it alive and the captain was exonerated.

I went to Monk's at nine a.m. the next morning, ready to face the issue of our unemployment head-on. I was still driving the Lexus and would continue doing so until someone showed up to repossess it. Intertect owed me at least that much for what Slade put me through.

My plan was to start contacting local police departments to see if any of them were interested in our services.

Monk's plan was to contact the Diaper Genie people and see if he could become their West Coast sales rep in charge of developing and encouraging broader use of the gizmo. The living room was filled with the extra Diaper Genies that he'd bought.

Before either one of us could dive into our pursuits, there was a knock at the front door. It was Captain Stottlemeyer. He looked surprisingly rested and relaxed, considering what the last few days had been like for him.

"I've got some good news for you," he said.

"The police department has agreed to replace all of their trash cans with Diaper Genies," Monk said.

"Almost as good," Stottlemeyer said. "You're back on the payroll as a consultant."

"It's a pleasure to be working with you again," Monk said.

"The feeling is mutual," Stottlemeyer said.

"How did you get the chief to change his mind?" I asked.

"Blackmail," he said.

"That's illegal," Monk said.

"Not this kind," Stottlemeyer said. "It's called political blackmail. I told the chief if he didn't restore my budget to what it was before, I'd go to every TV station and reporter in town and tell them how I was falsely arrested for a murder by an incompetent police department and freed by the efforts of a consultant they fired. I would also remind the reporters that one of the mayor's biggest campaign contributors was Linda Wurzel."

"Ouch," I said. "Speaking of lovable Linda, how's the case going against her and Slade?"

"They're each trying to cut a deal with the DA to testify against the other in return for taking the death penalty off the table. I think Slade's got the edge. Turns out he was wearing a wire when he met with Wurzel ten years ago and he kept the tape of their conversation as insurance."

"Slade wouldn't have taped the meeting if he'd gone into it intending to take the job," Monk said. "He was going to arrest her but something must have changed when he heard her proposal."

"It's called greed, Monk. He saw a way to bankroll his dreams."

"Why did she want her husband killed?"

"Remember all those women who came forward demanding a piece of Steve Wurzel's estate because they claimed that he'd knocked them up?" Stottlemeyer said. "Well, he did."

"I could see why that would make her furious," I said. "But why did she go shopping for a hit man at Peschel's tavern of all places?"

"She didn't know where else to go. She picked the sleaziest, most dangerous bar in the seediest neighborhood she could find and figured there was bound to be someone inside who was desperate and immoral enough to take the job."

"It's hard to believe that a police officer would ever fit that description," Monk said.

"It's an ugly world out there," Stottlemeyer said.

"I know," Monk said, and handed the captain a Diaper Genie. "We can change that."

"With this?" Stottlemeyer asked.

"Every revolution has to start somewhere," Monk said.

Don't miss another exciting book
in the *Monk* series!

MR. MONK
IN TROUBLE

Available from Obsidian

Adrian Monk dreaded Halloween.

He didn't like people coming to his house, he was afraid of children—whom he called "two-legged rats" and "plague carriers"—and he considered trick or treating a form of extortion. So I always tried to be around on Halloween night to keep him out of trouble.

Actually, it's also what I do every day as his full-time assistant. Monk has an obsessive-compulsive disorder and an encyclopedic list of phobias that make day-to-day life a challenge for him, and everybody around him, especially when he's out solving murders as a consultant for the San Francisco police department.

But staying with him on Halloween went far beyond the call of duty.

It wasn't as much of an imposition now that my daughter, Julie, was well into her teens and past the age of trick or treating herself, but it still wasn't much fun. I would have much preferred to be at a Halloween party somewhere, like Julie was, or even sitting at home answering the door to trick-or-treaters.

Of course, it could have been worse. At least we

weren't spending Halloween with Monk's agoraphobic brother, Ambrose, like we did a few years back. That night, Ambrose was nearly murdered by poisoned candy from a deranged killer, but that's another long story.

The point I'm trying to make is that you don't want to spend Halloween with Adrian Monk if you can avoid it. You are guaranteed to face embarrassment or murder, usually both.

I hoped that this Halloween would be different. He wasn't looking forward to it much, either. From the moment it got dark, Monk stood in the entry hall, staring warily at his front door.

"You don't have to stand there like that," I said.

I was curled up on the couch reading trashy magazines that I'd brought along so I could catch up on all the news. There was a big, important feature in the *National Inquirer* on what Hollywood stars look like without their makeup and another in *Star* on who had what done where to their bodies.

"They're coming," Monk said. "I just know they are."

"You don't have to be a detective to know that," I said. "It's Halloween."

"It's a night of unremitting terror," he said.

"That's the general idea," I said.

It would be easy to dress up as Monk on Halloween because his clothing style is so rigid and consistent that it's practically a uniform. His 100 percent cotton shirts were always off-white, with exactly eight buttons and a size-sixteen neck, which he buttoned at the collar. He wore a brown sports coat and Hush Puppie shoes tied with perfect bows. His pants were crisply pleated and had eight belt loops around the waist.

Monk lived in a ground-floor, street-front apartment in a Deco-style, two-story apartment building, which he admired for its streamlined look and perfect symmetry.

His neighborhood had somehow retained its homey

charm, eclectic mix of architectural styles, and middle-class affordability even though it was only a few streets away from Pacific Heights, an old-money neighborhood known for its elaborately ornate Victorian houses, manicured gardens, and extraordinary bay views.

Most of the families on Monk's block knew better than to stop by his door on Halloween, but there were always some newcomers each year who didn't get the word.

I hoped that the word would spread fast that night.

"The streets are full of little monsters," he said, peering anxiously through his peephole.

"They're children wearing masks."

"Of course they are," Monk said, looking back at me. "So nobody can identify them."

"They aren't doing anything illegal," I said.

"They're terrorizing me," Monk said. "Terrorism is a crime. This is probably how Osama bin Laden got started."

"Trick or treating," I said.

"It's possible," Monk said.

The doorbell rang and he went to answer it. I jumped up and joined him as he opened the door.

Two little kids, around five or six years old, stood on his doorstep dressed as a ghost and a mummy. They were absolutely adorable. Their parents stood behind them, all smiles. The mother held a tiny camcorder.

"Trick or treat," the ghost said and held out her bag of candy. She had a slight lisp because she was missing some of her teeth.

"I choose treat," Monk said. "But I want you to know that I am doing it under duress."

"You don't have to choose, Mr. Monk," I said, standing behind him.

"They wouldn't make the demand if they didn't expect an answer."

"It's not a demand," I said.

"You're right," Monk said. "It's a threat. You have to perform for them, or pay them off, or you'll have to bolt the door, turn out all the lights, and hide in your closet until they stop tormenting you or the sun finally rises."

I smiled at the parents, who had a shell-shocked look on their faces.

"Your children are adorable," I said. "Cherish it while you can. Pretty soon they'll be surly teenagers who are embarrassed to be seen with you."

I was talking too much. I do that when I am nervous. I should have stopped at *adorable*. Now they were looking at me as if I were as strange as Monk. I stopped myself before I started to explain that I wasn't like him at all, that I was a rational, normal, psychologically stable parent just like them.

Monk picked up a bowl from a side table and held it out to the kids.

"You can each take two," Monk said.

"What kind of candy is that?" the mummy asked, peering into the bowl.

"It's not candy," Monk said. "It's something much better."

The parents took a step forward and looked suspiciously at what he was offering to their kids.

"You're giving them Wet Ones?" the father said. The bowl was full of packets of moist towelettes.

"Your kids really lucked out this year," Monk said. "I got the party size."

"We like Snickers," the ghost said.

"They will rot your teeth and make you fat," Monk said. "Haven't you lost enough teeth already?"

"It's not from candy," I said. "It's normal for children at her age to lose their teeth."

"What about that flab?" Monk said, gesturing to the little girl's tummy. "Is that normal?"

"That's not flab," the mother said indignantly. "That's baby fat."

"Fat is fat," Monk said. "And she's a fatso."

The mother gasped. So did I.

The father scooped up his daughter protectively and tugged his son away from door. "C'mon, let's go."

"What about our candy?" the mummy whined.

"The awful man doesn't have any," the mother said.

The mummy started to cry. So did the ghost. Monk immediately closed the door, practically slamming it in their faces. Crying children terrified him—too many tears and too much mucus.

"My God," Monk said. "What is wrong with those people?"

"You called that little girl a fatso."

"She is," he said. "And if she keeps knocking on doors without disinfecting her hands, she'll be a sick little fatso."

"You can't talk to children that way," I said. "You'll traumatize them."

"That makes us even," he said.

"You're not going to endear yourself to them by calling them names and giving out disinfectant wipes."

"I'm stopping the spread of disease," Monk said. "They'll thank me later."

"They'll egg you," I said.

"See?" Monk said. "That's what I've been saying all along. It's extortion."

There was a knock at the door. Monk opened it. Two teenage boys stood outside. One looked like he had an ax in his head, with dried blood all over his face. The other kid had a very convincing alien bursting out of his chest in a spray of internal organs.

I was impressed. Monk was repulsed.

"I choose treat," Monk said before either one could speak. He threw two packets of disinfectant wipes in each of their bags and slammed the door shut, throwing his back against it in case they decided to come in after him.

"You know that's just makeup, right?"

"They're a disgusting mess," Monk said. "How can they go out in public like that? They should be ashamed of themselves."

"It's Halloween," I said.

"It's insanity."

"A little insanity is good sometimes," I said. "It keeps you sane."

"That is the dumbest thing I've ever heard," Monk said.

"Haven't you ever wanted to just let loose and do something wild? It can be exhilarating."

"You mean like drinking water out of the tap?"

"I was thinking of something a bit more reckless than that."

"You mean like putting a loaded gun to my head and playing Russian roulette?"

"There's a big middle ground between drinking tap water and playing Russian roulette."

"No, there isn't," he said. "They are exactly the same thing."

"One can kill you," I said.

"They both can," he said. "I don't see anything fun about suicidal behavior."

"Who said anything about suicide?"

"You did," he said.

"I didn't say anything about risking your life. I meant doing something wacky and outrageous, just for the fun of it, without caring what anybody might think of you. Haven't you ever wanted to do something like that?"

"No," he said.

"I think that's sad," I said.

"I've never stuck my hand in a blender and switched it on, either," Monk said. "Do you think that's sad, too?"

"I'm talking about dressing up in costumes and having a good time on Halloween."

"You're talking about insanity," he said. "You'd have to be crazy to dress up as a corpse, knock on a stranger's door, and demand a performance or candy. On any other night, we'd arrest people for doing something like that."

"This isn't any other night," I said.

"It should be," he said.

I felt the onset of a throbbing Monkache in my head. I decided to stop arguing with him before I had a stroke.

There was another knock at the door. Monk opened it. A young man stood outside. I pegged him to be in his twenties. His white shirt and blue jeans were splattered with blood. He held a bloody knife in one hand and a grocery bag full of candy in the other.

"Trick or treat," he said.

"Aren't you too old to be out trick or treating?" I asked.

"It's like Christmas," he said. "You're never too old to act like a kid."

He had a good point.

"I choose trick," Monk said and decked the man with a right hook.

The man dropped like a rock, out cold.

I stared at Monk in shock. "What did you do that for?"

"Call Captain Stottlemeyer," Monk said, taking a disinfectant wipe from the bowl and tearing it open. "Tell him there's been a murder."

"Don't worry," I said. "He's unconscious, not dead."

"I'm not talking about him," Monk said, wiping his hands with the moist towelette. "I'm referring to the woman that he stabbed to death twenty minutes ago."

Obsessive.
Compulsive.
Detective.

MONK

The mystery series starring the
brilliant, beloved, and slightly
off-beat sleuth from the USA
Network's hit show!

by Lee Goldberg

Available in the series
Mr. Monk in Trouble
Mr. Monk Is Miserable
Mr. Monk Goes to Germany
Mr. Monk in Outer Space
Mr. Monk and the Two Assistants
Mr. Monk Goes to Hawaii
Mr. Monk and the Blue Flu
Mr. Monk Goes to the Firehouse

Available wherever books are sold or at
penguin.com